the
CONSEQUENCES

Books by Colette Freedman

The Affair

The Consequences

Published by Kensington Publishing Corp.

the
CONSEQUENCES

Colette Freedman

KENSINGTON BOOKS
www.kensingtonbooks.com

KENSINGTON BOOKS are published by

Kensington Publishing Corp.
119 West 40th Street
New York, NY 10018

All Kensington titles, imprints, and distributed lines are available at special quantity discounts for bulk purchases for sales promotion, premiums, fund-raising, educational, or institutional use.

Special book excerpts or customized printings can also be created to fit specific needs. For details, write or phone the office of the Kensington Special Sales Manager: Kensington Publishing Corp., 119 West 40th Street, New York, NY 10018. Attn. Special Sales Department. Phone: 1-800-221-2647.

Kensington and the K logo Reg. U.S. Pat. & TM Off.

ISBN-13: 978-0-7582-8102-9
ISBN-10: 0-7582-8102-1
First Kensington Trade Paperback Printing: February 2014

eISBN-13: 978-0-7582-8103-6
eISBN-10: 0-7582-8103-X
First Kensington Electronic Edition: February 2014

10 9 8 7 6 5 4 3 2 1

Printed in the United States of America

To my brother David,
one of the good guys. The really good guys.

Acknowledgments

I'd like to thank several people for making this happen:

Mark Troy, the funniest man I ever had the privilege of knowing

Audrey and Martin and Adeola and the wonderful team at Kensington

Mel Berger at WME

Barry and Melanie at BKM

My *sisters* for their unconditional support and love: Franny, Nickella, Jade, Susan, Nessa, Elise, Robyn, Pat, Koni, Lynn, Lynne, Alli, Sundeep, Natalie, Taylor, Diana, Christian, Myra, Amy, Christine, Marilee, Rebecca, Julie, Rooney, Maureen, Keb, Clair, Steffa, Schweitz, Emilie, Jenn, Ellen, and Hannah Hope

My amazing family: Mom, Dad, David, Zack, Dylan, Moses, Miriam, and Diane

My surrogate family: Fred and Jill

And, of course, Michael, for absolutely everything else.

Book 1

The Mistress's Story

When did I decide to give him up?

When I discovered that his wife still loved him . . . and he still loved her?

Or was it earlier, when I saw how I'd be remembered: as the woman who destroyed a marriage and seduced a man away from his wife and children?

Maybe it was when I caught a glimpse of my future as Robert's wife/lover/housekeeper . . . and I didn't like what I saw.

Yes. It was in that split second of clarity that I decided to let him go.

But I still loved him.

God help me, I still loved him. And I didn't think that would ever change.

CHAPTER 1

―――――――――― ❦ ――――――――――

Tuesday, 24th December
Christmas Eve

As the car pulled up to the curb outside Logan's Terminal C, Stephanie Burroughs leaned up toward the passenger's seat, grabbing Izzie's hand. "Thank you," she whispered, her breath warm against her best friend's ear. "I don't know what I would have done without you."

Izzie Wilson turned back to Stephanie. "You don't have to go," she said quickly, blinking away sudden tears. "You could stay with Dave and me over the holidays. You wouldn't have to be alone."

Stephanie shook her head. "What! And ruin your Christmas too? No, thanks. I've already decided: I'm going."

As Dave got out and popped the trunk, Stephanie smiled conspiratorially. "Besides, I thought Mr. Romantic was going to propose at midnight tonight?"

"Ssssh!" Izzie pressed her fingers to Stephanie's lips and glanced over her shoulder to where Dave was negotiating Stephanie's large suitcase out of the trunk. He glanced up, spotted the two women looking at him and smiled his gap-toothed grin before he won the war with the Vuitton. They both saw him glance quickly at his watch. "He doesn't think I know about tonight,"

Izzie added, "though he's done everything except update his Facebook status."

"A Christmas Eve proposal is very romantic," Stephanie reminded her.

"Just stay with us," Izzie begged. "Please! I hate the thought of you leaving."

"I'll be fine," Stephanie protested. "Thank you. I have to go; you know that. I want to go. I mean, I don't want to spend another Christmas alone. I swore after last year that I'd never go through that again."

A Boston cop tapped on the car window, motioning for them to move on.

"When will you be back?" Izzie watched Stephanie gather up her large purse and open the car door.

"I don't know. I could only get a one-way ticket into Milwaukee. I'll call you before the New Year." She kissed her friend quickly, then jumped out of the car and collected her suitcase from Dave, gave him a quick peck on the cheek and wished him a Merry Christmas, before darting into the terminal.

"It'll take us forever to get home," Dave grumbled as he got back in, cranking up the heat as far as it would go. "She could have taken a taxi," he muttered.

Although Izzie was dwarfed by Dave's size and bulk, she wasn't intimidated by him. "No, she couldn't. She's my best friend, and she's just had an incredibly traumatic experience. I can't even imagine what it was like when she opened the door and found Robert's wife standing there!"

"If she hadn't been playing around with the wife's husband, she wouldn't have found herself in that situation," Dave suggested mildly.

Izzie opened her mouth to reply and then closed it again. She couldn't argue with Dave; he was right, and she'd said as much to Stephanie on more than one occasion. She drew a pattern on the window with her finger as her warm breath fogged up the cold glass. She didn't envy her best friend: If you date a married man, you eventually get burned. And she guessed that Stephanie's misery was just beginning.

* * *

An airport on Christmas Eve: This was not how she'd planned to spend her holiday.

Stephanie Burroughs grabbed her iPad off of the security belt, and shoved it into her purse. She tugged on her black leather boots, gathered up her bags, and made her way through the chaos toward the gate.

She'd been hoping to spend Christmas Eve in the company—and the arms—of her lover. About this time, they should have been sitting in front of a crackling fire, sharing a nice bottle of Bordeaux between them, the house smelling of pine-scented candles, with Ella Fitzgerald singing Christmas carols low and muted on the stereo. After they'd had a glass or two, they would make love and then open their Christmas presents and maybe make love again.

She had started to build the fantasy a couple of weeks ago. She'd even bought the bottle—a ridiculously expensive 2001 Château Léoville Poyferré—and spent ages choosing the right CD and scented candles to help create the mood. But even as she'd been putting the various elements of her perfect Christmas Eve in place, she knew—deep in her heart—she knew that it wouldn't happen.

Her lover would never be able to get away from his wife and children on Christmas Eve. He would want to spend the evening with his family.

His family.

And she was not part of that family. Part of his life certainly, but not part of his family.

But she'd accepted that, secure in the knowledge that Robert Walker, her lover of eighteen months, had finally agreed to tell his wife that he was going to leave her. He was going to tell her after Christmas, and then he and Stephanie would spend New Year's Eve together. So, if she couldn't have her Christmas Eve fantasy, at least she could make a New Year's dream come true. A new start to the New Year with the man she loved.

Of course, that was before her encounter with Kathy Walker. Before Robert's wife had come to Stephanie's door and confronted her about the affair.

Which left her . . .

Which left her walking through Logan Airport, purposefully ignoring loving couples who were leaving on their well-planned Christmas vacations, whereas she was about to head off to see the family she had only recently told that she wasn't planning to visit.

Stephanie turned into a gift shop; she needed to bring something back home, something Boston-ish. She'd already sent out her Christmas presents to her parents, four brothers, and two sisters, but she couldn't turn up empty-handed. Most of the shelves were bare, and there were lines at the cash registers. She grabbed a box of saltwater taffy and a tin of fudge with a Red Sox logo. You couldn't get more New England than that. It took almost fifteen minutes to be served. Then, she turned and headed down to gate 19.

Gate 19 was jammed.

Stephanie Burroughs looked around at the grim-faced men and women impatiently waiting for the last United flight of the day to Chicago and wondered who they were and why they were traveling. With Christmas falling in the middle of the week, she assumed most were office workers condemned to work right up to the last minute and then race for the plane to be home with their families for Christmas.

She never imagined she'd be one of them.

A few hours ago, it had been a normal Christmas Eve. She'd been happy—no, happy was too strong an emotion for what she'd been feeling. She'd been content. Yesterday, she hadn't been sure how she felt about Robert's telling his wife about their relationship. On the one hand she knew it had to be done: Robert had been stringing the two women along, lying to them both, lying to himself. So, he had to tell Kathy. According to him, relations between them had broken down a long time ago and Stephanie got the impression that the announcement might even come as a relief to the other woman. And Stephanie had felt a great deal of sympathy for the woman who was about to be told that her husband of eighteen years was going to leave her.

Then, six hours ago, Kathy Walker had appeared at Stephanie's door. Forty-five minutes later, Robert had turned up.

And in the interim between Kathy's and Robert's arrivals, Stephanie had discovered several things. She had found that Kathy still loved Robert and, shockingly—terrifyingly—that Robert still loved Kathy. Stephanie also caught a glimpse of her own future as Robert's partner. And it wasn't something she liked. She realized that whereas she had been happy to be Robert's mistress when she believed that his relationship with his wife had irrevocably broken down, she was not content to remain so knowing that Robert and Kathy still had feelings for one another. She wanted to be loved exclusively. She did not want to share Robert's love with another woman.

And it was only now, a couple of hours later, that the enormity of the decision she'd made was sinking in: She'd told Robert and Kathy that she'd made a mistake, a terrible mistake. "I love you, Robert. As much as Kathy loves you. But I cannot have you. Go back to your wife. If she'll take you, that is."

And he had. Without an argument. Without a fight. With barely a word of protest.

But she'd been lying: She did love him as much as Kathy did . . . maybe even more.

After Kathy and Robert Walker left, Stephanie wandered around the condo for a few minutes, arms wrapped tightly across her stomach, which was suddenly cramping with tension. She felt light-headed and breathless, and there were tiny black spots dancing before her eyes.

She stepped into the tiny, sterile kitchen and made herself a cup of camomile tea—she definitely hadn't needed caffeine at the moment—and she knew that if she had a single alcoholic drink it would go straight to her head, and right at that moment she needed to be thinking clearly.

Cupping the steaming cup of aromatic tea in both hands, she wandered back into the room where, only moments before, her lover and his wife had been sitting. She could see the depression in the cushions at each end of the couch. Robert's Christmas presents to her lay abandoned on the floor, a bouquet of flowers already drooping in the overheated condo. Above them a single pink balloon bobbed against the ceiling.

What was she going to do? She looked around the room. With the exception of the presents Robert had brought, and the small Christmas tree, there was nothing festive about it. She hadn't had a chance to hang decorations this year, and the few cards she had received she'd stuck haphazardly up on the fridge. Was she now sentenced to sit at home over Christmas . . . just as she had done last year? She'd been miserably lonely, and though she would admit it to no one, she'd cried every day.

What was she going to do?

Her last words to Kathy had been that she was going to go home to her family. She'd said the words quickly, casually . . . but even as she was saying them, she guessed that it was impossible. It was too late to book tickets. Or was it? How many people really wanted to travel on Christmas Eve?

And once the thought had entered her mind, Stephanie suddenly knew that she wanted to go home, back to Madison, Wisconsin, and spend Christmas surrounded by light and life, too much food, and too many children.

Anything but spend Christmas alone in an empty house in Boston.

Leaving her tea on the arm of the chair, she raced upstairs and powered up her laptop. Sitting on the edge of the bed, she had waited impatiently for the Apple icon to blink.

It had taken her only a few seconds to log into Orbitz. Stephanie rarely booked her own flights—whenever she had to travel, the company made all the arrangements, and electronic tickets and an itinerary landed in her in-box. She navigated quickly through the site. All she had to do was choose her starting city, her destination, the dates she wanted to travel on and enter her credit-card details. Simple. Maybe she would make it home in time for Christmas dinner. Her parents would be thrilled.

She quickly discovered there were no flights directly to Madison.

Her cell rang, and she jumped, almost knocking the laptop to the floor. It was Izzie.

"Merry Christmas, Merry Christmas! Dave and I are going for a drink, and we wanted to know . . ."

"I can't."

The tone of Stephanie's voice instantly alerted her friend. "What happened?" Izzie demanded.

"Kathy Walker was just here. She found out . . . about Robert and me."

The phone crackled with Izzie's gasp of horror.

"Then, the triangle was completed when Robert turned up."

"Oh, Stef!"

Stephanie suddenly found herself smiling. "Talk about a nightmare scenario."

"What . . . what happened?"

"What you always said would happen: He went back to his wife."

"Bastard!" Izzie said grimly. "That's what they all do. Bastard!"

"Well, actually, I sort of pushed him in that direction. I didn't want him, Izzie. I suddenly realized I didn't want to become like Kathy Walker. So, he's gone."

"And you. What about you? How are you doing?"

"I'm doing okay," Stephanie said, and was surprised to find that it was the truth. It was as if a great weight had been lifted off her shoulders. "But you know what I'd really like to do: I'd like to go home for Christmas. I want to spend Christmas with my family."

"Well, do it," Izzie said decisively.

"I'm trying. I'm sitting here looking at Orbitz, but there are no flights left to Madison," she said bitterly. "So I guess I'm stuck."

"No, you're not. What's the closest airport to Madison?"

"Milwaukee."

"What's the closest big airport?"

"Chicago. But that's a really long drive."

"You really never make your own arrangements, do you?"

"No, not really." Stephanie's fingers danced across the keys.

"There are a bunch of seats left on flights to Chicago: United, Delta, US Airways, American. . . ."

"Good. See if you can get a flight into Milwaukee that connects in Chicago," Izzie said decisively. "This late, it'll probably cost a lot. . . ."

"Izzie, I'll pay for first class if I have to."

"Then you'll definitely get a seat. Look, find a seat. Book it. Dave and I are on our way over. We'll drive you to the airport."

"It'll ruin your Christmas Eve. I'll get a cab."

"On Christmas Eve!" Izzie snapped. "Don't be ridiculous. We're on our way." And she hung up.

By the time Izzie, with a sullen Dave in tow, had turned up at Stephanie's condo in Jamaica Plain, Stephanie had managed to book a United ticket to Milwaukee's General Mitchell Airport with a quick layover in Chicago. She'd bought first class—an outrageous extravagance of over a thousand dollars—but after what she'd been through, she deserved it. Her only concern was that the timing of the two flights was incredibly tight. If the Boston flight was delayed by even an hour, she would miss her connection, and then she'd be doomed to spend Christmas Eve and probably Christmas Day in a grim hotel near O'Hare Airport.

It had taken her less than ten minutes to pack, throwing in underwear, a couple of pairs of jeans, a few sweaters, a yoga outfit, and a little black dress . . . just in case. She didn't need to take much more; she had a closet of clothes in Wisconsin. When she'd initially come to Boston, she'd been desperately homesick for the first two years and had taken every opportunity to head home, often twice or even three times a year. It simply didn't make any sense to keep dragging the same bulky clothes back and forth, so she'd finally left a huge suitcase full of clothes in a closet. Her mother had been delighted, and the last time she'd been home, she'd discovered that her mother had hung up the clothes and laid out the rest in her childhood bureau, which still sported a scuffed Pippi Longstocking sticker on one of the drawers.

Stephanie had just finishing dressing in her preferred traveling outfit—black jeans, black polo-neck sweater, and three-quarter-length black leather coat, all chosen to show no stains and splashes—when Izzie arrived.

When Stephanie opened the hall door, Izzie hugged her.

"Don't take this the wrong way," the petite blonde said softly, "but I'm glad it's over. You're finally free. Now you can move on with your life."

"I'm glad too," Stephanie whispered. And, in that moment, she had meant it.

CHAPTER 2

Stephanie was settling into her window seat when she felt her cell vibrate in her pocket. Probably Izzie. She pulled out the phone, leaned against the window, and hit the Answer button without looking at the caller ID.

"Hello?" she whispered, cupping her hand over her mouth.

"Stephanie? Stephanie? Is that you?"

The voice stopped her cold. It was Robert. She felt her breath catch, and her mouth was suddenly filled with cotton.

"Stef . . ."

She hit the End button, abruptly aware that her heart was racing. A couple of hours ago, he hadn't been able to look her in the face as he'd slunk from the room. And now he had the gall to phone her!

The phone buzzed again.

Stephanie hit the Decline button and shoved the phone in her pocket. What did he want? To apologize? Possibly. To get her to reconsider? Probably.

The phone buzzed again, but this time she knew it was a voice mail alert. It could stay there until after Christmas, she decided. In fact, she might just as well delete it without listening to it, because she was finished with him. Finished with his big lies and small promises.

Abruptly her throat closed, and her eyes stung with bitter tears. Were they all lies? It had only been a few days ago that he'd asked her to marry him, and he'd sounded genuine. She had believed him.

She'd also believed him when he said that his wife didn't love him. She'd been wrong then.

Stephanie reached into her pocket for the phone.

One Missed Call.

It would be the easiest thing in the world to turn the phone off and put it away. The doors were about to close, and the flight attendant would remind passengers to ensure that all electronic devices were turned off. Stephanie wanted to ignore the voice mail message until after the holidays. She wanted to, but she couldn't.

Pressing her head against the fuselage, feeling it cool and solid against her hot pounding head, she dialed into her voice mail.

"You have one new message."

Then she heard his voice: "Stephanie? Stephanie, it's Robert. Look, we need to talk. We have to talk. About today. About us. About everything. Please call me back. I'm on my cell."

Of course he was on his cell, Stephanie thought savagely. He wouldn't want her calling the house, would he? She deleted the message and turned off the phone.

There was nothing to talk about. Their relationship was over. She should never have gotten involved with him in the first place. Stephanie settled back into the seat, closed her eyes, and popped noise-canceling earplugs into her ears. Instantly, the world grew muffled and seemed to go away. She breathed deeply and did a mental inventory of their relationship.

It was difficult now, looking back over the past eighteen months to remember what she'd seen in him—and really it was only in the last six months that things had turned very serious and she'd begun to think that he might indeed be the one. He was handsome, in an ordinary sort of way, sixteen years older than she was, though there had been many times that she felt she was the more mature partner in the relationship. He ran his own business, a small production company, now making shorts, fillers, and ads instead of the groundbreaking documentaries he had once aspired to. His job certainly wasn't an attraction for Stephanie, who drew a bigger salary than he did and with much better benefits.

So what was it? What attracted a thirty-three-year-old, single, unattached, attractive woman, with her own mortgage and car, to a man with the ultimate baggage: a wife, two teens, and a struggling business?

It wasn't a question she'd chosen to ask herself too often in the past, though Izzie had asked it of her often enough, usually phrasing the question slightly differently, reminding her friend just how one-sided the relationship was. Stephanie brought much more to the relationship than Robert: She was a younger, prettier, slimmer version of his wife, who now had the cares and struggles of raising two teens etched into her face and body.

Stephanie was someone able to bring business to his company. She shook her head slightly. No, it wasn't just that. She refused to believe that it was just that. Certainly that was an additional benefit for Robert, but all that had come later.

Besides, thinking back to those early days, she had actively pursued him, and she had certainly made the first move.

What had attracted her to him, with all of his faults?

When she first met him, over six years ago, he had seemed so lonely. She'd been hired as a research assistant for a documentary that R&K Productions had been working on. Little by little his story had come out as they had trekked up and down the East Coast scouting locations. Although he shared joint ownership of the company with his wife, Robert had been struggling to grow the company alone, because Kathy had stepped away from the business. He was working fourteen- and sixteen-hour days just to make ends meet. Stephanie had no time for him then; she thought he was ignorant and arrogant and completely absorbed in the company. But, she had gotten her first break in the advertising business from Robert, and for that she would be eternally grateful. That first job had paved the way for the rest of her career.

When she met him again about eighteen months ago, that loneliness still radiated from him. He was still working ridiculous hours, scrambling from job to job and, from what she could gather, the relationship between him and his wife seemed to have broken down irrevocably. He'd also insinuated that when the children were grown, he was going to leave Kathy.

Once she knew that, Stephanie had felt no compunction about letting Robert know that she was available . . . if he was interested.

And he was interested.

But that still didn't answer the question. What had attracted her to him?

Stephanie was vaguely aware that the engines were revving up and that the plane was moving. It looked like it was taking off on time; that was a good omen. Maybe she would make the O'Hare connection.

What had attracted her to him? That was going to bother her now until she had worked out a satisfactory answer.

She could feel the sensation in her feet and stomach as the plane took off, and with the sudden lift came an answer: It was the sense of loss that he carried around him. The loss, the hurt that clung to him and perhaps the desperation too. That had appealed to her. He was someone in trouble, and she could help him. Fix his problems. Make him happy again.

How wrong she'd been!

She hadn't made things better; in fact, she'd made it worse, so much worse. Because of her—and Robert too—his family was condemned to a difficult and bitter Christmas. She'd already disrupted her friend's Christmas Eve, and she was doing something she really didn't want to be doing: flying to the Midwest to a family she didn't really know anymore. She'd already been censured at work because of her relationship with Robert's company, and she knew she'd have a lot of bridge building to do to repair that damage.

Everything had a price; she knew that. You just had to be prepared to pay the price.

And she had a feeling that she was only now beginning to pay for her relationship with Robert Walker.

CHAPTER 3

———————

Stephanie made her connection with less than ten minutes to spare. Although it had taken off on time, the United flight had circled O'Hare for the better part of thirty minutes before it had finally been permitted to land. Stephanie then had a mad dash to make it to the connecting flight.

"You're the last one," the flight attendant said, as Stephanie came panting onto the plane.

"I thought I was going to miss it," she gasped.

"Take a deep breath. You made it." She directed Stephanie to the right, into the first-class cabin. "Although, if you'd missed this flight you'd have ended up stuck in Chicago over Christmas!"

"I can't think of anything worse!"

"I can." The flight attendant smiled.

Stephanie heaved her suitcase up into the overhead storage, slipped into one of the large comfortable seats, and only then allowed herself to relax. She sighed deeply. For the first time since Kathy Walker had appeared at her door, she felt a little of the stress slip out of her system, though her stomach was still cramping with tension.

"That was a close call. . . ."

Stephanie buckled her seatbelt and glanced sidelong at the overlarge balding businessman in the three-thousand-dollar suit beside her. He exuded the faintest whiff of whiskey with every movement.

He stretched out his hand. "I'm . . ."

Stephanie held up her right hand, palm outward. "Please don't take this the wrong way. I don't care. I'm really not interested, and I don't want to talk to you between now and Milwaukee."

The fat man blinked, frowning slightly, trying to decide if she was joking or not.

"I'm just trying to be friendly!" he began to bluster.

"Don't be. I'm not interested."

"Well, I never. . . ."

"I'm glad we got that clear," Stephanie continued. She pulled her earplugs out of her pocket and popped them in. She could hear them hiss and crackle as they expanded and the world slowly went away. She opened the novel she'd shoved in her bag. It had been sitting on her bedside table for months, and over the past few months she'd only managed to read three chapters, and she'd forgotten those already. Of course it might not necessarily have been the book; maybe it was just her state of mind.

Stephanie closed the book, tilted her head back against the seat, and closed her eyes. The flight attendants were going through the emergency routine. Stephanie made a point of never watching them. If the plane crashed or fell out of the sky, she didn't think she'd have much chance to put the techniques into effect anyway.

She'd gotten out of the habit of reading during her time with Robert. He rarely read—claimed he never had the time—and he seldom listened to music. That should have been her first clue that their relationship would never work: She loved books and music.

However, it also made her realize just how much time an affair consumed. Before she met Robert she would have lunch at her desk or in one of the small restaurants close to her office, and read, and in the evenings she'd come home, set up a long, hot bath, and lose herself in her current book. She could get through two and sometimes three books in a week, more if it was something from one of her favorite authors.

But that was before Robert. . . .

Once she started the affair with Robert, they ended up having lunch together most days, often in his office or in one of the nearby cafés. Driving to his office and finding parking had cut her lunchtime in half, and she'd often ended up with a quick sandwich—even though she'd been determined to give up refined white flour—rather than the salads she preferred. Then, Robert would come to her place two or three times a week. When they were together, there was little time left for reading. The last book she'd read right through was . . . She couldn't remember.

Well, all that was about to change.

When the plane took off, she kicked off her shoes, tilted her seat back, and closed her eyes for the fifty-minute flight.

And when, exactly, was she going to return? Before or after the New Year? It really depended on when she could get a flight, she supposed. If she got back to Boston before New Year's Eve, there was bound to be a party she could go to—start off the New Year on a high note. Then she wanted to go through the house and strip out everything that belonged to Robert; she was determined to keep nothing of his. There wasn't much: some clothes, a toothbrush, a razor, a pair of shoes, a spare tie. She'd stick them in a bag and drop them—no, messenger them—to his office. She wasn't petty enough to send them to his home. She wondered briefly about the jewelry he'd given her. Should she return it or keep it? But if she kept it, she would never wear it because it reminded her of him. She wasn't sure she wanted to return it to him however; she didn't quite like the idea of him passing it on to his wife to wear. Then she smiled, quickly, fleetingly. She'd grabbed her jewelry case when she was packing. She guessed that most of the pieces were in it. She could always give them away as presents to her sisters and mother.

Stephanie dozed off and drifted into a sleep in which the events of the past couple of hours cycled and recycled through her consciousness, twisting and turning into a dream that was not quite a nightmare, in which she was the woman going to face her husband's lover. She came awake with a gasp, and for a brief moment didn't know where she was. Realization came slowly, but the emotion in the dream—that combination of terror and rage—remained. The more she thought about Kathy Walker, the more respect she had for the woman. What courage must it have taken to face her husband's mistress? A lesser woman would have been inclined to wait until after Christmas, so as not to disturb the status quo.

What would she have done, Stephanie wondered. She liked to think she would have done the same thing—confronted the other woman—but she wasn't entirely sure.

Stephanie's stomach lurched when the plane touched down. As soon as the seat-belt sign went off, she was out of her seat and had pulled her bag out of the overhead. The man sitting beside her opened his mouth to say something, but the look on her face silenced him. She was one of the first people off the plane, and as the blast of chill air hit her face, she was determined to leave her complicated past behind and enjoy returning to the simplicity of her childhood home.

CHAPTER 4

———————⧉———————

At least half a dozen flights, the last of Christmas Eve, had landed within the past forty-five minutes, and the arrivals terminal in General Mitchell Airport was heaving with people. Airport security were desperately attempting to keep the area clear, but it was an impossible task, and the refrains of "White Christmas" were lost beneath loud reunions.

Stephanie wound her way through the crowd, heading for the Hertz desk. She walked past couples embracing, families locked together; she saw tears and laughter, and she was overwhelmed by a deep sadness. She'd flown in and out of airports throughout her adult life and had rarely been met by anyone, and it had never bothered her. Now, for the first time, she felt incredibly lonely.

"Stephanie . . . Stephanie!"

Right at the very edges of her consciousness, she caught the sound of someone calling out what sounded like her name. But that was impossible; no one knew she was coming in, except her parents, and they'd hardly drive all the way out from Madison to collect her.

"Stephanie . . . Stephanie!" The voice was coming nearer.

She fixed a smile on her face as she turned. It would be just her luck to bump into someone she didn't want to see only moments after landing.

"Stephanie?"

It took a heartbeat to recognize the rather plain-looking young woman standing before her, head tilted to one side, smiling quizzically.

"You walked right past me," she said.

"Joan? My God, Joannie, I didn't recognize you."

Joan Burroughs was Stephanie's baby sister, six years her junior, and the last person she had expected to see waiting for her in the airport. Stephanie wrapped her arms around her sister and hugged her.

"Well, it's no wonder I didn't recognize you," she said with a grin. Joan was bundled up in a bulky down jacket and black cargo pants over thick boots and was wearing a woollen cap pulled low over her forehead and covering the tops of her ears. Her exposed cheeks and the tip of her nose were bright red.

There were seven children—four boys and three girls—in the Burroughs family, and Stephanie had never been especially close to any of her siblings. Most of Stephanie's brothers and sisters had stayed close to home, married young, and started families early, whereas Stephanie had left for college at eighteen and had never moved back. Now, at thirty-three, she was the only one left unmarried. The last Stephanie had heard of her sister, Joan had been working as a graphic artist in a Milwaukee design studio.

"Wait, how did you know I'd be here?" Stephanie asked, then answered her own question: "Mom."

Joan nodded. "Mom called me and told me you were on the way." She stepped away from Stephanie to regard her older sister critically. "You've lost weight, and you look tired."

"Thanks," Stephanie said sarcastically. "I'll take the weight loss as a compliment. The last couple of days have been tough, and I had to take two flights to get here. I'm exhausted."

"Well, I was still in the city, so I thought I'd hang around and wait for you."

"I'm so glad that you did." Stephanie linked her arm through her sister's, and together they moved through the crowd. "I really wasn't looking forward to the hour and a half drive home."

"Luckily, I-94's empty, so I can probably get us home faster than that." Joan smiled as she took Stephanie's suitcase. "I spoke to Mom yesterday, and she was complaining that you weren't coming home. Then she called me today to say that you were on your way."

"Yeah, Mom called weeks ago and tried her usual subtle cocktail of blackmail and encouragement on me. I told her I was tied up over the Christmas period . . . but . . . well, things changed."

"Well, she sounded thrilled on the phone. Looks like all the family will be there, and you know how much she loves that."

The two women traversed the skywalk to the parking garage, where the air was thick with the stench of gasoline and bitter with the acrid tang of car exhausts. There were frozen patches of water on the ground, and Stephanie felt the chill seep up through the too-thin soles of her comfortable shoes.

"Here. I guessed you wouldn't have anything with you." Joan pulled a wool hat from an inside pocket and produced a pair of gloves. "I didn't have boots in your size," she added.

Stephanie pulled on the extremely unflattering green and yellow Green Bay Packers hat, grateful that no one she knew could see her now, and tugged on the gloves that were one size too small. But she was grateful. The air was so bitterly cold that it took her breath away. She'd momentarily forgotten just how freezing Wisconsin could be in December.

"We're here," Joan said, stopping in front of a slightly battered VW van. The remains of dozens of stickers were still visible on its rear; in some places they had been removed so forcefully that paint had peeled off, leaving dappled rust spots in their wake.

Stephanie blinked in surprise. "You and Eddie were driving an SUV if I remember. . . ."

"The Cherokee. Yes, Eddie still has that."

"Isn't he coming with us?" Stephanie asked, as Joan wrenched open the door of the van, revealing its disheveled interior.

A scrap of carpet covered the metal floor, and the back of the van was packed with cardboard U-Haul boxes, suitcases, and black garbage bags obviously stuffed with clothes. One had burst and spilled shoes across the floor. Joan snatched Stephanie's single suitcase off the ground and shoved it in between two boxes.

"No, Eddie will not be coming with us. Haven't you heard—or did Mother conveniently forget to tell you that piece of family gossip?" Joan indicated the back of the van. "I'm moving back home. I've left him." She looked at her older sister. "Don't give me a lecture," she added quickly.

"I wouldn't dream of it," Stephanie said quietly. "When did you leave him?" she asked.

"Tonight."

CHAPTER 5

⸺❦⸺

They sat in silence while Joan maneuvered the sluggish VW through traffic. The heater lost the battle against the chill radiating through the thin floor. Every few moments, Joan would pluck a filthy rag from the dashboard and lean forward to defog an arc of window.

Stephanie huddled in the seat, arms wrapped around her body, gloved fingers tucked into her armpits. She was desperately trying to remember what she knew about Joan and her husband, Eddie. They hadn't been married long—twelve months, fourteen maybe. Yes, a little over a year. Stephanie hadn't been able to come to the wedding because it clashed with a week Robert had taken off. And, given the choice between spending a week away with her lover—their first real vacation—or attending a Catholic-Italian wedding complete with a Friday night fish-fry in downtown Milwaukee, she had chosen the vacation. At one point she had gently suggested to Robert that they might go to the wedding together, but he'd pointed out that it would raise too many difficult questions. She had sent an outrageously expensive set of Waterford crystal cut-glass goblets as a wedding present to ease her conscience.

"I'm really sorry," she said eventually. "I had no idea."

"Didn't you? I'm surprised that Mother didn't tell you." This time Joan was unable to disguise the bitterness in her voice. "She thrives on my misfortune. She's told just about everyone else I know."

Stephanie frowned. She didn't think that her mother had mentioned anything . . . and yet Joan was right. There was no way that Toni Burroughs would not have shared this tragedy with her other two daughters, discussing and analyzing it to death and wondering where she had gone wrong. Because of course, it was always going to be about her.

Somewhere at the back of her mind, Stephanie remembered her mother's talking about Joan and Eddie's problems. "Okay, yeah . . . now that I think about it, Mom might have mentioned something about you and Eddie not getting along . . . but I wasn't really listening. Was it about kids? He wanted them, and you didn't." Stephanie shut up; there was more, she was sure of it. She had the vaguest of recollections that her mother had told her a long and complicated story about Joan and Eddie. But she'd been too wrapped up in her relationship with Robert to really listen. Also, she knew she had a habit of tuning out when her mother was talking about her siblings.

"Sorry, do you want to talk about it?" Stephanie asked.

Joan shook her head. "I'm all talked out."

Stephanie kept quiet, knowing that Joan would not be able to resist the temptation to give her side of the story to a new audience.

Traffic was moving steadily as they cruised along the highway. Snow had been forecast, but none had fallen. However, the temperature had plummeted, and ice was beginning to creep across the road in broad sparkling sheets. There was a sound of sirens in the distance, and the van slowed to a crawl. Joan Burroughs leaned forward and tapped the dashboard, where the temperature gauge was beginning to edge upward. "I hope we don't overheat before we get home," she muttered.

"I'd be more worried this van would fall apart before it overheated," Stephanie said.

"What do you want to hear?" Joan asked suddenly. "The truth or the version I told Mother?"

Stephanie took a moment to consider. "Which version do you want me to hear?" she said eventually. "I'm sure I'll get Mom's version anyway."

Joan nodded and smiled. "I'm sure you will." Then she hit the brakes hard and leaned on the horn as a truck cut into her lane. The sound was an anemic whine. Then, unexpectedly, she said, "I've always been a little jealous . . . no, jealous is the wrong word, envious is better. I've always been a little envious of you."

"Envious of me? Why?" Stephanie frowned, unsure at the sudden change of topic.

"You live in Boston, you have a great job, a nice house, awesome car . . . at least that's what Mother keeps telling us all. She keeps hinting that you've got a man, but we all know that's untrue."

"Why?" Stephanie blurted, surprised.

"Because we all know you're a lesbian. Well, she knows too, but she doesn't want to admit that two of her three daughters are gay."

"What! What?" For a moment, Stephanie didn't know if she had heard correctly.

"CJ's gay," Joan said matter-of-factly.

"I know that. I've always known that. But why do you think I am?"

Joan turned awkwardly in her seat to look at her sister. "There's no need to be embarrassed. You're thirty-three, pretty, successful, and single. It's kind of obvious. And Mom says you're always talking about this Izzie friend of yours. It was CJ who suggested that she must be your partner. And she should know!"

Stephanie started to laugh. It began as a giggle, then grew into a full, bellyaching laugh that came remarkably close to hysterics. She could feel the tension of the past hours seep away with the laughter. The thought of her rather straitlaced mother thinking that her daughter was a lesbian simply because she rarely spoke about men was hilarious. The only reason Stephanie rarely spoke about the man she was dating was because for the past eighteen months she had been involved with a married man. And that was hardly something she could share with her conservative Catholic mother on the telephone. But because of that her mother had assumed . . .

Pressing the heels of both hands against her cheeks she wiped away the tears. "I'm not gay. My friend Izzie is just that—my friend, my best friend, who is getting engaged tonight. To a man. And the reason I don't talk about men is because first of all, it's not something I want shared on Mother's weekly e-mail blasts, and secondly, I am concentrating on building a career and I don't have a lot of free time. It's why I don't have goldfish. Too time consuming. But—and please don't tell Mom—I have been seeing someone, a man," she emphasized, "on and off for about a year and a half. But that's over," she added, not saying just how recently it had finished.

"Mum's the word." Joan laughed as she craned her neck, seeing something in the darkness. "There's the accident. Happens all the time on this stretch," Joan said. Ignoring the sudden blaring of car horns, she floored the accelerator, and the VW lurched forward and managed to crawl across two lanes of traffic. There were flashing blue and red lights ahead and a trio of police cruisers were parked at an angle, blocking two lanes. Beyond them, ambulance lights rotated over a traffic accident. Just at the exit off the bridge, a small, nondescript Japanese import had run into the side of a white stretch limo. Half a dozen young men in tuxedos and women in evening gowns stood shivering on the sidewalk, while ambulance crews struggled to cut the driver out of the smaller car.

"Their Christmas party is ruined," Joan remarked, nodding at the partygoers.

"Not as much as his," Stephanie said, looking at the bloody driver of the small car, now being laid out on a stretcher. "I wonder if there's a family waiting for him to come home?" She suddenly glanced sidelong at her sister. "Is Eddie waiting for you? Does he know what you're doing?"

Joan drove in silence for a minute, then said suddenly, "No."

Stephanie straightened in the seat. "You mean, he's expecting you at home tonight?"

Joan checked the clock on the dashboard, not entirely sure if it was accurate or not. "Yeah, he's probably home by now. I left him a note."

"Joannie, he's probably frantic. Call him now!"

"No," Joan said stubbornly.

"You have to talk to him."

"I don't have to do anything. You have no idea what it's like to have a man lie to you for weeks on end."

Stephanie opened her mouth to respond, then closed it again. "Tell me what happened."

"He lied to me," Joan snapped.

"All men lie," Stephanie murmured. And women too, she added silently. "But let's be honest, we wouldn't want them to tell us the truth about everything, would we?"

"We were married for a year in October. We were starting to talk about having a family."

Stephanie was freezing. She was beginning to feel a headache—a combination of stress and recycled airplane air combined with jet lag and the bitter weather—pulse at the back of her eyes. Her stomach still felt queasy. She'd just flown halfway across the country, running away from her own affair; the last thing she needed to hear was that her brother-in-law was also behaving badly.

"We were doing fine: Eddie was working as a beer distributer for Miller Brewing; I had a part-time job in a graphics studio in Riverwest. We were even managing to save a little every month. We talked about buying a house and getting a dog. I really wanted to adopt a greyhound. I've always loved greyhounds."

And Eddie got bored with this little domestic idyll, Stephanie thought, found himself a woman, made her some promises, told her some lies. . . .

"And for six weeks afterward, morning after morning, he went out to work. He even came home at the right time."

"Stop, stop, stop! I think I missed something between beer distributer and greyhound." Stephanie reached out to touch her sister's arm. "And would you mind slowing down a little—you're speeding."

"Oh." Joan eased up off the accelerator. As she'd been telling the story, she'd unconsciously been pushing her foot to the floor.

"I'm sorry, I'm a little edgy. What do you mean he went out to work?"

"After he was fired," Joan snapped. "He pretended to go out to work. I only realized it when the bank statement came in and his salary was no longer directly deposited."

"I'm sorry.... I thought ... when you said he'd lied to you ... I thought there was another woman involved."

"An affair! No way, Eddie knows what I'd do to him—and her—if I ever caught him with another woman!"

"So you're leaving him because he lost his job?"

"No, I'm leaving him because he lied to me. More than once. He pretended to go to work for six weeks—and every day I'd ask him how things had gone at work, and every day he'd spin me a tissue of lies. One lie leading to another leading to another ..."

Stephanie closed her eyes. Her own affair was built upon a series of half-truths, each one tugging her farther and farther into an intricate web. She hadn't fully realized until today just how deep and twisted that web was, just how limiting her relationship with Robert had been. A smile curled the corners of her lips: It had even made her mother think she was a lesbian!

"Maybe it was pride that prevented him from telling you that he'd lost his job," she suggested cautiously.

"Maybe. But he told me that he'd been let go because they were cutting numbers. That was a lie—another one. He was fired for claiming overtime that he hadn't done. I only found that out today. Once I realized that, I knew I couldn't live with him anymore."

"Why?" Stephanie wondered.

"Because I knew I could never trust him again. Once you catch your man lying to you about one thing, you know he'll lie to you about others. I didn't want to live with that mistrust."

"What will you do?"

"Go home for Christmas. Talk to a lawyer in the New Year."

"All because he lied to you?"

"Once the trust goes, what's left?"

Stephanie nodded. What was left? She suddenly felt bitterly sorry for Kathy Walker.

CHAPTER 6

Conversation had dried up.

Stephanie drifted in and out of troubled sleep, and Joan concentrated desperately on holding the old van on the road. It started snowing: huge silent flakes that quickly coated everything in a festive blanket. But both women knew how dangerous the snowfall could be. There was a very real danger that they could get caught on the highway and be forced to spend Christmas in a sleazy motel or, worse still, become trapped on one of the minor roads and run the risk of freezing to death in the car.

Stephanie wondered how Robert would react if he read about it in the newspapers. How would he feel? Relief that "the Stephanie Burroughs problem" had gone away? Would he feel even vaguely guilty that it was his fault she was driving through a snowstorm on Christmas Eve in a gasping van that sounded like it was about to conk out at any moment? However, since he rarely read a newspaper and she doubted that the deaths of two women in a snowstorm would make the *Boston Herald,* he'd probably never know.

Maybe she could haunt him.

The heater in the van suddenly decided to work and now pumped over-hot and vaguely acrid air into the van. The combination of the heat and exhaustion drove Stephanie into a light, uncomfortable doze in which ominous thoughts of Robert and Kathy were never far away.

The crunch of gravel and grit under the tires brought her awake. They had turned off the freeway and onto a narrow country blacktop. As she struggled to straighten and sit up, Joan said, "Nearly there."

Stephanie rubbed her sleeve against the side window and peered out into the night. It had snowed here recently, and the world had lost all shape and definition. The streets were deserted, but in the majority of the Craftsman and bungalow houses, set well back from the road, she could see a Christmas tree winking in the gloom. Some of the houses had been decorated with thousands—tens of thousands—of lights, but most of the lights had been turned off now, and the displays of Santas and reindeer, snowmen, and Christmas trees seemed rather forlorn.

It was close to midnight as they turned onto Lake Mendota Drive where a single house was ablaze with sparkling lights. Stephanie craned forward to look. This was the home of their childhood. The wan lights of the van washed across the front of the pale yellow house. An enormous Christmas tree dominated the living room's bay window, and Stephanie knew it would be festooned with the same balls and trinkets it had always been decorated with. She knew she would find the silver-foil and pipe-cleaner angel she had made in first grade; she knew that the crown her eldest brother Billy had worn when he'd played a wise man in the Christmas pageant in kindergarten would adorn the top of the tree. She'd once found such traditions rather petty and almost embarrassing, but as she got older she'd come to realize that there was something comforting in them, and the trinkets on the tree symbolized simpler times, happier times.

Climbing out of the car, she was surprised to discover that there were tears on her cheeks, and she tried, unsuccessfully, to convince herself that it was just the chill wind on her face.

The front door opened wide, and the long shadows thrown by the sisters' parents danced across the snow. The two women grabbed their bags and hurried out of the icy night air.

At fifty-nine, Toni Burroughs was a tiny woman, standing an inch under five foot.

To Stephanie's eyes, Toni looked the same as she had when Stephanie was growing up. Her features were all planes and angles: a pointed chin, sharp nose, prominent cheekbones, and skin that looked almost unnaturally smooth. Stephanie doubted that her mother used Botox and knew that a face-lift was simply out of the question, so she put her mother's perpetual youthfulness down to good genes and hoped that she would look as good as her mother when she was her age.

Toni met Stephanie on the step and reached up to wrap her arms around her daughter. "I can't begin to tell you how happy you've made me," she breathed in Stephanie's ear.

"I'm happy to be home," Stephanie said. And in that moment, she meant it.

"What made you change your mind?"

"Maybe I just wanted to be home with my family for Christmas," Stephanie murmured.

"Maybe," Toni said in that tone of voice that suggested that she didn't believe a word of it.

Matt Burroughs released Joan and gathered Stephanie into his arms. "Now this is the best Christmas present an old man could have."

"Dad . . ." Stephanie could feel tears prickling at the back of her eyes, and her throat felt unaccountably tight.

"Come inside now. You both must be freezing."

Matt Burroughs looked every inch the college professor. Tall, potbellied, and now beginning to stoop a little, he still possessed the thick mane of jet-black hair that, even now in his seventieth year, was showing remarkably little gray. But Stephanie noticed the extra lines around his eyes, the creases in his brow, the more pronounced stoop when he walked. He'd aged since she'd last seen him.

Matt ushered his daughters into the hall and closed the door. The small, cramped hallway was made even smaller by the addition of the second Christmas tree—the kid's tree—that was put up every year for the grandchildren to showcase their handmade decorations. This year the greenery was almost lost beneath a confection of silver and crepe paper, pipe-cleaner stars, and papier-mâché balls.

After the chilly drive, the house was luxuriously warm, rich with the smells of Christmas cooking, scented Yankee Candles, and pine. In the surprisingly deserted living room, a log fire was burning down to embers.

"Where is everyone?" Stephanie wondered. She'd been expecting to find the entire clan still up.

"Gone to bed," her mother announced, with just a hint of disapproval in her voice. "I thought they'd wait up for you."

"They'll be up early with the children," Matt said softly. He nodded toward the pile of brightly wrapped boxes piled haphazardly around the enormous tree that filled the window. "This is the first time in I don't know how many years when the entire family will be home for Christmas," he said with a smile. He reached out and squeezed his daughter's arm. "I'm so glad you could make it."

"So am I, Dad."

Toni caught hold of Joan's arm and pulled her out to the kitchen, leaving Stephanie alone with her father.

"No doubt your mother is pumping Joan for information right now," Matt said with a grin. He opened the antique rolltop drinks cabinet. "I know you don't really drink hard liquor," he said, opening a bottle of Maker's Mark with its distinctive red wax top, "but I think you might need this." He poured a double and handed it to Stephanie. "You look like you need it."

"Usually I don't, and normally I wouldn't, but tonight . . ." She tilted her head and threw back half the bitter liquor in one gulp. She felt it sear the back of her throat and then explode, warm and soothing, into the pit of her stomach. "It's been a really long day."

Matt poured himself a tiny drop into a cut-glass goblet that was older than he was, swirled it in the bottom of the glass, and breathed in the sweet aroma. Placing the goblet on top of the mantelpiece, he poked at the crumbling remains of the blackened log with a fire iron, watching red-black and yellow-white sparks spiral up into the chimney.

"You were lucky to get a flight," he said, without turning around. "It must have been very last-minute."

"It was. I didn't book flights until this afternoon . . . well, afternoon East Coast time."

Matt retrieved his glass and turned to face his daughter. Concentrating on the liquor, he asked, "Didn't you have Christmas plans?"

"I had," Stephanie said softly, but refused to elaborate.

For a moment it looked as if Matt were about to push for an answer, then he simply raised his glass to his daughter. "Welcome home!"

"Thanks, Dad."

"Stef . . . you're not in any sort of trouble, are you?"

"Dad!" she exclaimed, immediately reverting to her fourteen-year-old self. "What sort of trouble?" she asked, curious as to what he was thinking.

"Oh, I don't know. Job trouble."

"No, Dad, I'm not in any sort of job trouble."

"Man trouble?"

"There's no man in my life right now," she said quickly, determined not to lie to her father, and equally determined not to tell him what had happened. Her parents were devout Catholics. She wasn't sure how they'd react if they discovered that their daughter had been having an affair with a married man. "There's no secret, no big mystery, I promise you. I made a last-minute decision to be with my family for Christmas. The alternative was staying at home alone in Boston. I think I made the right choice."

"I know you did," Toni Burroughs announced from the doorway, where she was standing with a tray laden with a tea-cosy-wrapped pot and a huge plate of sandwiches. Joan hovered behind her. Without the heavy coat and concealing hat, the resemblance of her sister to her mother was remarkable. "Now eat up—you must be starving—then you can head up to bed. I've given you your old room; I thought it might bring back memories of childhood Christmases. Joan, you've got the spare room." She stopped, looked up, and tilted her head to one side, listening.

The room fell silent.

In the distance, a church bell had begun to toll midnight, the sound crisp and brittle, lost and lonely on the night air. Stephanie Burroughs blinked away tears; she was home for Christmas. When she'd awakened this morning, she'd had no idea this was how the day was going to end.

CHAPTER 7

Wednesday, 25th December
Christmas Day

It was almost two in the morning when she finally gave in and realized that she wasn't going to sleep.

Stephanie sat up in bed, pulled the heavy embroidered quilt up to her chin, and looked around the tiny room: a surreal piece of déjà vu. This was the room she slept in through her entire childhood. It was more or less identical to the room she left fifteen years earlier, and it looked as if her mother had deliberately set out to keep it that way. Costumed dolls from every country in the world faced her from the deep shelf across the room. She'd never really collected them, but every birthday and most Christmases her mother or an aunt would give her another blank-faced doll dressed in an intricate homemade, hand-stitched ethnic costume. They were always too delicate, too "special" to be played with, and Stephanie quickly grew to loathe the dolls. Below them were two shelves of books and, even in the gloom, she knew she would find *Little Women, Anne of Green Gables, The Adventures of Tom Sawyer* and Dr. Seuss, alongside about three generations of ink-splotched schoolbooks and a collection of *Mad* magazines. As with the dolls, she had never really liked the magazines, but her father used to buy them for her every month, and she hadn't the heart to disappoint him. In the corner, just as scary as she remembered it, was the rocking horse that her grandfather had hand-carved from a solid piece of elm. He had then lovingly painted the horse, and Stephanie knew if she climbed out of bed and examined its belly, she would see her name scratched into the wood. Really the only things missing were the intricate and ornate doll's house—given away to one of her nieces—and the posters that had once adorned the walls.

The house was a decent size, but with so many siblings, Stephanie was always surprised that she had gotten her own room. The basement had been converted into an enormous, almost dorm-like room that her two oldest brothers Billy and Little Matt had shared. Now, it was called the grandkids' quarters—where anyone under the age of adulthood slept and played. Growing up, Joan and CJ shared the room down the hall from Stephanie, across from their parents, and Jack and Christopher shared the large attic.

Stephanie swung her legs out of bed. The floorboards were warm and smooth beneath her bare feet. Taking the quilt with her as she got off the bed, she padded over to the window and rubbed her hand on the glass to peer out into the night. It was snowing: huge silent flakes that reminded her of her childhood and, for a moment, made her feel safe.

She wondered—fleetingly—what it must be like in Boston.

She pulled the quilt protectively around her shoulders and wandered out into the hall. She needed some water. She'd had a headache and stomach cramps ever since she'd gotten off the plane, and although the cramps had eased, the headache had never quite gone away. She could feel it pulsing now, throbbing dully behind her eyes.

The house lights were still on, but turned to dim, in case any of her nephews or nieces needed to go upstairs to the bathroom in the middle of the night. Her entire family was home for Christmas: her four brothers, Billy, Little Matt, Jack, and Chris, and her two sisters, CJ and Joan. With the exception of herself and Joan, everyone had arrived with partners, and her brothers had brought their children.

She reckoned that tomorrow—no, today, Christmas Day—was going to be that special nightmare that is a family Christmas.

She wandered downstairs, suddenly feeling incredibly guilty. She became the six-year-old girl sneaking downstairs in the middle of the night to see if Santa Claus had come. She remembered being devastated when she had discovered the truth about Santa. That was the moment when her innocence was shattered, and she began to look at the world through a more pragmatic lens. She paused at the door to the living room and looked in. The only light came from the fat wax candle burning in the window and the glowing red and gray ash from the fire, with the occasional spark spiraling upward. It looked almost magical. And Stephanie was suddenly glad circumstances had forced her to come home. While her mother looked exactly the same, her father was definitely aging, and with that thought came the realization that time was slipping by and every Christmas could be their last one.

The door to her father's study was partially open, and she peered inside. It was a room she'd always loved. One of her earliest memories as a very young girl was of standing at the doorway, staring into the dark cavern of the room, awed by the books that lined every wall, from floor to ceiling. Now there were piles of newspapers scattered around the floor; despite the advent of the Internet, Matt liked to read articles in newspapers before cutting them out and putting them in innumerable folders he'd store in the closet. Regardless of Toni's constant complaining that her husband was a hoarder and his room was a fire hazard, Matt took no notice. He had published several academic books and was considered one of the leading scholars in his field. He was happy with his "system" and refused to cave to technology. He used the computer to communicate with his students, to Skype his grandchildren, and to do research, but he refused to read articles online and even regifted the Kindle that Jack had bought him the previous year.

The room was dominated by a spectacularly ugly slab of a desk, carved by the same Grandfather Burroughs who had created the rocking horse. Behind the desk stood her father's high-backed leather armchair. The red leather was cracked in places now, some of the studs were missing, and the two arms were polished smooth by years of use. When Stephanie was growing up, she used to find comfort in the clicking keys of her father's old, battered Smith Corona; however, ten years earlier it had been replaced by an iMac. The computer was still on. A vibrant aquarium screensaver was active, colorful tropical fish swimming lazily through coral reefs.

On impulse, Stephanie slipped into the room and closed the door behind her. She purposely hadn't checked her e-mail for hours and, although she very much doubted she'd have anything other than junk mail, she decided she'd grab the opportunity just in case anything important had come in.

And was that the only reason? Ignoring the thought, she curled up in her father's leather chair, tucked her feet under her body, and settled the quilt around her. Then she tapped the space bar, and the screensaver dissolved.

She quickly logged into her company mail through the mail server. There were half a dozen virtual Christmas cards sent by people too lazy to send the real thing, and a couple of "see you next year" e-mails from colleagues.

Next, she logged into her personal mail. There were fifty-two messages.

The spam filters had caught most—but not all—of the special offers, the free money, the Viagra substitutes, and the Genie Bras. Stephanie scrolled down the screen, quickly deleting the remaining e-mails without opening them, and then rolled on to the next screen.

New e-mail from robert.walker@R&KProductions.com.

Stephanie was unsurprised.

Sitting in the chair, she stared at the e-mail for a long time. There was no subject, and it had been sent at 2:43 a.m., but that was his local time, Eastern Standard Time. Stephanie glanced at the clock. About fifteen minutes ago.

She could delete it. It would be so easy. Just highlight it. Click Delete, and it would be gone. She clicked once on the e-mail, and then she rested her hand on the keyboard, index finger brushing the Delete key.

There was nothing Robert could say to her, nothing she wanted to hear from him. . . .

But she was also curious. What had happened when he and Kathy got home? Had they argued, reconciled? . . . How had that terrible Christmas Eve finished?

She hit Enter, and the e-mail opened.

> *Dear Stephanie,*
> *I don't know what's happened to you. I am desperately worried. I've tried calling you at the house and on your cell, but it goes straight to voice mail. You've just disappeared.*
> *Please get in touch with me. Let me know you're okay.*
> *I even went over to the house earlier this morning. I let myself in. I'm concerned there's no sign of you, and yet I know you haven't gone away. I looked in the closets, and your clothes are still there.*
> *I am at my wit's end.*
> *I have no idea how to contact your friend Izzie, and I realize I don't know any of your other friends. If I don't get in touch with you soon, I might try to contact Charles Flintoff. I'm half thinking I should contact the police and report you as missing.*
> *If you get this, then please, please, please contact me.*
> *I love you.*
> *Robert*

"Oh shit!"

Stephanie's first reaction was one of anger—how dare he attempt to contact her, how dare he invade her home in the middle of the night, how dare he rummage through her closets, how dare he even think about contacting Charles Flintoff, her boss! And how dare he say that he loved her!

There was a tightness in her chest; she could feel her heart pounding hard enough to make her body shake. Her stomach clenched and boiled and, for a moment, she thought she was going to vomit.

Why couldn't he just accept that they were finished? That their affair was over?

When she had stood at her door earlier that day and watched Robert and Kathy climb into their cars, she never expected to see or communicate with Robert again.

Obviously, she'd been wrong.

Somewhere in the back of her mind, an alarm bell was ringing furiously. Barely a few hours after they broke up, not only had Robert attempted to contact her, he'd been inside her home.

A sudden smile curled the corners of her lips.

It was brought on by the thought of Robert's desperately attempting to get in touch, failing, then rushing to the condo to find it abandoned. All her clothes, her shoes, even her computer were still there. He'd no idea where she was; and he obviously imagined the worse. Was he arrogant enough to believe that she'd been so upset by the course of events that she'd done something stupid like thrown herself into the Charles? A lovelorn suicide. She realized— not for the first time either—that he didn't really know her at all.

She read the e-mail again, and the smile faded. The last thing she needed was for Robert to talk to her boss or to the police.

She'd have to talk to him.

A sudden thought struck her, and she checked the time of the message again. Maybe he was still online. She could IM him in Google Chat. Stephanie glanced at her father's desktop and laughed. Like most people his generation, Stephanie's father subscribed to AOL. She smiled at the distinctive yellow walking-man icon at the bottom of the screen and clicked on the Safari icon next to it. She logged into Google and waited while her personal contacts loaded into the address book. She knew the chances of finding Robert logged in on Christmas morning were probably slim indeed. . . .

Online: robertwalker.

Stephanie moved her mouse over the name, but didn't click on it.

Online for nineteen minutes.

Well that, if nothing else, told her something about the state of affairs in the Walker household. She grinned at the unfortunate phrase. What was he doing on his computer so early on Christmas morning?

Stephanie double-clicked on the name, and the message box popped up. It was divided into two halves: Outgoing messages were written in the bottom half, while the response appeared in the top half of the screen. She hesitated, looking at her name glowing on the screen: stephanieburroughs, then her fingers moved lightly across the keyboard, four characters:

Yes?

Almost instantly, she saw a note appear on the bottom of the screen: robertwalker is typing. A moment later, Robert's text appeared on her screen.

Thank God. Are you all right? I was worried sick.

I'm fine.

But where are you?

I'm fine.

Are you not going to tell me where you are?

No.

Tell me you're all right?

I'm all right.

Stephanie, please talk to me. We have a lot to talk about.

We've nothing to talk about. I want my key back. Don't go near the house again. Stay away from my boss. I don't want to see you again.

It doesn't have to be this way.

Actually, it does.

Please. I need to talk to you. About today. About the future.

We have no future together. Go back to your wife, Robert Walker.

Stephanie hit the button that signed her out of Google Chat. She knew Robert would get a message on the other end, saying that stephanieburroughs was offline. Jesus, the arrogance! The sheer, breathtaking arrogance of the man.

"Everything okay, sweetheart?"

Stephanie jumped. She looked up to find her father standing in the door. She wondered how long he'd been standing there.

"I'm sorry, Dad. I couldn't sleep. I was just checking my e-mail."

"Anything important?"

"Just spam."

CHAPTER 8

"I'm fine, Mom. Seriously I'm fine."

Stephanie Burroughs was sitting up in bed, her hands wrapped around a bowl of steaming soup.

"You don't look fine." Toni Burroughs sat on the edge of the bed and carefully inspected her daughter. "You look worn, and the bags beneath your eyes are so black they look like bruises."

"Thanks for not sugarcoating it, Mom."

"You know me; I say it like I see it. Keeps life simpler that way." She watched Stephanie take a sip from the bowl of soup.

"Not chicken soup?" Stephanie asked. Her mother's chicken soup was one of the great abiding memories of her childhood. Every illness from strep throat to chicken pox, every cut, scrape, and toothache received the chicken-soup treatment. It usually worked too.

"There wasn't any chicken in the house, so I thought I'd make it out of turkey instead. Seasonal chicken soup."

"Tastes great." And she meant it.

"Bit too salty," Toni said dismissively. "How are you feeling?"

"I told you, I'm fine."

"Billy told me you fainted, went right out cold. . . ."

"I did not. I . . . I was sitting down on the front porch, having a cup of coffee after breakfast. The kids were going crazy opening their presents, so I thought I'd sit outside for a second of silence. Billy came out to have a cigarette. Who smokes anymore?"

"Billy does."

"Yeah, well, I think it might have been the smell of the death stick that made me feel a bit woozy. That, plus all the travel yesterday and the fact that I was still awake at three thirty this morning."

"Your father said he'd heard a noise. He thought it might have been one of the children peeking at the presents, but instead he found you in his office."

"I was checking my e-mail."

"Still, lack of sleep doesn't make a person pass out," Toni insisted.

"I didn't faint."

But Stephanie knew that was a lie. There was a little slice of time she couldn't account for: One minute, she was sitting on the porch looking at the frozen lake, and the next, she was staring up into her brother's broad, pock-marked face, a cigarette dangling from his lips, his dark eyes pinched with concern. He had swept her up into his arms and carried her upstairs into her bedroom. Moments later her sisters had appeared and helped her into bed. Toni Burroughs stepped into the room moments after they left, carrying a tray with the deep bowl of soup and some Saltines on the side.

"I've had about three hours sleep in the past twenty-four hours," Stephanie said, "and most of that was on the plane. And I'm just a little run down, I guess."

Toni reached out and pressed the flat of her hand on her daughter's forehead. "You're hot."

"I'm drinking this soup, Mom," Stephanie reminded her.

"Are you pregnant?"

The question took Stephanie completely by surprise. Eyes and mouth opened wide, and she spilled some of the soup onto the tray. "What?"

Toni raised her eyebrows and tilted her head to one side. "You heard me," she persisted.

"How can I be pregnant if I'm a lesbian?" It gave Stephanie some pleasure to see a touch of color appear on her mother's cheeks.

"Well, I hear les . . . of gay couples having children every week. They let Jack adopt a little girl . . . even if he had to go all the way to Haiti to do it."

Stephanie put the bowl down, then moved the tray off to one side. She reached over to take her mother's hands in hers. Toni's hands were tiny, the joints beginning to knot and swell with arthritis, and each finger was bedecked with a ring. Gold rings on her left hand, silver on her right; it was her only eccentricity. Squeezing her mother's fingers gently for emphasis, Stephanie said, "Mom, I'm not a lesbian, and I'm not pregnant. I'm just exhausted. That's all. Now go and enjoy Christmas with your children and grandchildren. Let me get some rest, and I'll join you guys in a little while."

Toni Burroughs got up and fussed around the bed, smoothing down the coverlet. "I believe you," she said finally.

"Good."

"About not being gay."

"Mom!" Stephanie said, then smiled when she saw her mother's rare grin.

"I'll close the curtains," Toni said, loosening the curtain ties and pulling the heavy drapes across the window, effectively plunging the room into darkness.

"Maybe that's what I should have done last night," Stephanie said, suddenly a child again, lying in bed, watching her mother close the curtains as she had done every night of Stephanie's childhood before wishing her sweet dreams and love dreams.

Toni nodded. She took the tray with the barely tasted soup and leaned in to kiss her daughter on the forehead, the movement straight out of Stephanie's childhood. "Get some rest. This is probably the best place for you," she said, and then added, "Sweet dreams and love dreams."

The door clicked shut, and Stephanie heard her mother's light footsteps move along the hall and then the squeak on the third stair as she went down. Stephanie lay in the gloom, staring at the ceiling. As her eyes adjusted, the room began to reveal itself once more, but now the shadows were deeper, and what had once been comforting and familiar now seemed strange and just a little off kilter. Emotional exhaustion—that's all she was feeling: that horrible malaise that was a combination of the worst hangover and physical fatigue. A few hours' sleep, and she'd be fine.

Of course she wasn't pregnant. The very thought of it was ridiculous.

Or was it?

Stephanie lay back in the bed and stared at the ceiling, trying to visualize a calendar in her head. Her periods had always been irregular, anything from twenty-five to thirty-two days in between, and some months were heavier than others. She'd had her last period . . . She frowned, trying to remember.

Oh, it was ridiculous to even think about it.

But once the idea had entered her mind, it was impossible to dismiss. When had she had her last period? It had to have been some time in November, late in November. . . . No, it was earlier, because—she remembered now—her period had arrived just before the office Thanksgiving party had taken place. And that had been held on Friday the 15th of November.

Which meant . . . which meant that she was anywhere between eight and ten days late.

She slowly shook her head from side to side. She couldn't be pregnant. She and Robert were always careful. Except that the truth, the bitter, spiteful truth, was that they weren't always careful; she knew that. In the beginning, when they started making love regularly, Robert had suggested that she go on the pill. She refused. Her agency had just finished working on an awareness campaign about the various dangers of the contraceptive pill, and Stephanie decided that if she was eating right, not smoking, and had given up sugar, then there was no way she was introducing synthetic hormones into her system. Robert argued with her, reminding her just how safe and successful the pill was for the vast majority of people.

Stephanie advised him that she was not the vast majority of people, and if she had given up beef because most cattle ate food full of growth hormones and antibiotics, then she was equally giving up the pill if there was the slightest chance that it could have any adverse effects on her system.

Looking back on it now, she realized that it had probably been their first real argument. It was only later, much later, that she understood he was being selfish.

Reluctantly and with a lot of griping, Robert had gone out and bought his first box of condoms in nearly twenty years. And in the beginning, she'd been very conscientious about his using them. But as time had gone by, he'd started only using them on those occasions when it was "unsafe." Stephanie tried to remember the last time they'd had sex. . . . It had been last Friday, in his office. They hadn't used protection then. And she remembered thinking that it was safe because she knew her period was due. The time before that had been . . . it had been in her apartment, maybe a week earlier. Stephanie frowned. It had been a Saturday night. They'd been to the movies, had some sushi at JP Seafood Café on Centre Street, then had come back to her place. She'd run a bath . . . and again they'd made love with no protection. The box of condoms had been empty, and by that time they were in the throes of passion and the thought of getting dressed and heading out to CVS was unthinkable.

Almost unconsciously, her hand moved down to rest on her almost flat stomach. Her breathing was shallow, and her skin felt clammy, and she felt a bead of sweat gather in her hairline and trickle around to curl by her ear.

Pregnant.

Maybe.

Possibly.

Unlikely.

She tried to think of anything that might account for her late period. There were any number of factors: There was the pressure of her affair—she'd known for the past couple of weeks it was coming to a head, and that, coupled with the intense pressure at work to get everything finished for Christmas, certainly hadn't helped. She'd been traveling a lot—usually day-trips in and out of New York, D.C., and Miami, and she knew that air flight played havoc with regular periods. Too much exercise? She'd been going to the gym every Monday and Thursday night as well as religiously doing Tony Horton's DVD program, P90X. Or was it her diet? She'd gone on the Atkins Diet for a few weeks—could that have affected her system and knocked her cycle out of kilter?

Stephanie felt queasy again, and was it her imagination or did her breasts feel especially heavy and tender? And wasn't that supposed to be a sign?

Oh dear God. What if she were pregnant?

She was thirty-three years old; she knew her body, knew its rhythms and cycles. Her breasts often became tender just before her period. She was sure what she was feeling now was the onset of the delayed period coupled with extreme stress and exhaustion.

But what if it wasn't? What if she were pregnant?

Stephanie was exhausted and emotionally fragile, and she suddenly found that there were tears on her face. Tears of confusion and self-pity, mingled with fear. If she was pregnant: What about her career, her home, her lifestyle? She'd have to either give up her job or take maternity leave, probably have to sell the condo and irrevocably alter her lifestyle. What was she going to do?

And what would Robert think?

That sudden thought made her bolt upright in the bed. Would he have gone back to his wife so willingly if he knew she was pregnant with his child? Would she have allowed him—even pushed him away—if she had suspected that she was pregnant?

What would Kathy think? There were two children in the Walker marriage, a seventeen-year-old boy and a fifteen-year-old girl. Stephanie wondered if Kathy had ever wanted more. How would she feel if she knew her husband had fathered a child with his mistress?

Would she tell Robert, she wondered, and the answer was immediate. Of course she would; if she was pregnant, she wasn't going to do it alone. Robert had gotten her into this situation. She was going to make sure he knew about it and took financial care of the baby.

So much for trying to cut all ties with him, she thought ruefully.

Before she made any decisions, she needed advice.

And she needed to be certain.

CHAPTER 9

"Merry Christmas!" The phone was answered with a breezy chirpiness that immediately lifted Stephanie's spirits.

"That sounds like the voice of someone who got engaged last night," she said quietly.

"Stephanie!" Izzie Wilson's voice rose to a high-pitched squeal.

Holding the phone a little away from her ear, Stephanie asked, "Tell me everything. Are you officially engaged?"

"He got down on one knee, the whole nine yards." There was a clinking sound on the other end of the phone. "What you are hearing is the sound of a diamond in surprisingly good taste tapping the phone. We're officially engaged, and we decided not to have a long engagement, probably September. You'll be my maid of honor, of course."

"Of course." Although she was lying flat in bed, Stephanie felt as if everything had lurched. If—and it was still a big, huge, monstrous *if*—she was pregnant, then the baby would be due in September.

"Izzie, I'm so happy for you and Dave."

"I knew you would be. So what's going on? You got there all right? You must be zonked."

Stephanie had rehearsed her conversation. They'd chat about Izzie's engagement, talk about Christmas, compare presents and families and how crazy they were, and then, and only then would Stephanie indicate her fears to Izzie. That was the plan.

Instead she blurted out: "I think I'm pregnant." She was surprised to hear the crack in her voice. She was thirty-three; yet, she was sounding as scared as any teenager.

There was a long silence on the other end of the line. In the background, Stephanie could hear the muted explosions and gunfire of a Christmas Day movie and overloud and slightly drunken laughter. Abruptly the background noise went away as Izzie stepped into another room and shut the door.

"Talk to me."

Stephanie cupped her hand over the mouthpiece and dropped her voice to little more than a whisper. "I think I'm pregnant," she repeated.

"And I think I'm rich, but I'm not," Izzie said pointedly.

"I'm maybe ten days late. . . ."

"I've often been ten days late."

"I know. Me too. But, I'm also feeling very queasy."

"That could just be the stress of it all," Izzie said reasonably.

"I know. I thought of that. Or it could be my mother's cooking. But my breasts are heavy and sore, and I sort of fainted this morning."

"Sort of fainted! What does that mean? You don't sort of faint; you do or you don't." Izzie immediately went into her doctor mode.

"Just like I said. I was sitting outside on the porch having a cup of coffee and then next thing I know my brother is carrying me in. Plus, my mother asked me."

"Asked you? Asked you what?"

"If I was pregnant."

Stephanie could hear Izzie draw in a deep breath.

"She asked if you were pregnant?"

"Yup."

"Mothers always know," Izzie said glumly. "My mother could

always tell when my sister Rosie was pregnant. And that was usually weeks before Rosie herself knew. And she had four kids. What do you think? Is there any chance you could be?"

"There's a chance."

"Didn't you use protection?"

"Most of the time, but not all the time and not for the last two times."

"Oh, Stef!"

"I know, but in the throes of passion . . ."

"How do you feel about being a mother?"

Stephanie licked suddenly dry lips. A mother. Izzie would make a great mother; Joan, her youngest sister, would make a great mom, but no, not her. Not now. In a couple of years' time maybe, when she had a little more money saved, a bit of the mortgage paid off, and she was farther up the corporate ladder. The last time she and Robert had talked about children, she'd suggested in about two years' time. . . .

"I don't know. I guess I'm scared," she admitted finally in a whisper. "I'm scared, Izzie. What am I going to do?"

"First you're going to confirm that you are pregnant. You need to get a pregnancy test."

"I know, but if I am, what am I going to do? Do I tell Robert? Or do I leave him out of the picture completely?"

"You absolutely involve him! You tell that asshole."

"Izzie!"

"Jesus, Stephanie." Izzie's voice was loud, and her sentences were clipped with anger. "You tell him that you expect him to pay. Get some legal papers drawn up and, if he resists, slap a paternity suit on him."

"I know. I know. You're right. When should I tell him?"

Stephanie could almost feel Izzie smile. "Well, if it were me, I'd be on the phone to him right now, ruining his Christmas. He's certainly ruined yours."

It was the answer Stephanie had been looking for.

CHAPTER 10

———◆———

"Hello?" a man's voice answered, sounding slightly puzzled.

The same explosion and gunfire sound echoed tinnily in the background, and Stephanie knew that Robert Walker was watching the same movie as Izzie and Dave.

"Hello?" he repeated.

"You may want to move away from the TV and find someplace private where you can talk," Stephanie said softly. She was sitting up in bed, her chin propped on her knees, her right arm wrapped around her legs, while she pressed the chunky portable phone to her ear.

The line hissed and popped, but she could clearly hear Robert Walker swallow. She smiled. She could imagine him sitting at home, maybe surrounded by his wife, children, and relatives.

"Sure . . . sure," he said with forced joviality. "And a Merry Christmas to you too. Let me just step out of the room, away from the TV. . . ."

She heard the phone move away from his lips, and his voice, muffled, as he made an excuse to someone in the background. She

heard the two words "Christmas . . . dinner," and was unable to resist a grin. Izzie had been right; she was about to ruin his appetite.

There was a click, and then the ambient sound on the line
changed as Robert swapped phones, and his slightly fast, almost
panicked breathing was now clearly audible.

"Are you okay?" he asked immediately.

"Yes . . . no . . . I don't know," she answered truthfully.

"I've been worried out of my mind, and when I couldn't get
hold of you, I didn't know what to think, and then before, when we
were instant-messaging and you said you didn't want to see me
again, I was devastated."

Stephanie took a moment before she responded. He was devastated. And yet he'd lost nothing. His affair with her had cost him
nothing. Whereas the same affair had cost her so much more and, if
she really was pregnant, it had altered her future irrevocably. There
were a dozen responses she could have made—sad or sarcastic, bitter or angry—but in the end, she contented herself with the blunt
statement "I think I'm pregnant, Robert."

The silence that followed was so long that Stephanie was forced
to interrupt it. "What? No quick comment, no witty retort, no congratulations?"

"I . . . I . . . No. I don't know what to say."

"Well, think of something."

"How did this . . . I mean, when did this happen?"

"Who knows? We've had sex a couple of times without using
protection."

"I said you should have gone on the pill."

Stephanie bit back the snap of anger and swallowed hard. This
was not a time for scoring points. This was a time for decisions.

"Are you sure?" he asked. "Certain?"

"Reasonably," she lied. "My period is ten days late."

"Ten days isn't a lot, is it?" he said desperately.

"It's long enough."

"But you've taken a test, haven't you? Confirmed it?"

"It's Christmas Day, Robert, just in case you've forgotten.
Where am I going to get a pregnancy test kit today?"

She could hear him licking dry lips. "But you really think you could be?" He couldn't even say the word.

"Yes, I do."

There was a sound that might have been either a sigh or a moan. "Have you decided what to do about it . . . about the baby?"

"No. But you're the father. I wanted to talk to you first. Make some joint decisions. Real decisions."

"Yes, yes, yes, of course. Look, can we meet? Not today obviously . . ."

No, not today because he was having a Christmas family get-together and would not be able to fabricate an excuse to get out of the house.

"Tomorrow. Can we meet tomorrow?"

Stephanie allowed herself a smile. "Tomorrow might be a little difficult for me. . . ."

"I really need to see you, to talk to you," Robert protested. "I can meet you. Anywhere," he added.

"Anywhere?"

"I'll go anywhere," he insisted.

"Fine then. I'm at my parents' house."

There was a pause. "In Wisconsin?"

"Yes."

"What are you doing there?"

"Having a family Christmas," she said, unable to keep the touch of bitterness out of her voice. "Robert," she hissed, "what did you expect me to do? Sit around in an empty house on Christmas Day reminding myself just how stupid I'd been?"

"Look, about yesterday . . ."

"Not now," she snapped. "I don't want to talk about the past. I want to talk about our child." Something twisted inside Stephanie at the phrase "our child," and she was forced to take a deep breath. "You know, I had no intention of ever seeing you again, of ever having anything to do with you. But that's changed now. If I am pregnant, I have to see you."

"Yes, yes, of course you must." There was another pause, then she heard him draw in a deep shuddering breath. "How sure? I mean how certain are you that you're pregnant?" She could hear the desperation in his voice, the panic bubbling to the surface.

"You've asked me that already, and I'll give you the same answer: reasonably sure."

"When will you know for certain?"

"Tomorrow," she said, wondering if the local Target or Walmart would be open and guessing that they would.

"When are you coming home?" he asked.

"I don't know. I wasn't planning to come back until after the New Year, but I think this changes everything. I'll see if I can get back before the weekend. I'll check flights later."

"Let me know what flight you're coming in on. I'll pick you up. We can talk. Make decisions. See what you want to do about it."

Stephanie didn't like the way the tone of the conversation had shifted. "Robert, it's not what *I* want to do—this is our baby. It is all about what *we* want to do."

"Well, let's talk about options. . . ."

Stephanie frowned, feeling something sour at the back of her throat. "What do you mean by options?"

Something in Stephanie's tone must have alerted Robert, because he immediately changed tack. "I mean what's best for you and the baby." There was a pause, then he said, "Look, I've got to go. It's great to hear from you, and good to know that you're okay." He attempted a laugh, which sounded hollow. "Though how you got to Madison on Christmas Eve, I'll never know. What were you thinking?"

"I wasn't. Bit like when I began my affair with you, Robert. I simply wasn't thinking of the consequences." She hung up, dropped the phone on the bed, and flopped back on the pillows. Then she smiled. There was a certain grim satisfaction in ruining his Christmas. She'd dearly love to be a fly on the wall in his cozy Brookline home right about now.

Stephanie's practical nature kicked in. Maybe she was pregnant; maybe not. The first priority was to confirm that. If she was, then she needed to get back to Boston to confront Robert and decide what they were going to do. There was never any question in her mind that she was going to have the baby. An abortion was out of the question. Even if she had not been born and raised in a strictly Catholic household, she suddenly realized that she wanted this baby. There had been that moment during her conversation with Robert when she had thought he was going to suggest an abortion, but she knew that wasn't going to happen. Perhaps if she were younger, but instinctively, she knew that she wanted this baby.

There was the problem with her job. If she had a first love, it was her career. How would having a child have an impact on that? It would certainly restrict her free time and opportunities for promotion, that was for sure. Her particular position entailed a great deal of travel; she'd have to cut down, and she'd have to find a good nanny.

She hadn't really thought about children until Robert had proposed to her on Saturday. My God, was it four days ago? It felt like a lifetime. Some of her female colleagues had chosen to raise a child without the encumbrance of a man, and Stephanie had nothing but admiration for them. But, she knew she would never consider having a child unless she had a partner, someone to share the responsibility . . . and the burden.

Stephanie suddenly took a deep breath, held it for twenty seconds, and then slowly exhaled. My God, but she was getting way ahead of herself. Less than half an hour ago, the thought of pregnancy hadn't even crossed her mind; now she was thinking about managing a child and a career.

First things first: She had to find out if she was pregnant.

CHAPTER 11

———————— ⊗ ————————

Christmas dinner in the Burroughs household finished with their peculiar version of grace: It was said after the meal.

"Dear Lord, for all that we have received and eaten at Your table . . . ," Matt intoned.

Stephanie, sitting halfway down the long table, once asked her father why they didn't say grace before a meal like everyone else. Matt told her that he always thought that giving thanks for something you hadn't yet received was somehow presumptuous, whereas giving gratitude afterward was perfectly acceptable.

Sitting around the Christmas table, along with her four brothers and two sisters and their extended families, was a trial. The children were eating in the kitchen, but they were in and out of the dining room every five minutes, or one or the other of the parents kept hopping up to check on a particularly loud scream or bang from the other room. Stephanie came roughly in the middle of the Burroughs clan, but there was only a twelve-year difference between Billy, the eldest, and Joan, the youngest. The family remained remarkably close, with the exception of Stephanie, who had left home early and rarely returned. She felt slightly out of place—almost a stranger—sitting here surrounded by her Midwestern family. But it was better, infinitely better, than sitting at home in Boston in an empty, lonely house, she reminded herself.

After dinner, Stephanie and Joan found themselves in the kitchen, loading the dishwasher. The four boys and CJ, who'd always been a tomboy, were ferrying the dirty dishes in from the dining room, while Toni and Matt and the various spouses and partners played with the children. The kitchen still smelled wonderful—rich and warm with the aromas of meat and spices, herbs and liquors.

"God, I feel like I'm about ten again," Stephanie said. She breathed deeply. "These Christmas smells are the defining scents of my childhood."

"Mine was always the smell of tree sap," Joan said. "Remember when Dad would top the trees in the backyard, and the boys would drag the cut wood across the garden?"

"And the smell of burning leaves." Stephanie smiled. "The smell of autumn."

She looked out through the kitchen window. Most of the trees were long gone now. They'd simply grown too large for Matt to handle. Five years ago, the four boys had come over late in the summer with their chainsaws and cut down the larger ones. They'd then sliced the trunks into fire-sized pieces, and the dry shed beside the double garage was still packed with the circular and semi-circular sections. There was probably enough wood to last for another three years at least.

"I could get used to living here again," Joan said suddenly.

"Have you spoken to Eddie?"

"I had CJ talk to him for me. Told him where I was."

"Guess he had a lonely Christmas without you," Stephanie suggested, carefully stacking side plates in the dishwasher.

"Look, I missed him too. But he lied to me, Stef. And once a man starts lying to you, it's over. And when it's over, it's over."

"Maybe. Maybe not. Sometimes circumstances throw you right back at someone you've left," she said grimly. She looked up and caught her sister looking quizzically at her. "Did you ask Eddie why he lied to you in the first place?" she asked quickly, trying to forestall an inevitable question.

"He was ashamed that he'd lost his job and didn't want to worry me."

"That's fair."

Joan blinked in surprise. "You're taking his side."

"I'm not taking anyone's side; I'm just commenting. He was stupid, he lost his job. But he didn't want to worry you, so he got up every morning, got dressed, and went out and spent the day doing . . . What did he do?"

"Looked for a job, he said."

"So he spent the day looking for a job, because he loved you."

"And I forgave him that," Joan protested. "When I eventually discovered the truth, we had a huge fight. . . . Well, I screamed and he listened and finally admitted that he'd lost his job because they were laying crew off. But that was another lie. He was fired because he was claiming overtime he hadn't done."

"And you've never done that?" Stephanie wondered. "You've never padded an invoice, claimed for an extra hour, or slipped in a couple of additional expenses?" Before her sister could answer, she continued quickly, "Was he keeping this extra money for himself?"

"No, he wouldn't do that. It went into the joint account with everything else." Joan bent down to the dishwasher and loaded knives and forks into their little plastic container, before looking up at Stephanie. "Oh. I see what you mean. I never thought of it that way. Everyone here's telling me to ditch him."

"Everyone here doesn't know what happens behind closed doors. They just hear what they want to hear. See what they want to see. Besides, I'm not telling you to do or not do anything. I'm just giving you a different perspective."

"You were always so smart," Joan said. "Gosh, I look around this family and wonder how bizarrely we've turned out. Mom and Dad have been married forever, but . . . Jack, who's gay, is probably in the most functional relationship of everyone. There's Bill, who's now on his third wife; Little Matt and that strange older woman; Chris with his Thai wife, whose name I can't even pronounce; and CJ, who brought that woman with her today. At least I think it's a woman," she added, then fell silent as the very masculine-looking female appeared in the doorway at that moment, carrying the last of the plates. She nodded, smiled, and left the kitchen without say-ing a word. "That leaves just you and me," Joan continued. "And I'm married to a man who lies to me. . . ."

"Because he loves you and didn't want to upset you."

"And there's you. At least one of us is not a complete screw-up. The man who gets you is going to be so lucky."

"Oh, yeah, I'm a real prize," Stephanie murmured.

Joan looked across the stacks of plates at her older sister. "Do you think I should give him another chance?"

"Yes," Stephanie said without hesitation. "I think a man who loves you enough to lie to protect you isn't all bad." But what about a man who was having an affair and lying to his wife; was he doing that to protect her too, and did that suggest that he loved her? Stephanie shied away from the thought, unable or unwilling to fol-low it to its logical conclusion.

Joan leaned over and kissed Stephanie quickly on the cheek. "I'm glad you came home. If you weren't here, I'd have kicked him out. I'm going to give him a second chance."

"Just tell him: No more lying."

A heavy Sherpa fleece blanket settled over Stephanie's shoul-ders, making her jump. She was sitting on the back step, staring out across the rolling snow-white fields. She looked up to find her fa-ther standing beside her. He was tamping tobacco into his battered pipe. Fragments of the brown leaf flaked off and settled on the white snow, looking like tiny questions marks.

"This was always your favorite place when you were a child," Matt Burroughs said. "Whenever you were in trouble, I always knew where to find you. Sitting on the step." He lowered himself gently beside his daughter. She lifted the blanket off her shoulders and draped it around his too, sharing it. They sat together in si-lence while Matt packed the bowl of his pipe, but they both knew he wouldn't light it in her presence. "Are you in trouble now?" he asked softly.

Stephanie allowed her eyes to drift. There was the tree where the old tire had hung, and the tumbledown barn where they'd played when the weather was freezing, and if she followed the narrow path through the trees, it would end up at the tiny pool where she'd first learned to swim. This was a place of innocence, a place where she'd always been happy. And with the thought came the awareness that she wasn't happy now; she wondered if she would ever be happy again.

"I hope you won't be disappointed," she whispered, feeling like a teen again. "I think I'm pregnant."

Matt put the unlit pipe between his lips and nodded slightly.

"Did Mom tell you?"

"Your mother has many wonderful gifts, but reticence is not one of them," he murmured, "and don't you dare tell her I said so." He glanced sidelong at his daughter. "You will always be that seven-year-old girl running wild through this garden, chasing the skunk just to make it spray, because you were one of the few people in the world who loved the smell. You will be forever ten, coming to me with the injured cardinal cupped in your hand. I will always remember you in your Communion dress, and your prom dress, and your graduation gown. I will never be disappointed in you. You've always made me proud, sweetheart. Always."

Stephanie rested her head on her father's shoulder and remained silent, unwilling to trust herself to speak.

"Do you want to talk about it?"

Stephanie drew in a deep lungful of the icy December air. "The father's name is Robert Walker. He's sixteen years older than I am and runs a small production company in Boston. And he's married. With two children," she added.

"Still married?" Matt asked quietly.

"Still married. I know this goes against everything you've taught us and everything you believe in, Dad. But I fell in love with him. I allowed myself to fall in love with him, because he told me—and, in his defense, he genuinely believed it at the time—that his wife was no longer interested in him."

"But he didn't leave his wife?"

"No. No, he didn't." She sighed. "Last weekend I told him he had to choose." She shrugged. "And he chose me. Told me he'd leave his wife after Christmas, that we'd be together. There was about forty-eight hours, Dad, when I was never happier."

"Let me guess," Matt said, not looking at her, squinting out at the snow-capped field, now losing definition as the world drifted into night. "The wife shows up?"

"The wife shows up." She turned to look at her father. "How did you know?"

"Must have been something fairly dramatic that drove you back home on Christmas Eve. I can't think of anything more dramatic than that."

"She showed up yesterday. And then Robert turned up a little later."

Matt Burroughs's lips curled in a tight smile. "That must have been awkward."

"You have no idea. I found out that she still loved him. And talking to her made me really understand what my future with Robert would be like. So . . . I made him go back to his wife."

"How did he feel about that?"

Stephanie blinked in surprise. "I don't know. I didn't ask him. I suppose I thought since they both know there's a problem, surely they can work together to figure it out—get some counseling or something."

"And now?"

"I don't know what to do. If I'm pregnant, I'll need to keep in touch with him."

"Why?" Matt asked seriously.

"Because . . . ," Stephanie began and then stopped. She'd no idea why. "It just seems right. For me, for him . . . and for the baby."

Matt nodded. Then he asked Stephanie what she had been asking herself for months. "Does he love you?"

"I think so," she said eventually.

Matt stood up and fixed the blanket over his daughter's shoulders again. Then he leaned down and kissed the top of her head. "There are some questions that are like math problems. There should be no equivocation: only one answer—in the positive or the negative. So, I'll ask you again: Does he love you?"

The twilight cast long shadows on the snow, turning the pristine whiteness to gray. The familiar lines of the backyard were disappearing into the gloom. High and clear in the cold air, she heard a child's voice, raised in delighted laughter, the sound pure and inno-cent. When you are a child everything is so simple, so easy. You be-lieve what people tell you: Santa Claus and the Easter Bunny and the Tooth Fairy. And they are all lies. That is the ultimate betrayal of childhood. And is it any different for adults? When a man stands at the altar and promises, in front of witnesses, that he will love and honor the woman by his side for the rest of his life, it is probably a lie . . . whether he knows it or not.

So, last Saturday, when Robert had stood in the street and said, "I love you. I want to be with you. To marry you. Will you marry me?" had he been lying? She didn't think so.

She nodded firmly. "Yes, I believe he loves me."

"Do you love him?"

Yesterday, she would have said no. Yesterday, she had hated him, despised him. But that was yesterday. The day before that the answer had been different, and today . . . Well, she wasn't entirely sure how she felt about him today. "One of the reasons I let him go was because I loved him," she admitted slowly and deliberately. "I was angry with him because he went back to his wife so easily."

"But you told me you pushed him away."

"He didn't fight for me."

"Did you fight for him?" Matt asked, surprising her.

"No." Stephanie turned to look at her father. "I thought you'd be mad at me."

"Why?"

"Because I'd been stupid enough to get pregnant . . . because I'd been involved with a married man."

"Look, who knows how I would have felt ten years, or even five years ago. I'm not thrilled about it, but as you get older, you come to realize a simple truth: Love is the only thing worth fighting for." He turned and walked away, back toward the house. "Don't stay out too long—you'll catch a chill."

CHAPTER 12

Thursday, 26th December

There were four shelves of pregnancy-testing kits, all in neat, discreet boxes, most of them in a blush pink with the word *accurate* built into the title, and most promising instant results. The large print said ninety-nine percent accuracy, while the smaller print suggested that results might vary from person to person and to consult a doctor.

Stephanie walked up and down the shelves, picking up toothpaste and shampoo—which she didn't need—before she eventually grabbed the first box she looked at and walked toward the counter. The Walgreens was practically empty, and she was bundled up in a heavy coat she'd borrowed from CJ, so she knew she was unrecognizable, but she felt like a teenage girl buying a packet of condoms before the prom. On an abstract level she found her embarrassment almost amusing; where was the gutsy, ballsy executive who ran multimillion-dollar advertising campaigns?

The Hispanic girl behind the register checked the toothpaste and shampoo through the scanner without even looking at her, but stopped when she came to the pregnancy-testing kit and turned it over in her hands. Stephanie noticed that each nail had a tiny glittering stone set into it. "Oh, this one is very good," she said. "I used it myself."

Stephanie felt herself begin to color. "And is it accurate?" Her tongue felt too big in her mouth.

"I used it a week after I missed my period, and it was able to tell me that I was pregnant."

"Oh. Good. Congratulations." Stephanie didn't think the girl could be older than seventeen, maybe younger, but it was hard to tell.

"Thank you. Little boy, called him Chavez after his poppa." The girl bagged the items, took her cash, and made change in one smoothly practiced movement. "Have a nice day," she said, smiling brightly.

"Thank you," Stephanie said as she walked away. She chuckled at the girl's naïveté. Starting off the day with a pregnancy test was not her idea of having a nice day.

The second she got into the car, she opened the box and pulled out the single sheet of instructions. They were fairly straightforward, and she glanced back toward the store, wondering if it had a bathroom, then shook her head at the absurdity of the thought; she didn't want to discover if she was pregnant in a Walgreens restroom. Turning the key in the ignition, she gently eased her father's Buick out onto the road. The snowplow had been through earlier, and the streets had been salted, but she was still not entirely comfortable driving, and she crept home, the needle hovering just under thirty. Although home was only a three-mile drive, she felt the journey lasted an eternity.

Option one: If she were pregnant, she would need to return to Boston, meet with Robert, talk about the future.

Option two: If she weren't pregnant, she'd stay in Wisconsin through the New Year, enjoy her family, and return to Boston to start afresh. She would concentrate on her job, rebuild her boss Charles Flintoff's confidence in her. And ensure that she never saw Robert Walker again.

CHAPTER 13

———— ⟨⟨⟨⟩⟩ ————

Stephanie Burroughs waited for the plus sign to appear.

She sat on the edge of the bathtub with the plastic dipstick held delicately in her hands. She was intensely conscious of the moment. She remembered reading somewhere that in one's life there were a very few seminal moments—usually no more than five or six. She wondered if this qualified as one . . . or should it have been the moment she made love to Robert, which had placed her in this position?

The house was quiet. Everyone had gone out for a walk. She could hear floorboards crackling and settling, the water tank filling softly overhead, the hiss and thump as snow slid off the roof onto the ground outside. The bathroom was warm, lightly scented with someone's mint shampoo, and the edge of the bath felt hard and cold beneath her thighs.

If she was pregnant, she would book a flight—no matter how much it cost, no matter what route she had to take—and return home.

If she wasn't pregnant, she'd borrow a pair of boots and the heaviest coat she could find and run and kick her way through the snow. Then she would lie on the ground, and move her arms and legs to create a snow angel.

A positive sign appeared on the stick.

Stephanie looked at it for a long time and abruptly exhaled. She hadn't realized she was holding her breath. Her one overriding emotion surprised her: relief. At least now she knew. She then went downstairs, logged onto her father's computer, and booked a flight back to Boston.

CHAPTER 14

FROM: *stephanieburroughs123@gmail.com*
TO: *robert.walker@R&KProductions.com*
SUBJECT: *Returning to Boston*
Robert,
I'm coming in via Delta leaving Friday 27th (tomorrow), then connecting through Detroit with a flight into Boston, arriving around 9:30 in the morning.
You offered to pick me up. Does that offer still stand?
If you cannot meet me on Saturday, then make time on Sunday. This is important.
Leave an e-mail at this address. I can check it from the airport.
Stephanie.

CHAPTER 15

⬥⬥⬥

Friday, 27th December

Toni and Matt accompanied their daughter to the airport.

Madison's Dane County Regional Airport was just eight miles away, and Stephanie was thrilled she had managed to get the last available seat on a Delta flight to Detroit. The idea of spending another hour and a half in the car driving to Milwaukee with one of her family members suffocated her, and she had opted instead to fly out of the smaller airport, despite the ridiculously long layover she would face in Detroit. Still, she needed to get back to Boston and preferred a quiet overnight in a Detroit hotel to another claustrophobic night in her childhood home.

She saw her mother's head turn and, even before the words were out of her mother's mouth, Stephanie knew what she was going to say.

"Are you sure you have to go, Stephanie?"

"Yes, Mom."

"But you barely got here."

"Well, I did say it was a quick visit. And we did get to spend Christmas Day together."

"Leave her alone, Toni," Matt said.

Stephanie caught a glimpse of her father's eyes in the rearview mirror. He was watching her closely; he alone of all the family knew the real reason she was returning to Boston.

Her mother turned away to stare out to where the fields were giving way to houses. She surreptitiously—but very obviously—brushed tears from her cheeks. "And how are you feeling?" she asked, slightly emphasizing the last word.

"Fine, Mom." Stephanie had thought long and hard about telling her mother the truth about the test, but in the end had decided to keep it a secret for the moment. No doubt her mother had already told the entire family that she suspected Stephanie might be pregnant. She knew that her sudden reappearance home for Christmas had already been one of the main topics of conversation. She needed to get out of this environment, talk to Robert, make some decisions. Only then would she tell her mother, present her with the facts and the decisions.

"I wish you'd stay another couple of days," Toni grumbled. "I was really looking forward to spending New Year's together."

"Well, I've bought tickets," Stephanie said mildly, unwilling to argue.

"Could you change them?"

"The girl's going home, Toni," Matt said quietly.

"Her home is here."

"She's thirty-three now; she's lived away from us almost longer than she lived with us. Boston's her home now. But she knows she can always come back here. Always."

Stephanie saw her father's eyes in the rearview mirror again, and she nodded. He was speaking to Toni, but talking to her.

"Maybe you can visit me. Boston is beautiful in the summer," Stephanie suggested.

"Oh, where would we get the money?" Toni said instantly.

"I'd pay for the tickets."

"If we visit, we'll pay for them," Matt said firmly. His eyes moved to the mirror again. "You should be saving your money. Who knows what the future holds?"

Stephanie propped her chin on her fist and stared out at the approaching airport. She had a very good idea what the future held.

* * *

Although she wanted her parents to simply drop her off, they insisted on parking the car and accompanying her into the airport.

"We've a couple of hours," Toni said, looking at her watch. "Maybe we could get some coffee."

"I really feel I should go through," Stephanie said, nodding toward the check-in gates. "I want to see if I can get on an earlier flight."

"You should go through," Matt said. He turned and handed the car keys to his wife. "You go and sit in the car, and I'll walk Stephanie to the security line."

Toni blinked in surprise, unsure what was happening.

"You know you always get upset at the last minute, so say goodbye now, and then wait in the car for me. You don't want to upset Stephanie, do you?"

Toni Burroughs gave her husband that look that indicated that a full explanation would be required later, but obediently reached up to hug her daughter. "Be careful and travel safe," she said. Liquid danced in her eyes, making them huge. "And call more often. I know you're busy . . . but call."

"I will, Mom. I promise," Stephanie whispered, and kissed her mother's cheek. Holding her close now, she suddenly realized how frail her mother was, and she had the sudden, irrational thought that this would be the last time she'd see her. And now there were tears in Stephanie's eyes too. "I'll call as soon as I get home. I promise."

Stephanie stood with her hand in her father's, while they both watched Toni make her way across the concourse.

"I'm glad you're going back," her father said, surprising her.

"It's the right thing to do." She nodded.

"Take your time. There's no need to make any hasty decisions."

"I know." She took a deep breath and looked around the airport. "You know something, I want—I need—to have everything figured out by next Wednesday."

"New Year's Day?"

"I want to start the New Year with some sort of direction for my life. I just realized I've let things drift over the past couple of years. Even more so since I began my relationship with Robert." She smiled grimly. "Geez, this is a conversation I never imagined I'd be having with my dad."

"I've always loved your spirit, Stef. You remind me of myself when I was your age. You were brave enough to leave—first home, then America. When you backpacked through Spain, I was envious of you. And when you worked in London, I bragged to all of my students that I had an International daughter. Then your promotion in Miami and an even bigger promotion, which brought you back to Boston. You've never allowed anything to hold you back." Matt hugged his daughter close and kissed her forehead. "I've taught in college for more than thirty years now. I've acted as mentor and teacher for my students for most of that time. Nothing surprises me. Over the years, my students have come to me for all different kinds of advice. And they might have thought I was helping them, but in truth, they were helping me too, helping me to understand myself. What I've learned is that you have to face your problems—more is gained from acting than from ignoring the problem and standing still. Say yes more often than you say no. *Yes* keeps you in motion."

Stephanie nodded. "I stood still for the past eighteen months."

"Move on. Go forward. If you're pregnant, then you're moving forward with a baby. Accept that decision. Plan for it." He hugged his daughter again. "Now, you'd better go before your mother comes back to see what's keeping me. And Stephanie, I want you to do something for me."

"Of course."

"I want you to be selfish. I want you to think about what's best for you. And for the baby."

Stephanie nodded.

"You've gone nowhere over the past eighteen months because you were thinking of this man, being considerate of his situation and the world he was in. Now, it's time for him to starting thinking of your situation and the world you're in."

Stephanie nodded again. She knew there were tears on her face, but made no move to brush them off.

"I love you," Matt Burroughs said.

Then he kissed his daughter on the cheek, turned, and walked away.

"Now, go and be selfish!" he called back.

CHAPTER 16

Saturday, 28th December

So how do you greet your ex-lover?

Especially when you're about to bring him life-altering news?

On her layover in Detroit, Stephanie checked into the on-site Westin, showered, ordered room service, watched a pay-per-view movie, and ordered a massage. She wanted to be rested and refreshed for her confrontation ahead. In the morning, she put on a cream silk blouse and accessorized with platinum hoop earrings and a simple twisted-rope necklace, also in platinum. She carefully made herself up, removing the dark bruises from beneath her eyes with concealer, adding a layer of the lipstick that plumped up her lips, and massaging revitalizing cream into the tiny lines that appeared at the corners of her eyes and between her eyebrows. Finally, she dropped in some eyedrops to brighten and refresh her eyes, but the whites were still threaded with tiny broken veins she could do nothing about. When she was finished, she stepped back and looked at herself in the mirror: not bad, not too bad at all.

That's how you meet your ex-lover.

* * *

Stephanie strode out through the arrival gates at Logan and scanned the crowd.

There was no sign of Robert.

Stephanie kept walking, moving away from the throng pushing out from the arrivals area. She stopped by a row of seats and fished out her cell and turned it on, all the time scanning the crowd, looking for Robert.

Her cell blipped, signifying it was active, and she quickly saw that she had one new voice mail. From Izzie.

"Not sure when you're getting back, but just wanted to leave a hello-and-welcome-home message. Hope you had a fab time. Love you."

Stephanie smiled. Izzie could always be trusted to do the right thing. She was surprised she hadn't heard from Robert today.

Tugging her bag, she headed toward the taxi rank.

Maybe her phone call on Wednesday had frightened him. That had certainly been her intention. Maybe he now wanted nothing more to do with her. Funny, she'd thought he was a better man than that, but she'd been mistaken about him before; no reason why she shouldn't be mistaken about this too.

Stephanie stepped out into the crisp Boston air. The December sky was cloudless, the palest of blues, and the watery sunshine shed no heat. There were no taxis at the rank, and she had just resigned herself to a long wait when a taxi pulled in. She flung open the back door, slid her single suitcase onto the seat, and climbed in alongside it.

"Perfect timing." She smiled.

"Your lucky day, lady. Where to?" the cab driver asked in a thick Southie accent.

She gave the driver the address and settled back in the seat. "Someone let me down," she said.

Not for the first time either.

Even though she'd only been gone for a couple of days, Boston looked different. Fresher, brighter, cleaner. Living here, it was easy to forget how full of energy the city was. She remembered a recent article in the *Globe* about Boston residents being among the healthiest in the nation. The article came with a link to an online test that determined one's real age: It measured if one was physiologically older, younger, or the same as his or her chronological age. Stephanie had taken the test and had been three and a half years younger than her years. The report concluded with a list of the "youngest" American cities; Boston came out on top.

"Home with the family for a few days?" the driver asked. He was a pasty-faced man wearing a wool Red Sox cap.

"How can you tell?"

"One bag, which told me you weren't shopping. Then, I heard a Midwestern accent. But you gave the address like a local, so I knew you lived here."

"Right on all counts," she said.

"D'ya have fun?"

"I did," she said, and was surprised to discover that she really meant it. "It was good to see the folks again, and my brothers and sisters."

"Oh, I saw mine on Christmas Day. Once a year is enough for me. Got nothing in common now. As ya get older, ya create ya own family, and they're a lot easier to deal with than blood relatives."

"That's true." If she really were pregnant—and she needed to have it confirmed—who could she go to? She was surprised, and almost disappointed, when she realized just how few friends she had. Izzie Wilson certainly, but beyond that . . . ? There were colleagues of course, but they weren't friends. So if Robert had run scared from her, then she was going to have almost no one to rely on but herself. "Excuse me," she said, and lifted her phone out of the bag. "I've just got to make this call."

"Don't mind me."

She hit the speed dial for Robert's cell. The phone rang and rang before it was diverted to his voice mail.

"You've reached Robert Walker, R&K Productions. Please leave a message, the time you called, and the best number to reach you. Have a good day."

"It's me. I'm back in Boston. Maybe you didn't get my e-mail; maybe you did. Call me." Stephanie hung up and then, on impulse, went into the menu settings on her phone and deactivated the "Send Own Number" facility. Then she phoned the same number again.

The phone rang four times before it was picked up, and Robert's voice, muffled, very soft, said, "Yes?"

"Why didn't you answer my previous call?" she snapped.

"Sorry," he whispered. "The phone was in my inside pocket, and I had to pull my gloves off to unbutton my coat. By the time I got it, you'd gone. I was just putting it back in my pocket when you called again. Sorry."

Stephanie didn't know whether to believe him or not. It was a plausible excuse, but Robert was a good liar: After all, he had fooled his wife for long enough. "Did you get my e-mail, telling you I was coming home?"

"No, no, I haven't checked my messages."

"Bullshit," she snapped. He was permanently wired to his iPhone.

"Honestly." He sighed. "Things have been crazy. Look, I can't talk now. I'll call back later."

"You'd better!" Stephanie wondered exactly where he was. He was whispering, mumbling, and she could hear some background noise, so she knew there were people around.

"I'll talk to you later. I've got to go. I'm at Jimmy Moran's removal."

Stephanie frowned. "What? I can't hear you. What did you say?"

"I said I'm at Jimmy Moran's removal of remains. Jimmy's dead." She could hear the catch in his voice. "He died on Christmas Day."

CHAPTER 17

She'd been gone less than four days, but the apartment smelled stale and empty. She was surprised to find that it felt pleasantly warm, however, which suggested that she had left the heat on the timer. Dropping the suitcase in the living room, she stepped into the kitchen and filled the kettle. She pulled open the fridge and checked inside: As usual, it was almost empty, a half gallon of low-fat organic milk in the tray in the door, alongside an almost empty carton of orange juice and the bottle of champagne she'd planned to open with Robert when they'd something to celebrate. It had sat there for six months now. She lifted out the milk and sniffed cautiously; it smelled fine.

She returned to the living room, deliberately averting her eyes from Robert's Christmas presents, which were still sitting on the floor, and she checked the answering machine that sat on a tiny console table. She'd purposely not called in from Wisconsin to check her messages. The number "4" was illuminated in crude LED letters. How many were from Robert, she wondered as she hit the Play button.

"You have four new messages. New message. Message was left on Tuesday, 24th December."

"Stephanie . . . Stephanie, are you there? It's me. I want to talk to you; I need to talk to you. . . . Please call me back. I'm in the car."

"New message. Message was left on Tuesday, 24th December."

"Stephanie? It's me. I . . . I just need to talk to you. About today. About us. About the future. I know you're angry, but please call me, let me know you're okay."

"*New message.* Message was left on Wednesday, 25th December." "Stephanie. I don't know what's happened. I don't know where you are. It's just after two a.m., and I'm leaving your house. There's no sign of you. I'm leaving this message in the hope that you return, hear it, and answer me. I'm hoping you're with your friend, Izzie. I think I remember you saying that she was supposed to be getting engaged tonight . . . no, last night. My God, I've just realized it's Christmas morning."

"New message. Message was left today, Saturday, 28th December."

"Stef, it's your mother. I just wanted to make sure you got home safely and to see how you were. Give me a call when you get home. It was lovely to see you, even if it was a short visit. The good news is that Joan's husband, Eddie, is coming up for New Year's Eve. She told me you gave her some good advice. So, you see why you should come home more often. Your father sends his love."

"End of messages."

The kettle whistled, and she returned to the kitchen to make tea. Well, in Robert's defense, he had made the effort, and he did seem to be genuinely concerned for her. She rooted through her range of teas, looking for something soothing. In the end she chose a caffeine-free Egyptian Licorice. She wasn't too fond of the taste, but she loved the smell. Cupping the teacup in both hands, breathing in the spicy aroma, she wandered out of the kitchen and into the living room and allowed herself to take in the room, which still bore all the evidence of her terrible encounter with Kathy and Robert. The Christmas presents Robert had brought lay in an unopened pile on the ground. The flowers had wilted in the heat, curled petals everywhere, and the helium balloon lay deflated over the back of the chair.

Stephanie sank into her usual chair and sipped the tea. She looked at the unopened presents he'd brought and felt not the slightest twinge of curiosity about their contents. She'd give them back to Robert the first opportunity she got.

She wondered if Robert's wife had noticed the gold-and-silver-wrapped presents piled behind the sofa when she'd stepped into the room on Tuesday. They were gifts Stephanie had bought for Robert, and now she wondered what she was going to do with them. She certainly wasn't going to give them to him; maybe she could return them.

She glanced at her watch, wondering what time the removal of remains would finish. Would Robert come directly to her, or would he have to drop his wife home first? And if the removal was today, did that mean the funeral would be held tomorrow or Monday?

And then a thought struck her: Would she have to go?

She detested Jimmy Moran, though she'd always moderated her real opinion when Robert was present, because she knew the two men were great friends. Jimmy Moran had built a completely undeserved reputation through a combination of extraordinary arrogance tempered with too little talent.

The last conversation she had with Robert about Jimmy had taken place a week before Christmas. Jimmy's wife, Angela, was finally throwing him out because she'd discovered that he'd had a child by his long-term and much younger mistress, Frances. Angela had put up with a lot from Jimmy over the years—his constant drinking, none-too-discreet affairs, financial difficulties—but that had been the final straw. She was divorcing Jimmy and looking for her share of everything. Stephanie recalled that Robert had been outraged by what he saw as Angela's vindictiveness. He'd been unable to understand Stephanie's support for Jimmy's wife. She'd been surprised, and just a little disappointed, with his reaction. Surely he accepted that Jimmy had treated his wife abominably, and that while he had a duty to his girlfriend and her child, he was also morally and legally obliged to provide for his wife? Stephanie sipped the sweet, aromatic tea, and she wondered how this boded for her own news.

A sudden thought struck her, and she put down her tea and picked up the phone. She dialed a number from memory as she carried her suitcase into the bedroom. The phone rang once before it was picked up, and a brusque, cultured, and very British voice said, "Flintoff."

"Good afternoon, Charles. It's Stephanie . . . Stephanie Burroughs."

"Stephanie, how wonderful to hear from you!" If her boss was surprised, it certainly didn't show in his voice.

"I'm sorry to bother you on a Saturday," she began. She tossed the suitcase on the bed and snapped open the locks. She'd hadn't used half of the clothes she'd packed. Except for Christmas Day when she'd dressed up, she'd worn the clothes she'd left in Wisconsin on her previous visits. She lifted the unworn little black dress and decided she needed to drop it off just up the street at Classic Cleaners before she could wear it again.

"You can call me at any time. That's why I entrusted you with my home number." Charles Flintoff was the man who had discovered Stephanie, and he always treated her as a special protégée, but she knew her relationship with him had been damaged when he had discovered that not only was she having an affair with Robert—a contractor—but that she had awarded R&K Productions with three lucrative contracts. It would take her a long time to rebuild his trust in her.

"Thank you. I'm literally just back—I visited my parents for Christmas," she explained, also letting him know that she had not spent Christmas with Robert, "and I've just found out that Jimmy Moran died on Christmas Day. I wasn't sure if you knew."

There was a pause. Then Charles Flintoff cleared his throat. "No, I didn't. Thank you for telling me. Jimmy Moran—I got to know him when I first opened the Irish branch of the agency. We even worked together on a couple of campaigns, and of course I saw him all the time at various events, though I haven't used him in a long time. Poor Jimmy. So much talent and good, creative energy. Wasted. Do you know anything about the funeral arrangements?"

"The removal of the remains happened today, but I have no idea when the funeral will take place."

"Probably not tomorrow." She heard the sound of a page turning and guessed he was checking a calendar. "Monday or Tuesday." He sighed. "I should go and represent the firm. The funeral will be well attended. Despite his faults, or perhaps because of them, Jimmy had a lot of friends. I'd imagine some of his enemies will turn up too—just to make sure the old reprobate is in the ground." He paused. "If you have no other plans, perhaps you'd like to represent the firm with me?"

"Yes . . . yes, I would. Thank you." She was surprised by the offer, pleased too.

"Call me when you have the details. Now, if you've just come back from visiting your family, you probably need some rest."

"I'm going to do that now. Thank you."

Charles Flintoff hung up, and Stephanie sat on the edge of the bed, cradling the phone, wondering what he would say when she told him that she was pregnant.

And that reminded her . . .

She needed to get to her doctor. Would anyone be open over the weekend? Probably not. Maybe Izzie could convince one of her OB friends over at Mass General to examine her. She was just about to call Izzie when the wan afternoon sunlight flashed across the windshield of a car as it approached across the courtyard and pulled up outside the building.

Stephanie darted into the living room, scooped up the dead flowers, gathered up the curled and brittle petals, carried them into the kitchen, and dumped them in the trash. Then she grinned; now, if that wasn't a symbolic gesture, then she didn't know what was. She wondered if he would use his key or . . .

The doorbell rang.

CHAPTER 18

"Hi, Stef."

Robert's appearance shocked her. He looked terrible, skin pale and lightly sheened with sweat; his hair was greasy, and there were deep bags under his bloodshot eyes. His black suit was rumpled and creased. There was a dark stain around the collar of his pale blue shirt, and the knot on his pale charcoal silk tie—one she had bought him—was dark where grubby fingers had tugged it. When he stepped past her, she caught the faintest odor of stale perspiration. And that shocked her more than anything else: Robert was, if nothing else, fastidiously clean.

Stephanie closed the door behind him, took a deep breath to calm her suddenly thundering heart, and followed him up the stairs into her apartment, into the living room. She found him standing beside the chair, looking down at the Christmas presents he'd brought last Tuesday.

"It's good to see you again," he said, his voice flat, emotionless.

Stephanie nodded, unsure what to say. She finally fell back on the old reliable. "Would you like some tea or coffee or something stronger?"

"Tea would be great, thank you."

Stephanie disappeared into the kitchen, and Robert took up his usual position, leaning against the entrance to the kitchen, arms folded across his chest. It looked as if he was trying to hold himself upright. As she filled the kettle with water from the Brita pitcher, she was aware that he was watching her.

"You got back this morning?" he said finally.

"A couple of hours ago," she said shortly.

"I'm sorry I wasn't there to meet you. . . . Believe it or not, I didn't check my e-mails."

"I believe it," she said evenly.

"Flight was okay?"

"Fine. I booked a last-minute ticket and came in via Detroit, so I had to stay overnight, but I checked into the Westin and treated myself to a massage so I was able to relax a bit."

"Good. Good."

Stephanie found a cup for herself and a mug for Robert—he preferred mugs to cups—and hoped she had enough milk for the tea. It was low-fat, which he hated, but he would have to make do with it. Looking into the fridge, watching him out of the corner of her eye, she asked, "How was the removal? Were there many people there?"

"Yes. I was surprised by how many. Shocked. I think Jimmy would have been too. He made a lot of enemies over the years, but far more friends it seems. They all came out today." His voice broke then, and Stephanie saw him fumble in his pockets for a handkerchief.

The water in the kettle started to boil, and Stephanie concentrated on making the tea, deliberately not turning around, not wanting to look at him with tears on his face. She had imagined this moment a dozen times since she had decided to come back to Boston; she had rehearsed her speech, first in Madison, then on the plane to Detroit, and then again at the airport hotel, and knew exactly how she would handle this encounter. She would be cool, controlled, as unemotional as she could be. There would be no recriminations. They—she and Robert—had a situation to resolve, and all they were talking about was the most practical and logical way to go about it. That was the plan. But from the moment she had seen him standing on the doorstep, looking sick with exhaustion, she'd felt her resolve start to slip away. And now, listening to him trying to compose himself and not show emotion, to do that stupid thing men did, she felt all her carefully thought-out plans begin to fragment. And she suddenly—unaccountably—felt guilty that she'd been so hard with him earlier.

"Tea's ready."

He'd managed to compose himself by the time she turned and passed over to him the steaming mug of tea.

"I've added two sugars."

"Sorry," he mumbled. "Been an intense few days; I haven't had much sleep." He followed her into the living room, taking up his usual position on the couch facing her.

Stephanie made herself another cup of tea. She cradled the tiny porcelain cup in the palms of her hands and sipped. "Tell me what happened?" she asked. Although she really wanted to discuss her current situation, she recognized that he needed someone to talk to. She raised her cup to hide her wry smile. That was how their affair started eighteen months ago. Robert had simply needed someone to talk to.

Robert took a moment to answer. "I got a call on Christmas Day . . . not long after yours. Jimmy Moran had been taken to the hospital with a suspected heart attack. I immediately went to see him. Oh, Stef, he looked terrible. . . ." Robert breathed deeply and took a mouthful of tea. "He was awake. He said that at first he was trying to make light of it, thinking it was nothing more than indigestion. He had been cooking his own Christmas dinner and had sampled the turkey. When he got the pains, he thought that maybe the bird hadn't been cooked through. It was when he felt the pain move into his left arm that he realized it was serious and dialed 911. But it was Christmas Day, and it took the ambulance forever to arrive."

Robert sipped a little more of the hot tea. His eyes glazed, and Stephanie became aware that he was reliving the events of Wednesday.

"They'd put him in a private room. He looked old, so old and frail . . . and the moment I saw him, I knew he wasn't going to make it. It was almost as if he'd given up. The spark had gone. Turned out he'd tried calling Angela, but she wasn't taking his calls, nor was Frances. He asked me to contact Angela. She spoke to me, but she wouldn't come in to see him. She was finished with him, she said. He'd broken her heart with his lies and his affairs, and she was afraid that this was just another one of his tricks."

Robert fell silent. Stephanie could see the muscle twitching along his jawline and the sudden welling of tears in his eyes.

"I called Frances," he continued, his voice barely above a whisper. "She wouldn't come either. They'd had a fight, and she'd thrown him out. I think she thought it was a trick too. She told me that he was incredibly manipulative, and that this was just an act to get sympathy."

"So you stayed with him?" Stephanie asked.

"I stayed with him throughout the day and into the night until . . . until he died," he finished simply. "He died." There were tears on his cheeks now, but he seemed unaware of them. "He squeezed my hand and then . . ." He drew in a deep, sobbing breath.

"I'm sorry, Robert. So sorry." It took an enormous effort of will to remain seated in the chair. She had the urge to go to him, wrap her arms around his shoulders, and comfort him, but she knew that would be a mistake. "I know you and Jimmy were very close."

And Stephanie abruptly realized why Jimmy's death had affected Robert so strongly. Although he had three brothers, they were all estranged. Robert's parents had separated when he was fourteen, and he had gone to stay with his mother. He rarely mentioned his father, who had died fifteen years ago, and when he did, the comments were always tinged with bitterness and regret. Jimmy Moran had been Robert's mentor, friend, and father figure.

"He died alone, Stephanie," Robert said very softly.

"Not alone. You were there."

"But his wife . . . his mis . . . his girlfriend should have been there. Someone more . . . more significant than me. Someone who loved him."

"You loved him, Robert," Stephanie said firmly. "In the same way that he was very significant to you, then you too must have played a significant part in his life. Why else would he call you when he went into the hospital?"

Robert nodded. "Yes, yes, you're right. Thank you for reminding me." He finished his tea in one quick swallow and put the cup on the floor. "I'm sorry, I guess I'm all over the place. Since everything that happened here on Tuesday"—he waved his hand around the room—"then frantically looking for you, then your call on Wednesday, and then Jimmy's death, it's just been an incredibly emotional time."

"Yes, I can see that. And Christmas is the most stressful time of the year too."

He attempted a smile. "There were times I thought I was having a heart attack myself." He pressed the palm of his right hand against his chest. "I think it was just stress."

"You should get it checked out, just in case," she said immediately. Then she stopped, realizing what she was doing: She was assuming responsibility for him.

"Jimmy was fifty-two—only three years older than I am."

"He lived a completely different lifestyle," she reminded Robert.

"Not that different," Robert said quickly, unable to disguise the note of bitterness in his voice.

"He smoked."

"He did. And he liked rich food," Robert added.

"And he drank," Stephanie reminded him, "a lot more than you."

"Yes, Jimmy did that too. I'm only sorry now that we didn't get a chance to have that meal at Top of the Hub before Christmas. We had drinks around the corner in the Union Oyster House instead— You suggested that, remember? That was the last time I saw him until . . . until I saw him in the hospital on Christmas Day."

"At least you had the chance to see him."

Robert nodded. "Yes. I'm glad I did."

"Would you like some more tea?" Stephanie asked, filling the long silence that followed.

"Yes. Thank you." He picked his mug up off the floor, handed it across, then sank back onto the sofa, resting his head on the back of the cushion and closing his eyes.

Stephanie stepped back into the kitchen. She was unsure what to do: let him talk out his thoughts and feelings for Jimmy or raise the subject of her pregnancy? But she wanted him clear-headed when she was talking about that, and right now he was simply too emotional. As she filled the kettle again, she called out, "Jimmy's life was also incredibly stressful, and I can guarantee you he never exercised." Other than the horizontal kind, she thought, but didn't say aloud. She thought she heard Robert grunt in assent, and she continued on. "Plus, the whole situation with Angela and Frances must have taken its toll on him, and I'm sure the prospect of the looming divorce just added to the stress level."

There was no reply.

Stephanie turned and looked into the living room. Robert had shifted sideways on the couch, his head tilted onto his shoulder. He had fallen asleep sitting up. She replaced the kettle, but didn't switch it on, and returned to her chair. She sat down and watched Robert. Even in sleep the exhausted lines around his eyes and mouth didn't relax, and she could see his eyes darting madly beneath the closed lids. She wondered what dreams haunted him.

The events of the past few days twisted in the back of her mind, assuming a dreamlike quality all of their own. From the moment Kathy Walker had appeared on Christmas Eve and slapped her across the face, everything had just spun out of control. Even though she'd only been back home a couple of hours, her quick visit to Wisconsin was beginning to fade and recede into memory, and she was already beginning to feel like she'd never been away. Stephanie was concerned for Robert too; he looked like he might keel over at any moment, a combination of the high emotion of the past few days, too little sleep, and, she imagined, little or no food.

As she looked out the window, a shape passed below. Then she realized it was Mrs. Moore, the nosy neighbor whose condo was directly beneath hers. The old woman glanced up, and she managed a weak wave. It was impossible for anyone to see up into the window, but Stephanie still wondered what the scene must look like from outside: the woman curled up on the chair, the man dozing on the couch.

The irony of it was, of course, that she'd sometimes imagined a scene very much like this: It was from sometime in the future when Robert left his wife and Stephanie and Robert were living together. He'd come home from work, sit on the sofa, and nap. In her fantasy, the house would be warm and welcoming, smelling of baked bread or roasting meat. Some jazz—Etta James or Louis Armstrong—would be murmuring on the stereo. The couple would eat and talk, and he would tell her about his day, and she would fill him in on her activities. Then they would have a bath, and go to bed, making love into the evening before falling asleep comfortably wrapped around one another.

The reality had turned out to be different: While the house was warm, it smelled stale and slightly bitter with the scent of the desiccated flowers and just the hint of Robert's perspiration. There was no music, no sounds except Robert's shallow breathing.

Leaning forward, she propped her elbows on her knees, rested her chin on her fists, and looked at his face. He looked old and tired; he looked beaten. He was a workaholic, and the stress of trying to run a business was finally taking a toll on his body. If he kept working this obscene schedule, he would be dead in a few years. Just like Jimmy. And she did not want that to happen. Earlier that week she'd let him go, allowed him to return to his wife. But that didn't mean that she'd stopped loving him.

Stephanie knew that she still loved Robert . . . but Kathy loved him too. And Robert . . . ? Well, only Robert knew whom Robert truly loved. He said he loved her; he'd even proposed to her. But in this very room, last Tuesday, when his wife had asked him if he still loved her, he'd replied "Yes."

Nothing had changed since then.

Robert twitched and moaned in his uneasy sleep, and Stephanie suddenly realized that she had again, unconsciously, placed the palm of her hand across her stomach.

No: Everything had changed.

Last Tuesday, she hadn't known that she might be pregnant. She wasn't the sort of woman who was going to try to use the baby to trap Robert. He was the father, and she expected him to help her support the child. But if he was the man she thought he was, she would hope he would want to do more than just provide financial support. She hoped he would want to spend time with her and the child. His two children by Kathy were teenagers. Would they need him as much as a newborn? And even if he did leave Kathy and live with her, that didn't mean that he was never going to see his children again.

The thought stopped her cold.

That was the first time since the argument on Tuesday that she had allowed herself to even consider the possibility that he would want to leave Kathy for her.

Would she want him? Even after all that had happened?

Before she could work out an answer, Robert's phone rang, the sound shockingly loud in the stillness of the room, and she jumped. Robert mumbled, and slowly, groggily came awake. He blinked, trying to focus, obviously unsure where he was. Then he groped for the cell. "Hello . . . ," he began, then licked dry lips and tried again, "Hello . . ."

Even before he spoke the next sentence, Stephanie knew who was calling. She saw the look in his eyes—a combination of guilt and fear—before his entire expression turned shifty.

"Kathy . . . Yes, I'm fine. I'm at the office . . ." His eyes found Stephanie's face and darted away. "Yes, I'll be home soon." He hung up.

"Why did you lie?" Stephanie wondered aloud.

Robert straightened in the chair and coughed. "Well, I could hardly tell her the truth, now could I?"

"You could have said we had some unfinished business." She smiled, without humor.

"I promised Kathy I would never see you again."

"And yet you're breaking that promise," Stephanie said evenly.

"Well, I made that promise before . . . before I knew about . . . about you and . . . and . . ."

"About my being pregnant?"

"Yes. That."

Stephanie stood. "I'm going to make that tea now. Why don't you go grab a shower. I need you awake and alert when we talk, and right now you're barely conscious. You've got some clothes in the closet, and there's a toothbrush and a razor of yours in the bathroom cabinet. Shower and change; you'll feel much better."

"Yes, I will, thank you." He stood up and obviously caught a hint of his own stale sweat. "Gosh, I stink."

"Yes, you do," Stephanie said. And in more ways than one, she thought as she turned away quickly, before he could see the grimace on her face.

CHAPTER 19

She found him lying asleep on her bed, wrapped in her red flannel bathrobe. She stood and looked at him for a long time, trying to iron out her conflicting emotions. She wanted to make sure that the feelings she'd had for this man—still had—were not now colored by the pregnancy. And yet she knew they must be.

She had nothing but respect for those women who—either by choice or circumstances—brought up children on their own. It would be tough; she had no illusions about that. She would have to make changes in just about every area of her life—but she would make them. She might even have to sell the condo; she realized now she should never have converted the smaller second bedroom into a luxurious bathroom.

But if she had Robert's support, it would be a lot easier. He was working in a job that gave him great flexibility in his working regime and hours. He could work from home and look after the child while she returned to her job in the agency. It would make financial sense for her to continue working; she earned much more than he did.

Placing the hot tea on the bedside table, she opened the closet and took out a thick duvet that she gently spread over him. Then, turning off the light, she stepped out of the bedroom and allowed him to sleep.

"Robert? Robert?"

Robert Walker opened his eyes and looked around. And, for the first time since he'd appeared on her doorstep, he smiled. "Hi . . ."

"Hi."

Then the smile faded as his eyes moved toward the curtains, which were pulled against the night outside. "My God, how long have I been asleep?"

"A few hours. It's almost nine."

He jumped out of bed. "I've got to go. . . ."

"You've got to eat," Stephanie said firmly. She was sitting on the edge of the bed with a tray in her hands. It held a broad, flat pizza flanked by a bottle of ginger ale and two glasses. "I ordered from Zesto's. My fridge was empty, and I didn't want to leave you."

Robert looked at the ham and pineapple pizza and started to shake his head, but she distinctly heard his stomach rumble. "Just a slice then," he said with a wry grin.

They ate in companionable silence.

Although Stephanie poured herself a glass of soda, she barely touched it; her stomach was aching.

When Robert picked up his fourth slice, she smiled. "When did you last eat?" she wondered aloud.

He shook his head. "I've grabbed a few bites on the run. When Jimmy . . . when Jimmy died, I was left to make the funeral arrangements and contact his family. Two of his three brothers are coming home. They're spread all over the world: Lloyd is in Australia, Mikey's in Canada, and Teddy's in New York. I spoke to Mikey, the oldest. He told me to go ahead with the removal, but to delay the funeral until they arrived."

"When will the funeral take place?"

"Monday the thirtieth, at Forest Hills Cemetery."

"That's just a few blocks from here."

"I know. Teddy and Mikey are coming in tomorrow morning, but Lloyd's not going to be able to make it."

"That's a shame."

"True, but they've never been close. Jimmy never really told me the full story, but I know he went to live with his mother when the family broke up, while the older brothers chose to live with his father. When his parents separated, it destroyed all their lives and shattered the family. Almost exactly like my own experience." He glanced up at Stephanie and smiled that shy smile that always tugged at her heart. "I'm sorry; I've done nothing but talk about me. Tell me what you did over Christmas. You went home?"

Stephanie nodded. She lifted the tray and moved around the room to put it on the nightstand. Then she leaned back against the windowsill and folded her arms. "I went home. It was a last-minute rush, and I had to go via Chicago and Milwaukee, but I made it back late on Christmas Eve, and I'm glad I went. It was good to see Mom and Dad again. They're getting old, Dad especially. I know people say that time slips by—It doesn't; it races. I'm going to try to get home regularly, maybe every second or third month, to keep in touch with them."

"That's a good idea." Robert pushed away the duvet and slid his legs out over the edge of the bed. "I really should be going." He tugged on his underwear, pulled on his socks, and stepped into his trousers.

For a few moments, Stephanie was shocked speechless, then she exploded. "Hang on a second! We've talked about everything but the most important thing: us. Me. And the fact that I'm probably pregnant."

He opened the closet and pulled out one of the shirts he'd left there, then turned to her as he buttoned it up. "How sure are you?"

"Sure?"

"Sure that you're pregnant."

"Almost positive. I'm nearly two weeks late now."

"Did you do a test?"

"Yes. It came back positive. That's why I came home."

He nodded as he tucked his shirt into his pants, and Stephanie realized that he was doing everything but looking her in the eye. "So, let's say you are. What are you going to do about it?"

Stephanie came off the window ledge to stand directly in front of Robert. "What do you mean by that?"

He blinked in surprise. "I mean, you can't seriously be thinking of having it?"

Having it. It. It. Stephanie felt the single slice of pizza she'd eaten curdle in her stomach. "Of course I am," she whispered.

"But you can't. You've got this place . . . and then there's your job. You can't have all that and a baby."

"I could if I had a partner."

Robert concentrated on his cuffs. "If I'm the father of this child . . ."

She cracked him across the face, the force of the blow snapping his head to one side. For an instant something dark and ugly flared in his eyes, and she thought he was going to hit her back. "How dare you! You are the father. There's been no one else!"

"I'm sorry," he said, drawing in a deep breath, pressing the palm of his hand to his stinging cheek. "I'm sorry. I didn't mean to imply anything. It just came out wrong," he protested, but she didn't believe him.

Stephanie looked at him, saying nothing.

"I mean, let's be logical about this. I don't want to start again." She could hear him begging, emotion and fear driving each successive plea. Was he trying to convince her, or himself? "C'mon," he pleaded. "You don't either. You're on the corporate ladder—a child would stop that dead. Neither of us can afford to have a screaming baby in our lives." There was a pause, and he added grimly, "And what would I tell Kathy and the kids?"

She was seeing the real Robert for the first time. She was seeing the selfish, self-obsessed, arrogant bastard that he was. She didn't want to think it, didn't want to believe it, but the bitter conclusion now was that he'd only ever been interested in her for sex and the work she could bring to his ailing firm. She watched him now, mouth moving, words forming, and she knew with soul-chilling certainty what he was going to suggest.

"I'll pay for the abortion of course. And we'll go on with our lives." Robert smiled, but it was an artificial, patronizing curl of his lips, with no real emotion behind it.

When she spoke, her voice was so low it was barely audible. "Get out."

Robert attempted his quizzical smile again. "Well, what do you think?"

And then she screamed, the sound shocking them both. "Get out! Get out! Get out!"

Robert backed away from her. Stephanie reached for the nearest item—the pizza plate—and flung it at him. It missed and shattered against the wall, leaving a bloody smear of sauce.

"You bastard!" she gasped, suddenly breathless. "You bastard!"

"Stephanie . . . I'm just suggesting . . ."

"You've got a key to this house. Give it to me," she demanded. She reached into the closet and tore his other shirt off the hanger and flung it at him. She pulled his tie off its hanger, the silk catching and ripping on the metal, then snatched up his black patent-leather shoes and threw them across the room.

"Stephanie."

"Give me the key. Give it to me!" The vehemence in her voice frightened her.

Robert tugged the key off his key ring and dropped it on the bed. "Let's talk. I know you're upset—"

"Upset? I am way beyond upset. We're finished," she said icily. "Don't you ever speak to me again." There were tears in her eyes now, but she was determined not to cry. "I loved you. I loved you with all my heart. Now, I see you for what you are: an egotistical, arrogant bastard. This isn't a problem to be solved; this is a life and a future we're talking about. And you think an abortion will solve everything! A quick abortion, then we go on as if nothing has happened? I hate you, Robert. No, more than that. I despise you. Now get out. And don't come back. Don't ever come back."

She watched him, eyes blazing, arms folded across her heaving breasts, as he backed out of the room, and then she heard his feet on the stairs. It was only when she heard the door slam and then, minutes later, the car reverse away, that she allowed herself to lie back on the bed and cry, huge, heaving, racking sobs that took her breath away.

And buried deep among the other emotions, among the fear and loathing, the disgust and anger was another: relief. She was glad she was finished with him.

She was glad it was over.

Finally.

Book 2

The Husband's Story

I was glad Kathy knew, glad that the lies could now end, glad that we could both move on.

But then . . .

I'm not exactly sure what happened. The woman I was sure didn't love me claimed that she did, and the woman who claimed to love me pushed me away . . . as if she didn't want me anymore.

I realized I'd been given a second chance with my wife, a chance to make a new start, a chance to begin again.

But . . .

My relationship with Stephanie had given me a glimpse of how my life could be different.

So different.

CHAPTER 20

Tuesday, 24th December
Christmas Eve

His affair had been discovered.

When he'd stepped into that room and found Kathy standing there, it had taken him a couple of seconds to process exactly what he was seeing. There was no possible way that Kathy should be standing in Stephanie's living room. It was just *wrong*. And yet there they were: his wife and his mistress, standing together with identical expressions on their faces.

The pieces fell together quickly—especially when Kathy stepped forward and hit him across the face. He ran his tongue over the raw, chipped edge of his tooth. In the eighteen years they'd been married, she'd never raised her hand to him. He rubbed the palm of his hand against his jaw; she packed a fairly good punch too!

Kathy knew.

Initially, he had thought that Stephanie had contacted Kathy. She'd been putting him under increasing pressure of late to make a decision. She wanted him to choose—his wife or his lover. He knew that Christmas was a particularly hard time for her . . . but what Stephanie seemed to forget was that it was an equally difficult time for him. Stephanie wanted him to spend time with her, while he wanted to take the time to be with his children. They grew up so quickly—Brendan was seventeen already, and Theresa was fifteen— who knew how many more Christmases they would want to spend at home? Robert's own parents had separated when he was fourteen, and he remembered that first Christmas after the breakup of their marriage, sitting at home with his mother, a ragged artificial tree in the corner and the fire leaking smoke into the room, a hissing radio playing back-to-back Christmas carols. When his father and three brothers had left a few weeks earlier, his father had taken away the television set, and his mother had been too proud to admit any of this to either her sister or her neighbors. It had been a miserable Christmas—the first of several. But the one feeling that remained with him, the single abiding memory he had of that entire week, was the sense of loss. He missed his father. He was determined that his own children would never experience the same emotion. He was not going to leave his wife at Christmastime. But Stephanie was childless and couldn't understand that.

Robert got into his Audi, pulled out of the driveway, and eased onto the Jamaicaway. His hands were still shaking. He was grateful that the heavy traffic would slightly delay him. He needed time to think, to process what had just happened.

When he'd stepped into that room and discovered Kathy and Stephanie together, he had thought he was going to have a heart attack or throw up. Or both.

But Stephanie hadn't revealed the affair to Kathy; his wife had discovered it for herself. He didn't know how; maybe someone had spotted him out with Stephanie. But he'd always been careful, so careful. When he'd gone out to dinner with Stephanie, they always dined in restaurants in the steadily gentrifying south side of the city, where there was less chance of meeting any of his Brookline neighbors. Or they went to some of the hip new restaurants in the Financial District, where Kathy and her friends would never go. When they stayed away overnight together, it was always in an anonymous little hotel somewhere a few hours away on the coast, Portland, Maine, or the Cape, and Stephanie made and paid for the reservation in her name, so there would be no record on his credit card.

When he'd begun his affair with Stephanie, he'd justified these precautions as a way not only of protecting both of their reputations, but as a way of protecting Kathy. The last thing he wanted to do was to hurt her.

That must be it, he decided: Someone had seen them together and told Kathy. He remembered now the traces of suspicion he'd picked up in her voice recently. He was supposed to have had dinner with his old friend and colleague Jimmy Moran last week, but somehow the reservation at Top of the Hub had never been made. Kathy had quizzed him about it none too subtly. He remembered now that she'd even come into town that night and promised to drop by the restaurant.

She'd been checking up on him!

For how long had she suspected? And what exactly had she found out? Had she seen him with Stephanie? He knew that he acted differently when he was in Stephanie's company; he was more relaxed, more cheerful; he even felt younger. He tried to remember the last time he'd been out with Stephanie. It hadn't been recently. December was such a crazy month, and they'd both been extremely busy. He'd visited her at her condo, but no one really knew him there. Maybe someone in the business had spoken to Kathy? Only last week Jimmy Moran had told him that one of his rivals, Simon Farmer—sniveling little bastard that he was—had been spreading rumors that the only reason R&K Productions had received three major contracts from Flintoff's agency was because Robert was involved with their senior accounts manager, who awarded the contracts. The problem was, the rumor was true. Plus the business Stephanie brought his company had kept it afloat through a very difficult period. Was there any chance that Farmer had contacted Kathy out of spite?

All she would have needed would have been the barest hint to excite her suspicions. Kathy had suspected him of having an affair with Stephanie Burroughs years ago when he had first employed her. He'd never been so shocked, so startled in his life than when

Kathy had accused him. The irony, of course, was that it hadn't been true then.

If Kathy's old suspicions had been reignited, then this time she would have found they were fully justified. Once her suspicions had been roused, then she would have been watching him like a hawk, no doubt checking up on his excuses like any suspicious spouse. Also, he had to admit that lately he'd been just a little bit too casual with his lies. In the early days of his affair, he'd concocted elaborate, intricate fictions, based around potential contracts, meetings with possible clients, business seminars—anything that would take him away from home and allow him to spend time with Stephanie. More recently, however, he'd fallen back on those old reliable half-truths: overtime and pressure of work.

Not that it mattered too much anymore. With the affair out in the open, he felt an extraordinary sense of relief. No doubt he would discover how she'd found out when they finally got some time to themselves to talk. He grimaced with the thought; he was not relishing that conversation. He still didn't know how much Kathy knew and was unsure how much to reveal. But he knew he had hurt her enough, and he owed her the courtesy of the truth. If they were to start over, then he had to come clean. He'd tell her everything. Well, almost everything.

Robert crept along as Jamaicaway turned into Riverway, and he turned onto Huntington Avenue heading toward his home.

He'd told Kathy he wanted to come back; he'd told her he wanted to start again. He'd told her that he loved her. And he meant it, all of it. He'd never stopped loving her.

The only problem was that he also loved Stephanie Burroughs.

He made a quick U-turn. There was someone he needed to see before he would be able to talk to Kathy.

CHAPTER 21

Maureen Ryan was in her mid-sixties, but could easily have passed for fifty. She was a tall, masculine-looking woman, and her sharp features were dominated by almost translucent eyes and a shock of white hair that she wore in a single tight braid that hung to the small of her back. She had manned the front desk of R&K Productions right from the very beginning, and in that time she had come to regard Robert as the son she would never have and Kathy as the daughter she wished she'd had. The moment she opened the door and found Robert standing on the doorstep, Maureen knew that something was amiss.

"This is a surprise," she said carefully, standing back to allow him to step into the hall.

"I've been promising to come out and see you forever," he said, "but it's just been so manic." He gave her a polite hug. "Merry Christmas."

"I know what December's like; there's no need to apologize." Maureen had been on sick leave for the past month, and although Robert called at first and subsequently e-mailed her on several occasions—usually to ask questions about contracts and appointments—he'd never gotten around to visiting her.

"I'm sorry for dropping in unannounced."

"I'm delighted to see you." Maureen's tone suggested she was anything but delighted. If she'd known he was coming, she would have changed out of the off-white tracksuit that was too misshapen to do her figure any favors and slippers that had seen their best days at least five years ago. "You want some sherry?" she asked, leading him out into the circular conservatory that had been built onto the back of the house.

"I'd love a coffee, please. There are a lot of police cars on the roads, and I don't want to risk getting a DUI." He looked around the conservatory. "I like what you've done with this." R&K Productions had been commissioned to shoot a pilot for a reality makeover show a couple of years ago, and they had used Maureen's house for it, adding a conservatory to the rear of the property. Although the show had never sold, the conservatory turned out to be a huge success. "You've put in a new floor," he said.

"It got so hot in here that the original wood warped and buckled, so I replaced the floor and added the blinds," she said as she went into the kitchen.

Robert sat down in one of the enormous fan-backed white wicker chairs and breathed in soothing smoke curling from a slender purple candle. He thought it might be lavender. There was a book opened on the circular glass table, and he absently spun it around to read the title; it was a Stephen King book called *On Writing*. Robert thought that was an odd title for a horror novel.

Maureen appeared, carrying a wicker tray that held two bright green, Celtics-themed mugs featuring a cartoon leprechaun spinning a basketball, a tiny milk jug, and a small bowl filled with sugar cubes. Robert stood to take the tray, and Maureen set out the mugs, milk, and sugar on the table. She sat down in the wicker chair opposite Robert.

"So, why are you really here?"

Robert sat, facing her, and fixed a smile on his face. He was conscious that it had been only last week he'd talked with Stephanie about the possibility of letting the older woman go. But with Kathy back in the picture now, he knew that would never happen. "I really am sorry I haven't been around. . . ." he began.

Maureen held up her right hand, palm out. "Don't be. How's the temp—the Russian girl—working out?"

Robert shrugged. "I ask her to do something, then I end up doing it myself. It'll be good to have you back. You are coming back?"

"If you'll have me." Maureen smiled humorlessly.

"Of course—of course, there's no question about that. There would be no R&K Productions without you; you know that."

Maureen had spent twenty-five years in the city of Boston film bureau as a production assistant, before she went freelance. Her connections in the business were second to none, and everyone expected her to end up with one of the big independents; instead she had opted for the unknown start-up company. Her presence with R&K Productions lent it credibility in those early days when Robert and Kathy had been fighting to establish themselves.

"Do you have any idea when you might be back?" Robert asked.

"Early in the New Year, I'd imagine. Why?"

"No reason. I'll just need to give Illona notice."

"I'll be back when the doctor gives me the all-clear." Maureen sipped her coffee, carefully watching Robert. Waiting for him to broach the subject she knew he had really come to talk about.

Robert reached into his inside jacket pocket and produced a slim white envelope, which he laid on the table and pushed toward her. "A little Christmas bonus," he said, feeling vaguely embarrassed.

Maureen blinked in surprise. "I wasn't expecting anything," she said truthfully. "And especially not having been out sick for so long."

"I'm just happy I'm in a position to do it. There were a couple of months there in the summer when I really thought we were in trouble."

Maureen nodded. Out of force of habit, she added milk and two sugars to Robert's coffee and pushed it back toward him. She knew that this had been a particularly difficult year for R&K; at one stage, she'd even considered sending out her résumé. However she knew, if she did that, then word would get around the business, and R&K would be finished.

"If Stephanie hadn't managed to get us those jobs..." he added.

Something in his voice alerted Maureen, and she looked up quickly. "Is there a problem?"

"No," he began, then nodded. "Yes," he admitted.

"The DaBoyz contract?" she guessed.

"No, that's okay." DaBoyz was a boy band indistinguishable from any other boy band, but hoping to stand out with a cutting-edge music video. Stephanie had managed to steer DaBoyz' manager toward R&K Productions on the basis of a couple of sharp advertisements they had shot for her agency. "That contract is fine. I met with the band and their manager last week. They really like the new ideas, and it looks like we'll shoot in Hawaii early in the New Year."

"Great. Once that's in the can and aired, we're bound to get other music videos. And that's where the real money is nowadays."

"I know. Plus, I think we might get the new Zipcar ad, and I've just pitched for the new Sam Adams campaign. I think we have a very good chance."

"So what's the problem?" Maureen wondered.

"I... spoke to Stephanie recently. Apparently she won't be able to put any more work our way. Some people have begun to question why our company is getting so many contracts.... She had a difficult conversation with Flintoff, her boss. I think he told her: No more work for R&K."

Maureen sat back into the wicker chair. She stared at Robert over the rim of the brightly painted mug. "I know Charles Flintoff," she offered. "I know him well. I could speak to him."

"Thanks, but I don't think so. Not right now at least."

"What are you not telling me, Robert?"

Robert tasted his coffee, grimaced, and added another sugar cube. "I've been... involved with Stephanie Burroughs for a little while now. Romantically involved. It's one of the reasons we've gotten so much work. Some people in the business have started to gossip about it, and Charles Flintoff knows about the affair." He could feel some of the knot of tension ease as he confessed to Maureen. Maybe that old saying was true: Confession was good for the soul. He looked across the table toward her, unsure how she would take the news. Maureen was no stranger to the gossip pages of the Sunday newspapers and magazines; she had been romantically linked to several minor politicians and a B-list movie star. When the silence stretched unbearably, he said, "Well, say something."

"Say what? You're not telling me something I didn't know."

"You knew!"

"I've known for about a year."

Robert stared at the woman, mouth opening and closing. He thought he'd been so careful. "And you didn't say anything?"

"What exactly did you expect me to say, Robert?" Maureen smiled icily. "You're a big boy. I presume you're telling me this now because Kathy knows."

Robert nodded miserably.

"Do you know she came to see me last Saturday?"

"She mentioned it."

"She told me straight out that she suspected that you and Stephanie Burroughs were having an affair."

"And you told her!" Robert said, unable to keep the snap of anger out of his voice.

"She told me," Maureen said firmly. "She came to me straight from the office, where she'd just gone through the phone records."

Robert stared at Maureen in horror. "She was checking the phone bills. . . . Why?" he whispered.

"I imagine she was looking for proof. And she found it. She saw that your first call of the day and your last call at night were always to the same number. It didn't take a rocket scientist to figure out what was going on. I don't know how she connected the number to Stephanie—maybe she called it. The phone bills were the final confirmation she needed." Maureen put her coffee down. "You made the mistake of underestimating Kathy. And you got a little greedy."

"Greedy?" He tried to swallow, but his mouth was dry. How long had Kathy been checking up on him? It made him feel almost physically queasy, to think that someone was spying on him, checking up on his every move.

"Greedy," Maureen said. "Why didn't you get a pay-as-you-go phone and use that? No bills, no records. No, you wanted to be able to claim the calls as a business expense."

"I never thought . . . ," he muttered.

"So now Kathy knows. I take it she's spoken to you about this."

"I've just seen her . . . and Stephanie," he added glumly.

Maureen straightened in the chair. "The two of them? Together?"

"Kathy went to Stephanie's place to confront her face-to-face."

"Takes guts to do something like that," she murmured.

"I walked in on them. I was bringing Stephanie her Christmas presents," Robert said miserably. "It was . . . awkward. Then—and I'm still not entirely sure what happened—Stephanie sort of pushed me back to Kathy."

"Why would she do that?"

"Kathy said that she loved me."

"Was that ever in question?" Maureen asked.

Robert found he couldn't look her in the face. "I was sure she didn't. I think that's the only reason I allowed the affair to happen. Kathy had withdrawn from me. She was looking after the kids; she had no interest in me or the work. I was . . . I was lonely," he admitted. "That's the real reason I got involved with Stephanie."

In her life Maureen Ryan had indulged in three long-term affairs. In every case she'd known, right from the very beginning, that the man was not going to leave his wife for her. Nor did she want him to. And in every case it was not just sexual chemistry that had drawn the men to her—it was the fact that she was prepared to listen, to be interested in them, in their work, in their lives. Although they were married, the men had been lonely.

"I never set out to hurt Kathy," Robert continued.

"You have—you know that, don't you?"

"I do."

"Tell me how the conversation between the three of you finished."

"Stephanie rejected me; Kathy said she'd take me back," Robert said quickly. "That's it. Then I left. It all happened so fast."

"So you haven't had a chance to talk privately with Kathy yet?"

"Not yet."

"Then what are you doing here?"

"I . . . I wanted to talk to you first. To see how much she knew. To . . . be prepared before I spoke to her."

"When you do, you'll have to be honest with her, Robert. You know that. Totally honest."

"I know."

"Do you want to go back to Kathy?" Before he could respond, she held up a hand. "Think carefully before you answer."

Robert stared at the table, and even before he raised his head to look at her, Maureen had an inkling of how he would answer. If he truly, wholeheartedly, wanted to go back to Kathy, he would not have taken so long to formulate his response.

"I would like to get back together with Kathy," he said very carefully, "for the sake of the children. But I love Stephanie."

"Love or lust?"

He shook his head. "Love. I love her."

"You said you wanted to get back together with Kathy for the sake of the children. What about for Kathy's sake? For your sake? For the sake of an eighteen-year marriage?"

"Well, yes, of course."

"You don't sound positive," Maureen said softly.

"I love Kathy; I do. And I adore my children, you know that. But Stephanie . . . Well, I love her. When I'm with her I feel younger. . . . When I'm with her the world is full of possibilities. I don't get that feeling when I'm with Kathy." He looked at Maureen, "You don't get it."

"Bullshit." Maureen's voice had turned cold and distant. "I get it. But from the other side of the table. I was the mistress. More than once. I had affairs with men like you, men who thought they loved me." She shook her head quickly, and her eyes turned bright. "They didn't love me. They loved the freedom of being with me; it made them remember their youth, before they were married, had children, mortgages, commitments. For the few hours or days they were with me, they were free, existing in a little selfish bubble." She stood up, and Robert rose with her. "I want you to think about that. If you leave Kathy and go to Stephanie—that's assuming she'll even have you now—then how long do you think it will take for the gloss to wear off her?"

"I hear what you're saying."

Maureen came around the table and laid a hand on his arm. "You know, sometimes an affair can be a good thing. It forces a couple to reexamine their lives and see where things went wrong. I've seen marriages survive affairs and come out the other end stronger." Maureen looked into Robert's troubled eyes. "Is that what you want, Robert?"

"I . . . I don't know what I want. I love Kathy . . . but I love Stephanie too."

Maureen turned away so he could not see the expression of disgust on her face and began to gather the cups onto the tray. "Time to choose. Though from what you're telling me," she added with a wry smile, "Stephanie may no longer be available to you."

CHAPTER 22

———❦———

Robert sat in the car outside Maureen's house and cranked up the heat. He was tired of being so cold all the time. He turned on the radio. The traffic report on WBZ NewsRadio 1030 was describing heavy congestion near Logan. Robert suddenly wished he were at the airport, flying away for Christmas, spending it on some warm beach without a trouble in the world. He smiled wryly. Next year maybe. The smile faded. What would the coming year bring? Where would he be this time next year—still with Kathy, still in business? The next couple of hours and days were going to determine the course of his future.

And Stephanie. What about her? There was still so much they needed to talk about. It couldn't just end so abruptly. Only a couple of days ago, he had proposed to this woman. He'd been planning to leave his wife and start again with Stephanie, and she had been happy . . . but that was before she discovered that Kathy still loved him. That revelation had changed everything.

He needed to talk to Stephanie. He pulled out his cell and hit the speed dial that brought up her home number. The phone rang four times before the answering machine kicked in. Maybe she was screening her calls. Stephanie had recorded a new message recently; her voice sounded bright and cheerful, maybe even a little drunk.

"Merry Christmas, Merry Christmas, Merry Christmas! Leave a message."

"Stephanie . . ." He paused, waiting for her to pick up. "Stephanie, are you there? It's me." There was no response. "I want to talk to you; I need to talk to you. . . . Please call me back. I'm in the car."

Where was she? A sudden thought struck him, chilling him to the bone. My God, what if Kathy was still there with her? His fingers trembled slightly as he hit the speed dial that connected him to his wife's cell. It rang twice before it was answered, and he felt a wash of relief when he heard the background noise of traffic. She was in the car.

"Yes?" she said shortly.

"Hi . . . I was just wondering . . . just wondering how you are."

"I'm fine."

"Where are you?"

"Almost home. Where are you?"

"In Mission Hill. I stopped to give Maureen her Christmas bonus."

"Good."

"She told me you'd spoken to her."

"Yes, I have."

Robert squeezed the steering wheel in frustration. She was deliberately making no contribution to the conversation. "How are you feeling?" he asked lamely.

"How do you think I'm feeling?" Kathy snapped. "I've just been to see my husband's mistress. I've just learned some very ugly truths. We'll talk later." She hung up.

Robert started the car. He just needed to make a quick stop at EC Florist and pick up a present for Kathy. He'd spent weeks choosing just the right present for Stephanie, but had left his wife's to the very last minute. As always. He was sure there was something symbolic in that.

Where was Stephanie? Surely she hadn't gone out? He hit another speed dial key, this one for her cell phone. The phone rang twice before it was answered.

"Yes?" The voice was muffled, and for a moment, he thought he'd dialed the wrong number.

"Stephanie? Stephanie? Is that you?" He could hear background noise, voices, thumps. Where was she? "Stef . . ."

The call went dead.

Shit! He hit Redial. The phone didn't even ring; it just went straight to her voice mail.

"You have reached Stephanie Burroughs. Leave your name, number, and a brief message, and I will call you back. Thank you."

"Stephanie? Stephanie, it's Robert. Look, we need to talk. We have to talk. About today. About us. About everything. Please call me back. I'm on my cell."

Robert hung up, then sighed in exasperation. Five years ago, he wouldn't have panicked if he couldn't reach someone immediately. Now, people were all attached to some form of communicative device that made everyone naturally expect instant communication; they took it for granted. Why couldn't life be simple? There had been a time, a long time ago, when the world seemed to be a much easier place; he'd had no worries, no concerns . . . and of course, no wife, no children, no mortgage. Maybe Maureen was right: Maybe his time with Stephanie reminded him of what he'd once had . . . and lost. He'd been free—free of dependents, of mortgages and debts, free of worries. Then he had married. The mortgage on the first house was crippling; he struggled desperately to keep the business afloat, and then the children arrived. And as time went by the pressures increased, and he felt suffocated by bills and responsibilities. For the last eighteen years, he'd been running very fast just to stand still.

That wasn't to say that it had all been bad. There had been good times, loads of them, but somehow he found it harder to remember those. All that remained was the constant grind, the continual effort to just keep going. And the frustration of doing it alone, of watching Kathy step farther and farther back from the business, leaving him to manage on his own. Oh, he knew she was raising the kids and running the house, but she didn't have to worry about where the next contract was coming from. She didn't have to face the traffic each day; she didn't have payroll to worry about and crews to hire. He couldn't remember the last time she'd asked about the company—she'd even been shocked to discover that Maureen had been out sick. And he knew—just knew—that he'd mentioned it to her, though she claimed he hadn't. So, he'd ended up hiring a temp whose first language wasn't English when really Kathy should have been there to help. . . .

Robert took a deep breath and tried to ease the knot of tension he could feel gathering at the back of his neck. He worked his head from side to side and rolled his shoulders, hearing muscles pop and crack.

Actually, if he was being honest—truly honest—he'd hired the temp before he'd told Kathy that Maureen was sick. The last thing he needed was his wife working in the building where he was conducting his affair.

He stayed on Aspinwall Avenue, turned left on Harvard Street, and raced toward the flower shop. He needed to get there before it closed.

He'd been given a second chance.

He could choose to start again with Kathy. Come clean about his affair—and the reasons behind it—clear the air, and start again. Kathy wanted changes; well, so did he. Kathy said she would take him back, and no doubt there would be conditions, but he'd lay down some conditions of his own too. He might have had an affair, but Kathy had been just as much to blame. Naturally, Kathy wouldn't see it that way, but he'd be sure to remind her that she had first accused him of having an affair six years earlier, when he'd been perfectly innocent. She'd lost her trust in him when all he'd been doing was working every waking hour to care for his family.

Robert turned left onto Washington Street and pulled up to the shop. This late on Christmas Eve, he expected to find it filled to overflowing, but it was surprisingly empty. He pulled into a space, turned off the engine, and then sat, his head resting on the steering wheel. His thoughts were confused, whirling through dozens of permutations, and he felt dizzy.

No, this wasn't Kathy's fault.

He'd had the affair. It had been his choice. His decision. It was cowardly to even suggest that she'd somehow forced him into it. Circumstances, situations, and opportunity had encouraged him to enter into the affair with Stephanie.

And he couldn't deny that it had made him very happy. Happier than he'd been with Kathy in a long time.

CHAPTER 23

Bile bubbled at the back of Robert's throat as he turned onto the road that led down toward the house. He was frightened—no, terrified might be a better description—of what the next few hours would bring.

The temperature had been falling throughout the afternoon, and with the onset of night, ice had crept in, driven by a chill easterly wind. The roads were sparkling, and the weather guy on the news was forecasting light snowfalls later on, and promising the possibility of a white Christmas across New England.

Every house in the neighborhood was ablaze with lights. Many were decorated to a vulgar extreme with a combination of everything from waving LED rooftop Santas leading gold rattan reindeer to giant nativity scenes on the lawn, further enhanced by winking fairy lights. Most, however, had opted for dangling curtains of icicle lights running under the eaves, or had wrapped lights around trees in the garden.

In contrast the Walker house looked almost somber; there were no lights on the exterior of the house and none in the garden. Just a respectable wreath on the door. But the curtains in the living room had not been drawn, and the Christmas tree, lights winking, tinsel glittering, looked suitably seasonal. Robert slowed, feeling the heavy Audi slip on the icy street. Then he stopped: Kathy's blue Honda was parked in the driveway, while behind it, parked at an awkward angle that took up the rest of the space, was the enormous SUV belonging to Julia, Kathy's older sister.

Was she here by accident or invitation? Surely Kathy would not have asked her sister to come over for some sort of moral support? He shook his head slightly. He straightened the car and pulled it into the curb. No, he didn't think that Kathy would want her sister Julia—with her perfect twenty-seven-year marriage—to know about their problems.

Robert quietly let himself into the house and stood in the hall, head tilted to one side, listening. The TV was blaring in the family room with what sounded like a game show, and he could hear Brendan's and Theresa's voices rise as they shouted out the answers. He peered inside.

"Hi, guys," he said softly.

"Hi, Dad," they both said without looking up. Brendan was stretched out on the sofa, while Theresa was sprawled on the floor, chin cupped in her palms.

"Aunt Julia's here?" he asked, addressing no one in particular.

"In the kitchen with Mom," Theresa said. "Mom asked me to leave, so I think there's a problem."

Robert felt his stomach twist. Maybe he'd been wrong. Maybe Kathy had called on her sister for support. If she had, then he knew he was in deep trouble: Julia didn't like him and had made no secret of it.

"Keep the sound down, will you," he said, stepping out of the room. Then, taking a deep breath and twisting his lips into an approximation of a smile, he stepped into the kitchen. "Hello, Julia," he said pleasantly, though his eyes were fixed on his wife's face.

"Julia was just about to tell me about Sheila," Kathy said immediately, her eyes flat and expressionless, but at least letting him know that Julia's presence had nothing to do with their personal situation. Sheila was the youngest of the three sisters.

Robert felt a wash of relief surge through him. "Is she okay?" he asked, stepping around the table to lean against the sink.

"She's having an affair with a married man," Julia said in hushed, appalled tones and then stopped, waiting for a response.

"So?" Robert frowned. "What's that got to do with us?" He looked from Julia to Kathy and then back to his sister-in-law.

Julia Taylor was five years older than Kathy and looked five years older than that. Short and unprepossessing, she dressed in the same sensible skirts and cardigans that her late mother had favored and, since their mother's death, had assumed the role of the matriarch of the sisters.

"Oh, I should have known you would never understand," Julia said peevishly. "Men never do." Julia turned to look across the table at Kathy. "I called her today, just to confirm that she was coming on the 26th for dinner. Well, she said she would—on one condition: that she could bring her current boyfriend with her. I was thrilled, of course. Sheila's thirty-six; it's about time she thought about settling down, and if she's going to have children, then she'd better start soon. . . . Her eggs are drying up." Julia took a deep breath and pursed her lips. Glancing briefly at Robert, she turned back to Kathy. "Turns out her boyfriend is not such a boy; he's actually ten years older than she is. Ten years!"

Robert turned back to the sink. He knew what Kathy was thinking: Stephanie was sixteen years younger than him.

"And then she told me his name," Julia persisted. "Alan Gallagher. And I thought: I know that name. So I said to her, 'I know an Alan Gallagher—he's a chiropractor in Brookline who plays golf with my Ben.'" Julia nodded triumphantly. "And that was when she said that she didn't think she was going to be able to make it on Thursday after all."

Staring at Julia's reflection in the kitchen window, Robert asked, "So how do you know he's married?"

Julia sighed. "The Alan Gallagher who Ben knows has boasted about his little bit on the side. I put two and two together: The 'bit' is Sheila."

"Brookline is so small," Kathy murmured. "Everyone knows someone who knows someone."

Robert poured himself a glass of scotch, unsure if Kathy was talking to him or not.

"So I thought about it," Julia continued, "and I called her back."

"Julia, you didn't!" Kathy protested.

"I did."

"But it's got nothing to do with you!"

"Well, you may not think so, but I do, and I certainly didn't want an adulterer sitting at my table."

"Are you going to insist she stitches an *A* on all of her clothing?" Robert said evenly.

Julia looked at him coldly. "I called her. Asked her straight out. And do you know what she had the audacity to tell me?"

"That it was none of your business," Robert snapped, unable to keep the irritation out of his voice.

Kathy glanced at him, frowned, and shook her head slightly.

"No," Julia said, not hearing the tone. "She admitted it: Alan Gallagher is married. So I told her straight out that she would not be welcome in my house."

"Why are you telling me this?" Kathy asked.

Julia looked at her blankly. "Because . . . because . . ."

"This is Sheila's business. Hers alone," Kathy continued, surprising Robert. "Who she's seeing has got nothing to do with you or me."

"But he's married!" Julia protested. "She's breaking up a happy marriage."

"How do we know that?" Kathy asked. "How do we know the marriage is happy? Do you have some kind of psychic power that enables you to know what goes on behind closed doors?"

For one of the few times in her life, Julia was stunned to silence.

"There are three people in an affair," Kathy said. "The mistress, the husband, and the wife. Takes all of them to make it happen."

Julia pushed back her chair and stood up. "Well, this is not the attitude I expected from you. The wives are always the innocents in these situations, always the last to know. I don't know why these women—these mistresses—are attracted to married men; I really don't!" She lifted her coat off the back of the chair and pulled it on.

Then glancing at Robert, she was unable to resist adding, "I just hope you never have to go through what poor Alan Gallagher's wife is going through right now." Then, obviously misinterpreting the looks on Kathy's and Robert's faces as anger, she continued hastily, "Well, I don't think that came out the way I meant it to. I'm sorry, I didn't mean to imply..." Looking embarrassed now, she turned to leave. "I'll let myself out." She paused before she stepped out of the kitchen. "You will come over the day after tomorrow for dinner, won't you?"

"We'll let you know," Robert said firmly, before Kathy could respond.

Julia looked from Robert to her sister.

Kathy's smile was ice. "We'll let you know," she said.

CHAPTER 24

In the silence that followed Julia's departure and the slam of the hall door, they both clearly heard the high-pitched, squealing scrape of metal on stone.

"She's hit the edge of the pillar," Robert said, unable to keep the grin off his face. He glanced over his shoulder to where Kathy was also smiling. "She was parked at such an awkward angle," he explained. "I'm not sure I would have been able to get that big SUV out of the driveway without hitting something either." He brought the bottle of scotch to the table and sat down in the chair facing Kathy. Silently, he poured her a glass.

"I'm thinking I might have given her a different response a couple of days ago," Kathy said quietly. "There was a time—in the very recent past—when I might have agreed with Julia. But when you become part of an affair, you discover a different perspective. There are two sides to every story, but in an affair . . . there are three. And you never really know anyone's story but your own."

"Did you know?" Robert asked, just to make conversation. "About Sheila," he added hastily. In truth, he couldn't care less about how the youngest of the sisters was living her life.

Kathy held the heavy glass in both hands and looked into the amber liquid. "She told me on Monday. We were sitting in her car outside the Boston Sports Club. I sat there and watched my husband kiss another woman." She looked up, and her expression made him sit back, suddenly frightened that she was going to throw the alcohol in his face. She obviously had the same thought, because she carefully set the glass down. "I called you," she said, her voice little more than a whisper. "I sat in a car less than ten yards away from you and called you."

Robert nodded, remembering the call; he had been standing in the street, having just spoken to Stephanie about children, then he had leaned over and kissed her, deeply, passionately. He felt himself color, and beads of icy sweat gathered in his armpits.

"I asked you what time you were coming home," Kathy continued.

Robert nodded. The idea that she had been trailing him around, following him, spying on him, was unsettling, even frightening. This was a Kathy he didn't know.

"You told me you were just leaving the office and would be home in forty minutes." Kathy suddenly stood up, startling him. She threw the rest of her scotch into the sink and then began to clear off the kitchen table.

"How long . . . how long have you known?" he asked eventually. "About us? About me?"

"Not long. Why? Did you think I was the sort of person who would turn a blind eye to my husband's affair?" Kathy's voice was calm, reasonable, conversational. She pulled a cookbook off the shelf and flipped through it until she found the recipe she was looking for.

"No. I never thought that," Robert admitted.

Pressing the book flat on the table, Kathy scanned the contents, then started to gather the ingredients for the turkey stuffing.

"Will you please sit down and talk to me?" Robert asked. Kathy's constant movement around the kitchen, the banality of her actions contrasted so sharply with the extraordinary conversation that the whole experience was taking on a surreal, dreamlike aspect.

Kathy ignored his request. "I suspected the truth last Thursday, when I was writing the Christmas cards. Once my suspicions were roused, it was relatively easy to put it all together. There was a speeding ticket upstairs in your office. You got a ticket in Jamaica Plain on Halloween . . . even though you were supposed to be in Connecticut that night having dinner with a client."

Kathy pulled the blender out from the cupboard under the sink and plugged it in. In the pantry, she found the plastic bag of dried bread she'd been saving for the past couple of days. She started feeding the bread into the blender, grinding it to crumbs. When the blades were whirring, conversation was impossible, and she only spoke when she stopped and cleared out the breadcrumbs. "Then I remembered all the other nights you'd stayed away, meeting with clients, wining and dining them. . . . I don't remember the company getting contracts from any of these alleged clients. You were supposed to be having dinner with Jimmy Moran at Top of the Hub last week. But when I called to check, they had no record of your reservation."

"Jimmy and I really were supposed . . . ," Robert began, and then shut up. No matter what he said, Kathy was not going to believe him—and why should she? She had lost trust in him; everything he said was suspect.

Kathy stuffed more bread into the blender, and the blades whirred and stopped. "And then I found the phone records in the file cabinet. That was priceless." She turned to look at Robert. "Hundreds of calls, Robert. Hundreds. First call of the day. Last call at night. All to the same cell or the same house number. And I couldn't help but remember the mornings you left here without speaking to me, or the days when you were too busy to call to see how I was, or those days when you got back late and I'd be in bed. Whole days would go by, and we wouldn't speak more than a few words. And yet you always seemed to find the time to call your mistress several times a day. Every single day."

"Maureen told me you'd seen the phone bills," he muttered.

"She just confirmed what I already knew. She just gave me the time frame. She thinks it's been going on for a year. Stephanie said eighteen months. What is the truth?"

He nodded. "June of last year was the . . . the first time."

"The first time for what?" Kathy snapped.

Robert glanced over his shoulder toward the family room where the kids' voices were just audible over the sound of the TV. "Could we discuss this somewhere more private?" he asked.

"Right now, this is the most private room in the house. If we go upstairs, the kids will think that we're wrapping their presents and be in and out every five minutes. Right now, they know I'm prepping the stuffing for the turkey, and they've no interest in that."

Robert stood and came around the table to stand beside Kathy. "Can I help?"

"No," she said simply. She turned back to the blender. "I don't know what's going to happen between us, Robert. But it's going to take me a long time before I can trust you again . . . a long time before I can even look at you without feeling sick to my stomach."

He reached out to touch her, but she jerked away. "Don't!" she snapped.

Robert allowed his hand to fall loosely by his side. "I'm sorry," he said. "I know it sounds like a cliché, but I never wanted to hurt you. You have to believe me—that was never my intention." Folding his arms, he leaned against the counter and took a deep breath. "I allowed myself to enter into the relationship—"

"Affair!" Kathy snapped. "Jesus, Robert, call it what it is—an affair!"

Robert bit the inside of his cheek, the instant pain forcing him to focus on each word. "I began my affair with Stephanie last June. I was lonely, Kath, desperately lonely. I wanted someone to talk to, someone to share with, someone to show an interest in me. I tried to talk to you—God, I tried. But you never seemed to be interested. You never asked how things were going, never seemed to be in the slightest bit concerned with the ordinary day-to-day minutiae of keeping the company afloat. I'm not even sure you realized how much trouble we were in. We came very close to going under."

Kathy stepped around Robert to remove fat tubes of sausage meat from the fridge.

"I was lonely," Robert repeated, aware of her movements, but not looking at her. "We'd stopped . . . having sex. When I tried, you'd turn your back on me or you'd come to me so reluctantly that I felt like you were making love to me almost as a duty. You didn't seem to enjoy it. After a while I stopped making the effort; I'll admit it. But—and please don't take this as a criticism; it's just a statement of fact—you never made an effort either."

"So you're saying it's my fault you found yourself a mistress?" Kathy asked savagely.

"No," he sighed. "I'm not trying to score points here—I'm just trying to let you see how I ended up in this situation." When Robert had been driving home, he'd imagined several versions of the conversation he was having now. He'd visualized it taking place in the family room, late at night, with the TV turned off, or the pair of them sitting on either side of the big table in the dining room, or upstairs in the bedroom, with both of them standing on either side of the bed. He'd never imagined it taking place in the kitchen, while Kathy stuffed the Christmas turkey as if everything was normal. "I allowed myself to have the affair, Kathy, because I believed—genuinely believed—that you no longer loved me." He held up his hand as Kathy rounded on him. "I know. I'm just telling you how I felt, telling you how I saw things. When you stood in Stephanie's living room earlier and said that you loved me, no one was more surprised than I was."

"I never stopped loving you," Kathy said immediately.

"Even right now?" he asked, trying to lighten the somber mood.

"I'm not sure how I feel about you at this moment. But the very fact that we're both standing in this room, even after all that's happened today, should suggest something."

"What?" he wondered.

"That maybe I do accept some responsibility for what happened," she said, surprising him. "I wasn't paying attention. And if a marriage is going to work, then both parties have to keep paying attention. You stopped paying attention to me, and I stopped paying attention to you."

"Would it help if I said I was sorry, truly sorry?"

Kathy glanced sidelong at him. "Sorry for what? Do you regret the affair?"

"I regret the pain it caused you," Robert said carefully. In truth, he didn't regret the affair. His only regret was that he'd been caught and the affair was now at an end.

"Well, I'm glad you chose to tell me the truth," she said lightly.

"I would never knowingly hurt you," he continued.

"And yet you have hurt me, Robert. Hurt me and humiliated me. And it's going to take me a long time to forgive that."

"What's going to happen to us?" he asked.

"As I see it, we have two choices: We can stay together, make some new rules, start again, and really work at it this time. Or I can file for divorce."

If Kathy filed for divorce, what happened then? If she got herself a good lawyer, he could end up losing his home, access to his children, and possibly even his business. "Well, look, let's talk about this later, or tomorrow maybe. We're both tired and probably not thinking too clearly. I know I'm not." Robert licked his dry lips and glanced sidelong at Kathy. "I do have a favor to ask," he added.

Kathy looked at him, a mixture of amusement and disdain on her face.

"Kath, if you decide that you want me to go—and I understand if you do—then can we keep this from the kids for a while? I don't want to ruin their Christmas."

"I won't ruin their Christmas," she promised. "Let's try to get through the next couple of days like civilized people."

"Thank you," he said sincerely.

"When were you going to tell me, Robert?"

"Tell you what?" he asked.

"Tell me that you were going to leave me."

"I don't know for certain," he mumbled. "Probably over the weekend."

"You don't sound so sure."

"I'm not," he admitted.

"And yet Stephanie seemed convinced that you were going to tell me after Christmas so that you could spend New Year's Eve with her."

"Yes, we talked about that."

"Or were you going to give her an excuse and stay here?" Kathy guessed.

"Kathy," Robert said truthfully, "I have no idea what I would have done. But yes, the plan was to tell you, probably on Saturday or Sunday, that I was leaving."

"Bastard!" Kathy hissed. She pushed him away from her. "You callous, uncaring bastard!"

Robert stepped away from her and moved around the table. "I'm sorry, Kathy; I really am. But I made that decision believing that you didn't love me. Before I knew the truth."

Kathy turned back to the turkey. "If we're going to rebuild our lives and our relationship, we're going to have to be honest with one another." She looked up, seeing his reflection in the window. "Will you be honest with me, Robert? Can you promise me that?"

"Yes. Yes, I can," he said.

"Then you have to promise me something else."

"Anything."

"You have to swear to me that you'll stay away from that woman."

"I promise," he said quickly. "In any case, I think you can tell from today that she'll want little enough to do with me." When he realized that Kathy wasn't going to speak to him again, he turned and left the room, stepped out into the hall, and took the stairs two at a time. When he entered his office, he shut the door. Then he lay back against the door and slowly slid to the floor.

This was a day he would never forget.

Thank God it was almost over.

CHAPTER 25

———— ❦ ————

Sitting at his desk, Robert didn't think the papers looked like they had been disturbed; Kathy had obviously been very careful. He dug down through the pile of mail until he found the speeding ticket. It was a fixed penalty ticket, two points on his license, for driving forty-five miles per hour on a twenty-five mile per hour stretch of road in Jamaica Plain last October 31, at 11:12 p.m.

He remembered the night, clearly remembered seeing the white van parked by the side of the road with its blacked-out back windows as he shot past it. The irony of it was, of course, that he had met with a client in Connecticut, and the plan had been for him to spend the night there and drive back the following morning. However, within about fifteen minutes of starting the meeting, it had become obvious that what Robert had assumed might be a potential client was nothing more than a time-waster. It happened all the time. He had concluded the meeting as quickly as politeness allowed, canceled the dinner reservation, and had driven back to Boston. He was heading home to Brookline when he'd picked up the phone and, on impulse, called Stephanie and asked her if she wanted him to stay the night. She said yes; Stephanie always said yes. So he continued on to her house. Usually, he was so careful with his speed. He was in a business that depended upon a car, and his insurance premium was so high that the last thing he needed were points to drive it even higher. But his excitement to be with Stephanie had edged the speed over the legal limit.

He checked through the rest of the mail in his in-tray, but he could find nothing else incriminating; there was an MBNA bill, but it was for business expenses. He turned the page and frowned. Hmmm, had she seen this page? There were three items that might have given her pause. A purchase from QVC, a bouquet of flowers from ProFlowers.com, and a meal at the French restaurant L'Espalier. He could claim they were business expenses . . . but he doubted Kathy would believe him. Maureen was right: He had been greedy. He should have conducted his affairs—he smiled grimly at the irony—on a cash-only basis. But he never thought he'd be discovered; he never imagined that Kathy would come searching, looking for proof.

How much did she know?

He looked at the bill in his hand. He doubted if she'd seen this; she would undoubtedly have brought it up in conversation. He pulled the second page off the bill and was just about to feed it into the shredder when he realized that the sound might alert Kathy to the fact that he was shredding documents on Christmas Eve. And it wouldn't take a genius to work out what he was doing.

He stood and opened the filing cabinet, then pushed the page to the very back of a folder marked IRS. She'd never find it there, and next time the house was empty, he'd shred it and any other piece of evidence he could find.

How much had she discovered? He fully intended to tell her the truth, the whole truth, and nothing but the truth . . . or as much of the truth as he dared tell her. He knew one thing for certain: He could never tell her that he'd asked Stephanie to marry him.

Robert looked around the room, past the printers, faxes, scanners, a large desktop computer, the digital editing suite to the row of filing cabinets that took up the left wall. The files were all work related. There was nothing personal—nothing incriminating—in them.

And the computer?

Robert ran his fingers along the top edge of the screen. There was nothing on this computer. All of the files on the desktop were entirely business related. There were no e-mails, no romantic letters that could link him to Stephanie. Besides, the machine was password protected, and Kathy didn't have the password. When he wanted to send e-mails to Stephanie, he used an online account, or his cell, and when he talked to her using Google Chat, he never kept the IM logs. The laptop was also clean as far as he remembered. He'd check it out later. But it was also password protected.

Robert sat down at his machine and powered it on. Then he entered his password, Poppykoo—the name of his beloved childhood dog. As he did so he realized that the password offered little protection from Kathy—it was something she could easily guess if she thought about it. He really must get around to changing it.

He quickly checked his e-mail. Some spam, an offer from a Nigerian to share fifty-two million dollars with him, offers for Viagra and a Genie Bra, and a couple of e-mails from clients wishing him a Merry Christmas.

Nothing from Stephanie.

Pulling out his phone, he called her cell, but the call went straight to her voice mail. Lowering his voice, he said, "Stephanie, it's me. Please give me a call when you get this. I just want to have a few words about what happened today, about us too. Talk to me. Please."

Where was she?

He didn't think she'd had any plans for the evening. She'd told him that her friend Izzie was getting engaged, but she'd said it was a private party. He called the house. "Stephanie? It's me. I . . . I just need to talk to you. About today. About us. About the future. I know you're angry, but please call me, let me know you're okay."

Somewhere at the back of his mind, an alarm bell started ringing. Where was she? Why wasn't she answering? He glanced at his watch. He'd try again in a couple of hours.

CHAPTER 26

⁂

Robert opened the hall door and breathed in the icy night air. It was so cold it burned his nostrils. It had snowed earlier, the merest dusting of flakes, but the sky was now completely clear.

"Are you going out?" Kathy's voice sounded as chilly as the night air, and did he hear the faintest hint of accusation in it . . . or was it just his guilty conscience?

"I just want to bring the car in," he explained. "I parked it on the street earlier." The kitchen door closed behind him, and he thought he heard Kathy's voice talking on the phone.

He stopped to look at the pillar on the way out. The edge of the stone cap was missing, and there were flakes of blue metallic paint on the stonework. He grinned; he guessed Julia had caught the back bumper and probably the back door as well. Her little moral outburst had cost her a couple of grand at least. He hit the remote; the Audi's lights flashed, and he climbed in and turned on the engine. Ice crystals had grown like mold along the edges of the windshield, and he leaned forward to stare at them, suddenly a boy again, remembering—with absolute clarity—that first terrible Christmas when his father had left home. He'd spent Christmas Eve sitting at his bedroom window, fully dressed, with a flannel blanket thrown over his shoulders, watching, hoping, praying that his father and brothers would come home for Christmas. They hadn't, and he'd sat through the night, watching the same ice crystals, intricate and delicate, creep across the window until they completely obscured the night.

With the car wheels spinning on the ice, he eased the car into the driveway, turned off the engine, and then sat in silence, listening to the engine tick quietly to itself. He was beginning to realize that nothing was ever going to be the same again.

As he climbed out of the car, he caught the slightest flicker of the bedroom curtain moving, and wondered if Kathy was watching him. Was this how the future was going to be: forever watched and spied on? He experienced a brief snap of anger. Well, that wasn't going to happen. Kathy had every right to be angry with him, but, as she'd admitted herself, she was not entirely blameless. She was talking about changes that she wanted to see. . . . Well, he wanted to see some changes himself.

He popped the trunk and pulled out the large bouquet of flowers. He would hide them in the garage overnight and give them to Kathy in the morning. Perhaps they could start the day off on a good foot instead of with betrayal and suspicion. His gifts for Kathy weren't as thoughtful as the ones he'd picked out for Stephanie, because he'd barely managed to make it into the store before closing. His choices for Christmas presents for his wife had been limited. In addition to the necklace and scarf, he'd gotten her a lavish bouquet called The Martha's Vineyard, which was filled with white roses, fragrant lilacs, and lavender hydrangea. He'd scribbled on the card, one gift certificate for an all-expenses weekend on the Vineyard. He wondered: Would there be a next year?

Shivering in the chill night air, Robert hurried back into the house.

This was now the third call, and there was still no answer.

He'd been calling Stephanie every hour on the hour. The calls kept going straight to her answering machine. Where was she?

He was getting worried. Stephanie had always appeared to him as calm and sensible, not given to hysterics or emotional outbursts. She was the senior accounts manager in one of the biggest—if not the biggest—agencies in Boston, handling multimillion-dollar accounts and even bigger egos on a daily basis. She didn't strike him as someone who would do something stupid.

And yet . . .

And yet he had to admit that she had been slightly *off* over the past few weeks. He had known she wasn't looking forward to spending Christmas by herself, and they'd come close to an argument on more than one occasion when she'd put pressure on him to leave Kathy and spend the time with her.

Robert rewrote Kathy's gift certificate on a nicer piece of stationery. He absentmindedly started to doodle a caricature on it. He relaxed for a moment, enjoying the simple creative task of drawing, and he filled the card with funny Christmas vignettes of the family. When he first married Kathy, he had very little money to romance her, and he used to leave her cartoons like this all over the house. Why had he stopped doing that? Oddly enough, he never drew for Stephanie. Where was Stephanie? He'd tried to remember last Christmas. Stephanie had been a little down then too. They'd been seeing each other for six months, and it had honestly been the happiest six months of his life. He'd felt young again. Young and alive. He had a young woman who was interested not just in him as a person, but in every aspect of his life, someone he could talk to about the business, someone he could make plans with. And then Christmas had arrived. It was the first big test of their relationship.

Stephanie had wanted him to spend Christmas Eve with her— but he couldn't. She wanted him to come over on Christmas Day, but he couldn't do that either. And it was the same story with New Year's Eve and New Year's Day.

He'd spoken to her on several occasions over that week, and he had known how lonely and miserable she was. She promised she was never going to do it again. And yet here she was, a year later, in an even worse position. The future she had been happy to plan was in pieces; the man she'd hoped would move in with her and ultimately marry her had left her, and she was alone again over Christmas. He'd seen the look on her face earlier, a look of heartbreak, of absolute loss. He could only imagine how she was feeling right now: lost, lonely, alone, depressed.

She had to be at home. . . . Where else could she be? But if she were at home, then why didn't she answer the phone? Sly and insidious, the thought that had been lurking at the back of his head all evening finally surfaced. She wouldn't have done anything . . . anything foolish, would she?

CHAPTER 27

Wednesday, 25th December
Christmas Day

The house was still and silent.

The kids had gone to bed, and he'd heard Kathy move around the bedroom—funny, he'd always thought of it as her room, never their bedroom. A deep silence had fallen over the house. The heat had just clicked off, and a chill was beginning to creep into the air.

Robert came out of his study and crept downstairs as softly as he could, moving silently in his socks on the heavy, cream-colored carpet. He checked the front door and slid the security chain across it. He stood in front of the Christmas tree, realizing that he hadn't been part of the decorating. He bought the tree, but Kathy and the kids had done all the work. Brendan's and Theresa's presents were carefully arranged around the tree, and Robert was embarrassed and just a little ashamed that, apart from the books, CDs, and DVDs, he didn't know what Kathy had bought them for their major present.

In the kitchen, he checked the back door before turning off the lights. He stood in the darkened room and allowed his eyes to adjust to the gloom. The kitchen took on a vaguely milky glow, and when he stepped up to the window, he could see that huge, silent flakes of snow were falling, swirling and curling around the back-yard, painting one side of the trees in white, while leaving the other side black and shapeless.

It was going to be a white Christmas. He smiled. And then the smile faded. Where was Stephanie?

Standing in the kitchen, he pulled out his cell and hit Redial. Hers had been the only number he'd been calling all evening. As before it went straight to her voice mail, and he hung up without leaving a message. The snow hit the window, stuck briefly, then dissolved into icy tears, and he could see his own image reflected back at him, broken and distorted.

Where was she? He was getting seriously worried.

Maybe she'd drowned her sorrows in a bottle of wine and was even now sleeping it off. It would be totally out of character—he'd seen her tipsy, but never drunk—but today's events were totally out of the ordinary too.

Maybe she'd simply turned her phone off. He shook his head; he'd never known her to turn off her phone. Once she'd even stopped in the middle of sex to take a call from a client.

Was she at home, with her cell by her side, watching his number repeatedly come up on screen and choosing to ignore his calls? He went into the settings and selected "Show Caller ID" and turned it off. Then he called again.

It went straight to her voice mail.

He suddenly had a strong feeling that something was wrong. And he needed to see for himself. He looked up at the kitchen clock. Nearly one. But what was he going to tell Kathy? He couldn't exactly tell her the truth—I've gone to check up on my mistress—especially having just promised to stay away from Stephanie, could he? And yet he couldn't just walk out in the middle of the night. . . .

He suddenly remembered the last time he'd been called away in the middle of the night. Pulling a page from the notepad by the phone, he scribbled, "Office alarm has gone off; gone in to see if there's a problem." He was about to add "love, Robert," but didn't. He might be a liar and a cheat, but he wasn't sure he was that much of a hypocrite yet.

*   *   *

The roads were deserted.

Jamaicaway was dusted with a thin layer of white snow, pristine and unmarked ahead of him, only his rapidly-disappearing car tracks behind. Even with the windshield wipers doing double time, all they succeeded in doing was compacting the snow in either corner of the window, and despite the heaters on full blast, frost was forming on the bottom edge of the windshield. He could feel the heavy car shift and slide on the corners and kept dropping his speed until he was doing a little under fifteen miles an hour. Where were the snowplows and the salters? Maybe they didn't work at one fifteen on Christmas morning.

Even though he'd driven this section of road regularly over the last eighteen months, he found that the snow, now falling thick and fast, was removing all his usual landmarks. When it spun and eddied and blew directly toward the car, it gave the disconcerting impression that he was falling into it. And with the side and rear windows completely covered in a thick gray-white coating, his world was reduced to little more than an arc directly in front of his face. He was forced to pull off the road before he reached Jamaica Pond. He hated driving with limited visibility. Forcing open the door, he was shocked by the bitter chill in the air and even more shocked by the amount of snow on the roof of the car, and for the first time he wondered if he was going to make it back home that night. What would Kathy say to that? Using a furled umbrella he scraped the snow off the roof and cleared the back and side windows before climbing back into the car. The back and shoulders of his heavy leather coat were coated in snow, and he could feel wet, icy fingers clinging to the hair at the nape of his neck and beginning to trickle their way down his spine.

Christ, what a mess!

He slowed at the light on Pond Street where a late-night party was going on in one of the huge houses. He could hear the loud music through his windows and saw a group of young men on the upper balcony, smoking cigars. A young woman in a red dress, wearing a reindeer hat, ran out, reached her arms around one of the men, and pulled him back inside. Robert watched as the man flicked his half-lit cigar into a snowy drift below and allowed himself to be pulled into the party. That's what Christmas should be like, Robert decided: young and free, without a worry in the world, full of dreams for the future and Christmases to come. To his right, crouched in the doorway of the boathouse, a shapeless, indeterminate figure in a filthy sleeping bag was huddled out of the icy sleet. As Robert turned left, driving toward his destination, he decided that the latter was probably a closer approximation of what Christmas was: lost innocence and shattered dreams.

Robert lowered his headlights as he turned into the courtyard in front of Stephanie's building. Ice crackled and crunched beneath his wheels, and he swung into the parking space and parked beside her silver BMW. Her car was here, but he wasn't sure if that was a good or a bad sign. If she was going out to a party, she always left the car at home. Turning off the engine, he sat for a moment, composing himself.

Stephanie lived on the upper floor of the restored Victorian, and it was shrouded in darkness, unlike some of the other condos, which had miniature Christmas trees or menorahs in the windows. There was an illuminated Santa in the window box of one of her neighbors, a string of icicles hanging on another. It was close to one thirty, and there was no movement in any of the condos, and the cobbled courtyard was unmarked by tires or footprints. He pulled out his wallet and opened the little zip compartment. Nestled in the back of the pocket was a single unmarked key. Stephanie had given it to him for his birthday last October, just over a year ago. "So you can escape, whenever you need to," she had explained. "And who knows, maybe I'll even come home one day and find you waiting for me in bed." That had never happened.

Stepping out of the car, he gently eased the door closed. The last thing he wanted to do now was to slam the door in the small courtyard; he knew from experience that it would echo around the little square and no doubt bring Mrs. Moore, the nosy neighbor, to her window.

He slipped the key into the main door and silently let himself in. He crept to the door on the left, number 8, and turned the key. The moment he opened the door, he knew the condo was empty. It wasn't the cold—the house was surprisingly warm—but it was the ambience. It felt empty.

"Stephanie!" he called from the bottom of the stairs. If she was upstairs, he didn't want to panic her, maybe have her call 911 and have the police show up. He grinned humorlessly; now wouldn't that just be the perfect end to a perfect day? "Stephanie?" He climbed up the stairs and looked into the living room; it was exactly as he had left it several hours ago. The presents were where he had dropped them, the balloon floating close to the ceiling.

Robert looked at the closed doors to the bedroom and bathroom.

He was suddenly conscious that his heart was pounding in his chest. On the one hand he was hoping that the house was empty, because the alternative was almost too horrible to contemplate. What was he going to do if he did discover something?

He took a deep breath. And then he realized that he was also unconsciously sniffing the air, smelling for . . .

The air smelled dry and warm, faintly perfumed by the flowers he had brought earlier and a hint of something mint and floral from the bathroom. He couldn't smell anything else, anything noxious.

What if Stephanie had done something stupid in a fit of depression? Taken too many pills or slit her wrists in the bathtub or thrown one of his ties around the ceiling beam and . . .

Standing outside the bathroom door, he was conscious that his heart was hammering so hard he could feel the shake in his chest, his temples, even in his fingertips.

And what would he do if he found the body? He'd have to report it to the police, and then they'd want to know what he was doing here at one thirty on Christmas morning, and then Kathy would know that he'd gone back to Stephanie's, and then . . .

Jesus, what was he doing here? He'd called Stephanie; she hadn't answered. Why wasn't he satisfied just to leave it at that? Why had he continued to call and work himself up into a state of panic that had driven him out of the house in the middle of the night to check up on a woman who had rejected him only a few hours earlier?

The answer was very simple: He was here because he loved her. He still loved her, despite what had happened.

Pressing his hands flat against the bathroom door, he pushed it open. The bath was empty. Which left the bedroom. He took two quick steps toward the door and pushed it open.

The wave of relief that washed over him was a physical sensation that left him clutching the doorframe for support.

The bed was empty. It also hadn't been slept in, though the cover was rumpled as if Stephanie had sat on it, and it bore the outline of a rectangle. A small suitcase maybe? He pulled open the closet and checked through Stephanie's dresses, skirts, and coats. As far as he could tell everything was there.

But the purse she normally used was missing, as was her cell, though her company laptop was shoved under the bed where it usually lived.

Robert sat on the edge of the bed and looked around the room. He was totally confused now; he wasn't sure whether to be relieved or even more scared. At least he hadn't found a body, but there was no evidence that she'd gone away. Maybe she'd simply gone out to an all-night party and was even now enjoying herself in the arms of a new lover? The pulse of jealousy that rippled through him surprised him with its intensity. But if she'd gone out to a party . . . Robert stood and checked the opposite end of the closet where Stephanie kept her formal dresses. He remembered many happy occasions sitting or lying on the bed, watching her standing in her matching Agent Provocateur lace bra and panties as she riffled through her dresses looking for something suitable to wear. Inevitably, she ended up wearing black. There were four little black dresses, all with different combinations of neck and hemlines, on the hangers, all covered in eco-friendly dry cleaning bags. There didn't seem to be any noticeable gaps on the rail. He pawed through the rest of the dresses; most he recognized and, as far as he could tell, none were missing. Nor were there any spaces in the lines of shoes arranged on their little shelf close to the floor.

So, maybe she hadn't gone to a party. . . .

It looked like she had simply walked out of the house. Where was she? His only hope was that she was with her friend Izzie. If he hadn't heard from her by morning, he'd try to get in touch with

Izzie . . . and if Izzie didn't know where her friend was, then he might have to go to the police.

He moved through the house, turning off the lights and shutting the doors. After locking up, he climbed into his car and pulled out his phone.

"Stephanie. I don't know what's happened. I don't know where you are. It's just after 2:00 a.m., and I'm leaving your house. There's no sign of you. I'm leaving this message in the hope that you return, hear it, and answer me. I'm hoping you're with your friend, Izzie. I think I remember you saying that she was supposed to be getting engaged tonight . . . no, last night. My God, I've just realized it's Christmas morning."

It was two thirty by the time he reached Brookline. It was still snowing, quick flurries, followed by odd spiraling flakes, followed by another quick flurry, driven on by an increasingly icy wind. Driving alone, he felt as if he were the only soul in the world.

By the time he turned down the road to his house, he was desperately tired, both physically and emotionally exhausted. The snow was so bad he felt like he was crawling. At one stage he had cracked open the driver's window, slices of frozen snow caked on the glass falling into the car, and breathed in the bitter night air in an effort to stay awake. Climbing out of the car, he thought he saw the bedroom curtains twitch, but he was too tired to even care. Opening the door as silently as possible, he stepped into the hall, and climbed the stairs to his study, wincing as the third step from the top protested with a squeak.

Where was Stephanie?

Still fully dressed, wearing his heavy leather coat and gloves, he slumped into his office chair, started up his computer, and checked his e-mail. Besides the usual junk, there was nothing from Stephanie. He started to scroll through his contacts, looking for Izzie's name. He was sure Stephanie had given it to him. The problem was he could not remember Izzie's last name—Williams, Wilson, Wilton—something like that. He hunted under the word *Izzie,* but that returned zero hits. Perhaps Izzie was short for something. Isabelle? He tried every combination, but nothing came back. He knew she was a doctor, but her hospital would never give out her private number. Still, maybe he could leave a message for her if he hadn't gotten in touch with Stephanie by the afternoon.

Okay, so maybe she'd gone out to a party last night and stayed over. If her friend Izzie had gotten engaged then it was likely the party had gone on to the early hours of the morning. He knew Stephanie had her cell with her and that she could use it to retrieve e-mails. He'd tried calling the house and her cell; e-mails were all that was left.

Opening his Outlook e-mail program, he composed a message to Stephanie.

> *Dear Stephanie,*
> *I don't know what's happened to you. I am desperately worried. I've tried calling you at the house and on your cell, but it goes straight to voice mail. You've just disappeared.*
> *Please get in touch with me. Let me know you're okay.*
> *I even went over to the house earlier this morning. I let myself in. I'm concerned there's no sign of you, and yet I know you haven't gone away. I looked in the closets, and your clothes are still there.*
> *I am at my wit's end.*
> *I have no idea how to contact your friend Izzie, and I realize I don't know any of your other friends. If I don't get in touch with you soon, I might try to contact Charles Flintoff. I'm half thinking I should contact the police and report you as missing.*
> *If you get this, then please, please, please contact me.*
> *I love you.*
> *Robert*

He read it twice over before he sent it. There was nothing but the truth in it, and the only line that gave him any pause was the sentence, "I love you." That was the truth, but he wondered how Stephanie would see it. Surely she'd realize that if he'd driven through a snowstorm to check up on her, then he must have genuine feelings for her?

He hit Send.

He wondered how long it would take for him to get a response.

The computer pinged, the sound like that of a door creaking open, and then his instant message program, which usually ran silently in the background, popped up.

Stephanieburroughs123 is now online.

Would you like to send a message to stephanieburroughs123?

Thank God! Before he could type a letter, a single word appeared onscreen: Yes?

He was all fingers and thumbs, and practically misspelled every word in his haste to communicate with her. Thank God. Are you all right? I was worried sick.

I'm fine.

But where are you? Was she home? She must be if she was online with him now. Could he call her, would she answer?

I'm fine.

He frowned in annoyance. What game was she playing now? Are you not going to tell me where you are? he typed, fingers moving more slowly now.

No.

Tell me you're all right? Surely that was the least she could do. If she was online, surely she'd just seen his e-mail; surely she had to understand just how worried he'd been.

I'm all right.

Stephanie, please talk to me. We have a lot to talk about. Okay, so she was pissed off; he could understand that. But why couldn't she just answer his questions?

We've nothing to talk about. I want my key back. Don't go near the house again. Stay away from my boss. I don't want to see you again.

That was like a slap in the face. He flinched away from the screen. It doesn't have to be this way, he typed quickly.

Actually, it does.

Please. I need to talk to you. About today. About the future.

We have no future together. Go back to your wife, Robert Walker.

A message box popped up: stephanieburroughs123 has signed off.

Robert sat in front of the screen, watching the cursor blinking rhythmically after the last sentence she had written: *Go back to your wife, Robert Walker.*

He leaned his head back and closed his eyes, trying to think, to make sense of what had just happened.

The nightmare that followed was particularly unpleasant, although when he awoke, he could remember none of the details, only the incredible feeling of loss and searching, of traveling through a long gray-white tunnel where a figure seemed to be constantly running away from him. He thought the shape in the distance might have been Kathy, but it could just as easily have been Stephanie.

CHAPTER 28

Robert came suddenly awake.

He was sitting in his chair in his office, wearing his leather coat, gloves, and outdoor shoes. He groaned aloud. His feet were blocks of ice. Rising out of the chair and standing took an effort; he felt like an old man. Peeling off his gloves he dropped them on the floor, then shrugged off the heavy coat. He sank back into the chair to fumble with the laces of his shoes. His socks were damp, his shoes lined and stained from the snow. Padding barefoot into the bathroom, Robert found a towel and sat on the edge of the bath to dry his feet.

Christ, he felt hungover. He felt exactly as if he'd spent a night drinking with Jimmy Moran. He tried arching his back and rotating his shoulders, but it didn't help ease the tension.

He wandered down to the kitchen and glanced up at the wall clock as he made the coffee. He pulled out the Peet's French Roast and poured the beans into the coffee grinder. He grimaced at the noise. It was seven thirty, and he was surprised the kids hadn't come down yet; he smiled, remembering Christmases past when they would be up at three and four in the morning. He and Kathy would lie in bed, listening to Brendan and Theresa whisper excitedly together in the next room, wondering if Santa had come. They had been good times, happy times. But it had been a long time since the children had hurried downstairs on Christmas morning to fall upon their presents. It had been a long time since he and Kathy had been happy.

He measured out the ground beans and put them in the filter, adding enough water to make a full pot. As the coffee brewed, he reached up to the cabinet for a mug—the one Theresa had made for him at Color Me Mine years earlier. It was a ceramic mug with her handwritten scrawl, World's Best Dad. Most of the letters had faded, and the once bright red was now faded almost to a dull pink. He was about to pour a cup for himself, then, on impulse, he decided to pour a second cup for Kathy. He reached for another mug and then changed his mind. She liked hers in a cup and saucer. He added the soy milk she preferred and then carried both coffees upstairs. Leaving his World's Best Dad mug balanced precariously on the banister, he gently opened the door to the bedroom and peered inside. He immediately knew by the way she was lying that she was awake. Her posture was too rigid, and normally, when she slept, she'd kick the cover off, but now the sheets were tucked in tightly beneath her chin.

He moved around to her side of the bed and put the cup of coffee on the small nightstand, alongside the fat piece of historical fiction she was reading.

"Kathy," he whispered. "Kathy . . . ?"

Her dark eyes snapped open, and she looked at him.

"I brought you some coffee."

Kathy continued to look at him, saying nothing.

"Merry Christmas," he said eventually, and thought about leaning in to kiss her, but decided not to.

"You went out last night." The simple statement held a world of accusation in it.

"The office alarm went off; I got a call from the alarm company. I had to go in." He kept his face impassive, but the irony wasn't lost on him: lying to his wife first thing Christmas morning, having promised only a few hours previously to be honest with her.

"You were gone for a long time," she said, pushing up in bed, pulling the covers up to her chin.

"Roads were terrible. Mine was the only car out; I crept along. And then when I got there, I had to make sure everything was okay." That was the problem with lies: They built upon one another, a second lie bolstering the first, a third to add credence to the second.

"I take it there was no problem with the office."

He shook his head. "Probably snow or ice falling off a neighboring building, hitting our roof, and setting off one of the sensors. I could hear other alarms ringing out across Storrow Drive as I drove home." More lies. Did you lie to a woman if you really loved her, he couldn't help but wonder. And yet he had lied to Kathy every day for the past eighteen months . . . and to Stephanie too, he realized. He had lied to Stephanie when he'd led her to believe that he was going to leave his wife to be with her. Because in the beginning he'd had no such intention. It was really only in the last couple of weeks, when Stephanie began pushing him for commitment, that he'd been forced to really consider leaving Kathy.

"Drink your coffee," he said. "I'm sure the kids will be up soon." He padded silently out of the bedroom, retrieved his cup from the banister, and locked himself in his study.

Well—leaving aside the lies—that hadn't gone too badly. At least they were talking to one another.

Drinking his coffee, able to clear his head for the first time in days, Robert finally made a decision. Now that he and Kathy had gotten over the initial shock of discovery and had started to deal with it, he had slowly and inexorably come to the conclusion that he was not prepared to spend the next couple of years constantly looking over his shoulder, wondering if his wife was checking up on his every move. He'd lived like that six years earlier, when Kathy had mistakenly accused him of having an affair with Stephanie. He'd been conscious in the weeks and months that followed that she was spying on him. He remembered standing in the bedroom and watching Kathy climb out of the car with a pen and notepad in her hands. It took him a while to work out that she was noting down the mileage. He'd quickly realized that when he stayed away from home on business, Kathy always made a point of calling the hotel with some excuse. It was a horrible, horrible feeling. He didn't want to live like that. He didn't want to spend the rest of his life knowing that his wife was watching his every move, not trusting a word he said, spying on him.

He wanted to get through Christmas, clear the air with Kathy, then talk to Stephanie. Stephanie was his future, he'd decided.

Except now she wanted nothing to do with him.

If he could only talk to her, he was sure he would be able to convince her that he genuinely loved her and wanted to be with her. If she knew that he was going to leave Kathy, he was sure she would come back to him. Wouldn't she?

It was time to make changes, radical changes. At the age of forty-nine, he had the chance to start again. Over the next year, he'd concentrate on the business, build it up, really make it a force to be reckoned with. He'd work on those scripts he'd always been planning to write, maybe even apply for a film grant for funding. He'd talk to Jimmy; although they'd often worked together in the past, maybe it was time they formalized their relationship—entered into a partnership. Jimmy could run the business, and he could look after the creative end.

And he would work with Kathy to make the separation amicable, but she would have to be reasonable. He would do a deal with her for her portion of the house, if she was prepared to do a deal with him for her percentage of the business. He'd make certain to let the children know that he would always be there for them, that he would always love them. They were teenagers; he was sure they were old enough to understand.

And he wouldn't make the same mistakes with Stephanie that he'd made with Kathy. He'd pay attention to her, and he knew she'd pay attention to him. They worked in the same type of business, so work would be a shared interest. He'd move into her condo and help her with the mortgage. Although Stephanie had talked about possibly having a baby, she was thinking two or three years down the road. A lot could happen in that time. Frankly, he'd done all that, knew the amount of time and effort babies took, and he definitely didn't want to do it again. Once Stephanie started moving up the corporate ladder, she wouldn't want children to distract her. It would be just the two of them, no diversions, no interruptions. They would be happy together.

A new beginning, a new future: That would be his New Year's present to himself.

All he had to do was convince Stephanie that he was genuine. And the one way of doing that was to spend New Year's Eve together and start the New Year with her.

CHAPTER 29

―――――――――― ❦ ――――――――――

Half the country awoke to a white Christmas. Ten inches of snow had fallen across the entire East Coast, while certain areas of Connecticut and Providence, Rhode Island, were coated in fourteen inches, with more forecast for the afternoon. Parts of Massachusetts were impassable, and AAA was advising drivers only to venture out if it was absolutely necessary.

The sky had cleared with the dawn, and the sun was a flat gold disc that shed no heat, but touched everything with a thin veneer of amber light. The morning was spectacular, and Robert thought it ironic that the last Christmas they would spend together should be so memorable. Brendan and Theresa would be sure to remember that their last Christmas as a family was the time it snowed.

Robert and Kathy were outwardly polite to one another in the presence of the children, but when they were on their own, an icy gulf separated them. They went as a family to eleven o'clock Mass, the only time of the year when the four of them attended church together. Although both Robert and Kathy had been raised Catholic, they had lapsed and were unwilling to force their children to join any organized religion. They hoped that when the kids were old enough they would make their own decisions, though so far, neither showed an interest in any particular faith.

Robert felt deeply uncomfortable in church. He had never been particularly religious—but he did like to think of himself as spiritual. He believed in God; he just wasn't sure why it couldn't be a more private relationship, not molded by the church's principles. When he'd stood at the altar eighteen years ago with Kathy by his side, he remembered dutifully repeating the priest's words: "I, Robert Walker, take this ring as a sign of my love and fidelity. In the name of the Father, and of the Son, and of the Holy Spirit." He had disappointed not only Kathy and himself; he had disappointed God. Eighteen years ago he hadn't intended to break those vows. And yet, here he was standing in church on Christmas morning, actively planning to break those solemn oaths without causing his wife too much pain. Maybe he didn't love Kathy enough to want to spend the rest of his life with her, but he still cared for her; she was the mother of his children, and he wanted her to retain her dignity. There was no stigma attached to divorce anymore; in fact, most marriages failed.

"Let us share with one another the sign of peace...." The elderly priest's voice boomed across the loudspeakers.

Robert turned toward Kathy. While other couples around them were embracing or kissing, she stuck out her hand like a stranger. After a moment's hesitation, Robert fixed a smile on his lips and took her hand. "Peace be with you," he murmured.

Kathy didn't respond.

He was going to have to find himself a divorce lawyer. He'd call Jimmy Moran after Christmas; Jimmy would be sure to know.

"Dad, phone." Brendan didn't move from the couch.

Robert opened his eyes and blinked at the TV. His late night had finally caught up with him in the early afternoon, and, despite *Indiana Jones and the Temple of Doom* blaring from all five speakers, he'd fallen into a deep and dreamless sleep. "You get it," he mumbled.

"It'll be for you. It's always for you."

Robert rolled out of the chair, moved into the dining room, and grabbed the phone from its cradle before the call went to the machine. He licked dry lips and squinted at the clock, wondering who was calling them on Christmas Day. Julia probably. "Hello?"

The line echoed and popped, ghost sounds clicking and whispering.

"Hello?" he asked again, squinting at the caller ID. Unavailable, it read, so either the call was from abroad or the caller had withheld his or her number.

"You may want to move away from the TV and find someplace private where you can talk." Stephanie's voice, loud and clear in his ear, shocked him fully awake.

He swallowed hard. "Sure . . . sure," he said, forcing a smile onto his face, turning to look at the children, but they were both ignoring him. Kathy was working in the kitchen, and he saw her glance curiously at him, obviously wondering who was calling. "And a Merry Christmas to you too," he continued. "Let me just step out of the room away from the TV. . . ."

"It's Jimmy Moran," he said to Kathy, the phone pressed against his chest, "just calling to wish us Merry Christmas."

Kathy nodded. Wearing a striped cook's apron, she was staring into the open oven, slowly sinking a skewer into the turkey. "Don't talk too long; I'll be serving dinner soon."

Robert moved out into the hall. "I'll be just a minute." He hurried upstairs, heart pounding, stepped into his office, and locked the door behind him. Then he changed from the portable phone to his office line. "Are you okay?" he asked immediately, slightly breathless from his run upstairs and the shocking surprise of the call.

"Yes . . . no . . . I don't know." Her voice sounded strained.

He figured she was probably hung over. No doubt she'd only now gotten around to checking her messages; maybe she was even a little embarrassed about her outburst earlier.

"I've been worried out of my mind, and when I couldn't get

hold of you, I didn't know what to think, and then before, when we were instant-messaging and you said you didn't want to see me again, I was devastated."

There was a long pause, then Stephanie said simply, "I think I'm pregnant, Robert."

There was a moment, a long moment, as the words sank in. Thoughts tumbled through his mind—this was a joke; she was punishing him; she was lying—because he knew that she couldn't be pregnant. Simply couldn't.

Before he could reply, she snapped, "What? No quick comment, no witty retort, no congratulations?" She was unable to disguise the bitterness in her voice.

"I . . . I . . . No. I don't know what to say."

"Well, think of something."

His mouth was dry and felt like it was stuffed with cotton wool, and he had difficulty swallowing. He looked around the room, but could find nothing to drink. He finally cracked open one of the windows and dipped his fingers in the snow crystals, and then brought them to his mouth. Ice cold, they burned their way down his throat. Staring out at the backyard, now sheathed in snow, he asked, "How did this . . . I mean, when did this happen?"

"Who knows? We've had sex a couple of times without using protection."

Pregnant. Dear God. She was pregnant. "I said you should have gone on the pill."

Stephanie didn't respond. She'd refused to go on the pill, and they had ended up using condoms, which he hated.

"Are you sure? Certain?" he asked carefully.

"Reasonably."

Reasonably. Reasonably. What exactly does "reasonably" mean, he wondered.

"My period is ten days late."

"Ten days isn't a lot, is it?" he said desperately.

"It's long enough."

"But you've taken a test, haven't you? Confirmed it?"

"It's Christmas Day, Robert, just in case you've forgotten," she snapped. "Where am I going to get a pregnancy test kit today?"

He licked his lips. "But you really think you could be?"

"Yes, I do."

Taking a deep breath, he asked, "Have you decided what to do about it . . . about the baby?"

"No," she said icily. "But you're the father. I wanted to talk to you first. Make some joint decisions. Real decisions."

"Yes, yes, yes, of course." This was a nightmare. If she were pregnant, they would have do something about it. Soon. He wondered how far gone she was. "Look, can we meet? Not today obviously . . ." he amended quickly. Getting out of the house now, with Christmas dinner about to be served, would be impossible. There would be too many awkward questions. "Tomorrow. Can we meet tomorrow?"

"Tomorrow might be a little difficult for me. . . ."

Robert shook his head in frustration. Why was she making things so difficult? "I really need to see you, to talk to you," he said. "I can meet you. Anywhere," he added.

"Anywhere?"

He thought he heard a touch of amusement in her question. "I'll go anywhere," he insisted.

"Fine then. I'm at my parents' house."

Robert frowned, trying to make sense of the statement. "In Wisconsin?" he asked finally.

"Yes."

"What are you doing there?"

"Having a family Christmas," she snapped. "Robert," she hissed, "what did you expect me to do? Sit around in an empty house on Christmas Day reminding myself just how stupid I'd been?"

"Look, about yesterday . . . ," he began.

"Dinner's ready!" Kathy's voice echoed faintly up the stairs.

"Not now," Stephanie snapped. "I don't want to talk about the past. I want to talk about our child."

Our child. Robert felt a chill wash over him. Our child.

"You know, I had no intention of ever seeing you again, of having anything to do with you. But that's changed now. If I am pregnant, I have to see you."

"Yes, yes, of course you must." A child. Our child. Robert drew in a long breath. "How sure?" He licked dry lips. "I mean how certain are you that you're pregnant?"

"You've asked me that already, and I'll give you the same answer: reasonably sure."

"When will you know for certain?" He grasped at the straw: Reasonably sure was not the same as dead certain.

"Tomorrow," she said.

"When are you coming home?" he asked.

"I don't know. I wasn't planning to come back until after the New Year, but I think this changes everything. I'll see if I can get back before the weekend. I'll check flights later."

"Let me know what flight you're coming in on. I'll pick you up. We can talk. Make decisions. See what you want to do about it."

Stephanie's voice was flat and unemotional, almost businesslike. "Robert, it's not what I want to do—this is our baby. It is all about what we want to do."

"Well, let's talk about options. . . ."

"What do you mean by options?" she snapped immediately.

This was definitely not something they should be discussing over the phone; this was something that had to be handled face-to-face. If she'd just discovered that she was pregnant, then she was bound to be emotional and upset. He needed to give her a little time to think about things. "I mean what's best for you and the baby," he finished lamely.

"Dad, dinner's on the table!" Brendan called.

"Look, I've got to go," Robert said quickly. He didn't want the children coming up and finding the door locked, and he wanted to take a few moments to compose himself before he went down for dinner . . . though right now, he had absolutely no appetite. "It's great to hear from you, and good to know that you're okay." He attempted a laugh, which sounded hollow even to his ears. "Though how you got to Madison on Christmas Eve, I'll never know. What were you thinking?"

"I wasn't. Bit like when I began my affair with you, Robert. I simply wasn't thinking of the consequences."

The phone went dead before Robert could respond.

CHAPTER 30

———⁂———

They had just finished their soup when the phone rang again.

Brendan and Theresa turned to look at their father, but Kathy said, "Let the machine get it. This is one of the few meals this family sits down to together."

Robert nodded dubiously. What if it was Stephanie calling back? The last thing he needed was her voice calling out into the room. "I'd better get it. I'll just be a minute."

Kathy sighed as she carried the soup bowls out to the kitchen.

Robert snatched up the phone. "Hello?"

"Robert Walker?"

"Yes, this is Robert Walker," he said, puzzled. The caller ID showed a 617 area code.

"This is Sharon May Reed. I'm a nurse at Mass General. . . ."

"Hi," Robert said, more puzzled than alarmed. "What can I do for you?"

Kathy came to the kitchen door, eyebrows raised in a silent question.

"I'm phoning on behalf of Mr. James Moran. . . ."

"James . . . I don't know . . . Oh, you mean Jimmy."

"Yes. Jimmy Moran."

"Is he okay?"

"Mr. Moran has just been admitted for observation. He's asked me to contact you. He said he'd like to see you."

"Today?" Robert covered the mouthpiece and muttered to Kathy, "Mass General. Jimmy's been admitted."

"But you were talking to him less than half an hour ago," Kathy said, but Robert wasn't listening to her. The nurse was speaking again.

"Mr. Walker, are you there?" Nurse Reed asked.

"Yes, yes, I'm here. . . . It's just it's . . . Christmas, and I'm with my family. . . ."

"I fully understand," the nurse said, in a tone that suggested that she didn't.

"Is it an emergency?" Robert asked.

"Is Mr. Moran a friend of yours?"

"Yes, yes, a good friend."

"Then I think you'd better come."

"Tell him I'm on the way." He hung up and looked at Kathy. "It sounds really serious. I'm sorry, but I've got to go. . . ."

"I know. You should go. But how did he sound when you were talking to him earlier?"

Robert looked at his wife blankly, then remembered that he'd used Jimmy's name as the excuse for the previous call. "He sounded fine," he said lamely. Lies upon lies upon lies. Where did it ever end?

"Go. Get your coat and gloves. I'll fill a thermos with coffee."

The late afternoon sunlight was blinding, and Robert found himself squinting against the light as he drove to the hospital, wishing he'd brought his sunglasses. He could feel a headache—a combination of the light, lack of sleep, and stress—beginning to throb behind his eyes.

Robert sipped the hot over-sweetened coffee as he drove. What had happened to Jimmy, and why had he asked for him? Surely either Angela his wife or Frances his girlfriend would be with him?

He was surprised that Kathy had let him go so easily—though

he had seen the expression of distrust in her eyes when she'd been questioning him about the earlier call. Why had he used Jimmy's name? If he got a chance, he might have a quick word with his old friend and ask him for an alibi, just in case Kathy asked. He'd given Jimmy alibis often enough in the past, though he had never thought he'd be needing a similar favor in return.

He was happy to be able to get out of the house. The conversation with Stephanie had shocked him to his core, left him feeling slightly shaky, almost as if he were coming down with the flu.

He was also stunned that following the dramatic confrontation between Kathy, Stephanie, and himself yesterday, Stephanie had managed to book herself on a flight back to Wisconsin. It was all so improbable. Maybe she was sitting at home, or in her friend's house, or somewhere in a bar in downtown Boston, just spinning him this story to keep him away from her. That also begged the question: Was she really pregnant? They'd broken up only yesterday, and suddenly she was pregnant. It was too much of a warped coincidence. He'd tried to get a straight answer out of her, but all she'd said was that she was reasonably sure that she was pregnant. Well, either she was or she wasn't.

And if she was . . . Well, Robert couldn't help but wonder how this impacted his New-Year, New-Start fantasy.

There is no place more lonely than a hospital on Christmas Day, Robert decided, following the directions the young woman at the reception desk had given him. Although there were Christmas trees on every floor at the nurses' stations, decorations on the walls, and Christmas cards and flowers everywhere, it had all the appearance of a movie set—everything was in place, but nothing belonged. Many of the rooms he passed were half empty, or held a single occupant, usually surrounded by a large family group, and there were far fewer nurses than he would have expected. He saw no doctors.

Jimmy Moran was in a private room on the side of the hospital that overlooked the Red Line. Robert checked the number on the half-open door and peered inside. It took him a single shocking moment to recognize the shrunken, pallid figure in the bed as his friend and mentor. Jimmy's fine, elegant features were sharply outlined against his skin, giving his face a skull-like appearance, and his flesh was the color of off-white paper, which highlighted the threads of broken veins in his cheeks. His jet-black hair was spread out on the pillow in a greasy swirl.

Conscious that his heart was hammering, Robert fixed a smile on his face and tapped on the door as he stepped into the room.

Jimmy turned his head to look at his visitor, tired eyes struggling to focus. Then he nodded and stretched out his right hand. A tube attached to a drip was taped to his left hand. "Robert . . ." He licked dry, cracked lips. "Robert," he said a little more strongly, "thank you for coming."

Robert pulled over a chair and sat down beside the bed. He took off his coat and laid it across the back of the chair. Jimmy was fifty-two years old—three years older than himself—but today, he looked older, much, much older. "You knew I'd come."

Jimmy nodded. "I knew I could depend on you." He glanced sidelong at the bedside table. "Pass me some water, would you?"

Robert stood to pour a glass of water. "I'm sorry I didn't have a chance to get you anything—flowers or chocolate or something like that—but when the hospital called I just came straight here."

"I wasn't expecting you to woo me." Jimmy laughed feebly. "I'm sorry to have dragged you away from your family on Christmas Day."

"It's not a problem. Really. Kathy sends her love." He held the glass to Jimmy's lips while he sipped, then helped Jimmy lie back on the pillow. When his friend was settled, Robert sat back down again and took his hand. "What happened?"

"Looks like a heart attack." Jimmy grinned wryly. "I thought it was indigestion. I was cooking the turkey, and I'd been picking away at it all morning, just testing to see if it was cooked through. Plus, I'd had most of a bottle of an indifferent South African red."

"But, Jimmy, you can't cook! Do you remember that barbecue we had at your Quincy house when you'd finished renovating it? I spent a week with Montezuma's revenge after that."

Jimmy laughed. The laughter turned into a quiet, wheezing cough that seemed to catch in the center of his chest. "I remember. You and me both, though the women were unaffected."

"Yeah, because they didn't touch the sausages. I think both Kathy and Angela pretended to be vegetarians." Robert kept his tone light and the smile on his lips. The color of Jimmy's skin, the blue of his lips was frightening him. "So how did you get in here?"

"I knew there was a problem when the indigestion didn't go away, and then I knew there was a bigger problem when it moved into my left arm. I'd a good idea what that meant. Shit, Robert, how many people in our business do we know who've had problems with their tickers?"

"Too many," Robert agreed. The lifestyle combination of too much business conducted over too many rich meals, coupled with incredible amounts of stress, meant that heart problems, high blood pressure, and high cholesterol were endemic in the business. He'd been meaning to have his own cholesterol checked recently, but he'd never had the time.

"I dialed 911," Jimmy went on. "And then I waited. And waited. And waited." He attempted a shrug, which hurt. "Of course it's Christmas Day, and the roads are shite. I was waiting about forty-five minutes before they got to me. I could have walked to the hospital in that time." His eyes filled with tears. "It felt like an eternity. I think I might have had another attack sitting in the chair. Felt like I'd been stabbed in the shoulder."

"Where were you?"

"In the apartment in the North End."

"Alone?"

Jimmy nodded.

"Jimmy, why didn't you say something to me the other night? You could have spent Christmas with us. I didn't even think to ask; I thought you'd go to Frances or that maybe Angela would have you home for the day." Frances, a former actress, was Jimmy's girl-friend who had given him a son eighteen months earlier. Angela was Jimmy's long-suffering wife who was in the process of divorcing him.

"I didn't want to impose on you," Jimmy whispered. "Actually," he admitted, "I was hoping that Angela would have me back . . . just for the day, as you say. But she's done with me. Really done this time. I tried calling her from the apartment, but she wouldn't answer. Frances picked up her phone, but put it down again when she heard my voice." There were tears on his cheeks now. "All I wanted to do was to say good-bye . . . just in case."

"Why didn't you go up to Concord and stay with Frances?"

"I spoke to her yesterday morning and suggested it, but I could tell she wasn't too keen on the idea. She said she was snowed in and that I'd never make it up. I wasn't sure whether to believe her or not, but I got the impression that even if she wasn't snowed in, she didn't want me around. I've a feeling," he added with a wry smile, "that she's found herself a nice young man, with the emphasis on young. More power to her."

"Jesus, Jimmy—what a mess."

"I always did have a flare for the dramatic."

"Have the doctors seen you yet?"

"I was checked in about two hours ago by some young fella who looked like he was about twelve. All he'd tell me was there was some arrhythmia—as if I didn't know that—but that they'd take me in for observation and they'd have to do some tests, take some X-rays and scans to be sure. He said they'd have to wait for a little while because the alcohol in my system would mask the results, and it also means they couldn't give me any meds. Let me give you a piece of advice, son, don't ever come into the hospital on Christmas Day. Any other day of the year, you're fine—but not Christmas."

"I kind of figured that. How do you feel now?"

Jimmy pushed himself up in the bed. Robert adjusted the pillows and helped Jimmy to sit a little straighter. "Considering everything, not too bad. Better now that you're here. I'm feeling a little guilty now that I dragged you away from your family."

Robert shook his head. "I would have been annoyed if you hadn't."

Jimmy reached over and squeezed Robert's hand. "Waiting for the ambulance to arrive, feeling the pain in my chest getting worse, watching black spots before my eyes . . . You know, I thought I was going to die."

"Why didn't you call me?"

"Because if I did die, I didn't want you to find my dead body."

"Thanks . . . I think," Robert muttered. His own father had died

fifteen years ago. Although he'd been living on the other side of
Boston, less than an hour away from where Robert lived, they had
rarely seen one another. When Robert had seen his father laid out
in the open coffin in the funeral parlor, he hadn't recognized the
bloated figure.

Jimmy tilted his head toward the gray window. A train squealed
by, oblivious to the storm. The sky was leaden, and the snow was
falling heavily now, coating the piles of grimy slush in a new layer of
white; heavy, fat drops hit against the windows and curled slowly
down to gather at the base of the frame in a lattice of ice crystals.
"A white Christmas," Robert said, glancing over his shoulder. "I
don't remember the last one we had, do you?"

Jimmy shook his head. "Never forget this one though."

"Amen to that," Robert said grimly. He wasn't ever going to forget this Christmas.

"Will you do me a favor before you go?" Jimmy asked.

Robert spun around. "Go? Go where? I'm not leaving."

"It's Christmas Day, Robert. You should be with your family."

"You're also my family, Jimmy."

Jimmy nodded, suddenly unwilling to trust himself to speak. He
concentrated on finishing the glass of water, then said, "Will you
call Angela for me, please? Tell her where I am and that I'm okay."

"You're not okay," Robert reminded him.

"Aye, well, but there's no point in alarming her. Besides, what's
she going to do? She's probably snowed in, in Quincy."

Robert took the number from Jimmy and stepped out into the
hallway to call Angela Moran. He walked up and down the corri-
dors, ignoring the glares from the few nurses on duty and the signs
that said to switch off all cell phones.

Angela's phone rang nearly a dozen times before it was finally
picked up. He could hear the clink of glasses and low, muted music
in the background.

A voice boomed, "Hello, hello?"

"Oh, hello." It was a man's voice, and Robert had been expecting Angela to answer. "I'm not sure if I've dialed the right number.
I'm looking for Angela. . . ."

"Yes, she's here."

Robert heard the clunk as the phone was dropped onto a hard surface, and then a slightly drunk male voice calling, "Angela, darling, phone for you!"

Footsteps rattled on wood, then clicked on marble. There was a time when Robert had been a regular visitor to the historical colonial property Jimmy and Angela had bought on the outskirts of Quincy. Rumor was John Adams had lived there for a short period. The house was magnificent, and the couple had restored it in exquisite taste. Robert could just imagine Angela—tall, thin, an overly made-up, brittle beauty—walking across the black and white marble floor to pick up the phone. "Hello. Yes?"

"Angela. Merry Christmas. It's Robert Walker."

There was a pause, no doubt as Angela tried to remember who exactly Robert Walker was. It had been about four years since he'd last spoken to her.

"Oh, Robert. What a pleasant surprise." Angela's cut-glass diction was perfect; she'd been a reporter in the early days of NPR. "How's Kathy?"

"She's very good, thank you, Angela," Robert said quickly. "I'm calling you for Jimmy."

There was a slight pause, and when Angela spoke again, there was a definite chill in her voice. "Has he asked you to call me?"

"Yes, he . . ."

"I don't want to speak to him or about him."

Robert bit back an angry response. "I'm at Mass General, Angela," he said firmly. "Jimmy was admitted earlier with a suspected heart attack."

There was a pause, then Angela said, "I'm not entirely sure I believe you, Robert. Is this another one of Jimmy's pranks? He's broken my heart with his lies and his affairs, and I am afraid, Robert, that this may be just another of his tricks designed to fool me. I won't fall for it this time. If Jimmy's genuinely in the hospital, then please give him my best wishes for a speedy recovery."

". . . and then she hung up," Robert finished. "She believed it was some sort of joke. Where would she get that idea?"

"Ah, well...," Jimmy said quietly. "Last Christmas I might have told her a little white lie to get back home."

"A little white lie?"

"I said the apartment was flooded—a burst water pipe. I painted a very graphic picture of frozen icicles of water hanging from the ceiling. And Angela—God love her, but she has a big heart—asked me home for Christmas dinner. I think that was the last meal we had together."

"But it was a lie."

"A slight gilding of the truth perhaps. She wasn't very happy when she found out."

"Why didn't you stay with Frances last year?"

"The baby was only six months old, and her mother was there. I'm afraid that the potent combination of postnatal girlfriend, mewling baby, and girlfriend's mother was too much for me to contemplate, or bear. So I told her I spent Christmas in the apartment. And she was even less pleased when she discovered the truth, that I'd spent Christmas Day with Angela."

"I know you didn't ask me to," Robert said, "but I phoned Frances."

"Jayzus," Jimmy muttered.

"She seems to think you had a fight the last time you were with her and that she'd thrown you out and told you never to come back."

"Ah. There might have been some hard words said over her boyfriend," Jimmy admitted. "But you know me: quick to anger, even quicker to forgive."

"So the upshot of it is, Angela doesn't believe you're in the hospital, and your girlfriend doesn't care. How do you end up in these messes, Jimmy?"

"Stupidity," Jimmy Moran said simply. "Just honest-to-God stupidity. I didn't realize how good I had it with Angela. I loved her—in my fashion—and she loved me, but I was prepared to throw it all away because a young one flashed her big eyes at me ... made me feel young again." He patted Robert on the hand. "Learn from my mistakes, Bobby: You've a good thing going with Kathy; don't be a feckin' eeijet and throw it all away for the illusion of youth. It doesn't last."

Robert had opened his mouth to respond when the door opened and an extremely harassed-looking young doctor appeared. "Now, Mr. Moran," he began, then glanced at Robert. "If you could give us a few moments, I just need to run some tests on your father. . . ."

CHAPTER 31

"They took him down for tests about two hours ago," Robert said to Kathy. "I keep asking them for results or a progress report, but the nurses on duty can't tell me anything."

Kathy's voice cracked and hissed on the cell phone. "And how did he look?"

Robert ran his fingers through his hair and sighed. "Terrible. Kathy, when I first saw him, I thought he was dead."

"He's tough, Robert; you know that. He's going to pull through."

"I'm sorry for ruining your Christmas," he said eventually. He walked back into Jimmy's room and closed the door. In the darkness, he stood at the windows, watching the snow fall, invisible until the moment it whirled around the streetlights.

"It was ruined a long time before Jimmy got sick."

He nodded, his reflection in the glass mimicking the movement. Then he said simply, "Yes."

"If you'd stayed at home today, we would probably have ended up fighting."

"Probably," he agreed. He'd had the same thought. If Jimmy hadn't provided him with an excuse to leave the house, he knew he would have had to invent one. And he knew that if he left the house for no reason, Kathy would immediately suspect that he was going to see Stephanie. Maybe he should tell her that Stephanie had gone back to Wisconsin . . . though that might raise the awkward question: How did he know?

"Maybe this time apart has been . . . useful. Allows us both to get a little perspective."

"Yes, yes, you're right."

"Time to think," she added.

"I've been doing nothing but think," he said carefully, though he'd arrived at no conclusions. His head was still whirling with possibilities and opportunities—all he needed to do was find a little quiet time to think them through. His lack of sleep was catching up with him, and he felt fuzzy, disoriented.

"We'll talk when you get home. Maybe we'll have a little dinner together, just the two of us, and talk."

"That would be nice. . . . Yes, it's been a long time since we sat down and talked. It'll be just like the old days." In the early days of their marriage and for the first few years after the children came along, they would sit together every night and talk. It didn't have to be about important things—simply the mundane events in their days, items on the news, television shows they'd seen, gossip they'd heard. He wasn't sure when the ritual had begun to drift away—when the kids got a little older, he thought, or maybe when he started working later and later. Then, by the time he got home, he was so exhausted that the last thing he wanted to do was chat. Looking back now, he realized how important those conversations had been. The communication had bonded them.

"Do you think you're going to make it home tonight?" Kathy asked.

"I'd like to wait and see how Jimmy is. I don't want to leave him on his own."

"Why is he alone? I thought Angela or Frances would be there. They're not snowed in, are they?"

"Maybe, but that's not the reason they're staying away. They've both refused to come. Turns out Jimmy told them too many lies over too many years, and that's finally caught up with him," Robert admitted. "I'd like to stay for a while longer . . . if that's okay," he added.

"Of course it's okay. It's snowing heavily here. It's probably better if you stay there, rather than getting back on the road. The hospital staff isn't going to kick you out."

Robert leaned forward to stare down at the street. It was completely deserted. "Maybe I'll try to nap on one of the empty beds." His phone started blipping, and he swore softly. In his rush to get to Jimmy, he'd forgotten to bring his charger. "Shit, I'm down to one bar," he said quickly.

"Is there a phone in the room?" Kathy asked immediately.

Robert hit the switch over the bed, flooding the room with diffused yellow light, and squinted at the number taped beneath the telephone. "Here it is. . . ." Even as he was reading out the number, he felt sure that Kathy would phone him on it at some stage in the next couple of hours. It was her way of checking up on him, one she had used before when she suspected him of lying to her about his location. Surely she didn't think that this was some sort of elaborate ruse to spend time with Stephanie? He felt anger bubbling . . . and then he remembered that he had used Jimmy's name to lie to Kathy earlier. "Look, I'd better go and save what's left of the battery. You've got the number; call me anytime. I'll be here for the next couple of hours at least, and if I do decide to stay here, I'll give you a call."

"Give Jimmy my love," Kathy said and hung up.

"And what about me?" Robert whispered quietly, staring at the phone.

Robert was dozing in the chair when Jimmy Moran was brought back to the room by a trio of nurses in green scrubs. He smiled wanly at Robert and attempted to lift a hand to wave at him, but couldn't manage more than waggling his fingers.

Robert stood awkwardly in the corner and watched as the staff lifted Jimmy onto the bed. Two bustled away pushing the gurney while the third—a slender, Indian woman—filled in the chart at the foot of the bed. She glanced up at Robert and smiled, her teeth startlingly white against moist red lipstick. "I'm Doctor Sidhu."

"Good evening, Doctor." He came over to the side of the bed and squeezed Jimmy's hand in his. "How is he?"

"Don't talk about me as if I wasn't in the room," Jimmy grumbled.

"Behave yourself," Robert snapped.

"Your father had at least one and possibly two minor heart attacks today," Doctor Sidhu said, making the same mistake as the previous doctor, and neither Robert nor Jimmy corrected her error. "They weren't the first, I might add, though he might not even have been aware of the other ones. I would imagine the cardiac surgeon will want to discuss a bypass—certainly a double and possibly a triple—within the very near future."

"How near?" Robert asked.

"Within the next couple of months certainly. Maybe sooner."

Robert held a glass of water to his friend's lips and watched him sip. When Jimmy's lips were wet, he managed to ask, "When can I go home?"

The young doctor smiled. "Well, not today, and not tomorrow, that's for sure. Maybe before New Year's—on the condition that this will be the quietest New Year you'll ever celebrate. We'll keep you under observation for a few days, monitor your vitals, and then our heart specialist will have a look at you. He'll make the final decision." She looked down at the chart. "It says here you live alone."

"He can come home with me," Robert said immediately.

"I can't—" Jimmy began.

"I insist," Robert said.

"But Kathy—"

"Will be delighted to have you too," Robert said firmly. He looked at the doctor. "I'll look after him."

"Well, that makes it easier certainly." The doctor clipped the chart back onto the end of the bed and patted Jimmy's leg. "It's good to have family at times like this, isn't it?"

When she was gone, Jimmy muttered, "I hate doctors!"

Robert pulled over the chair and sat beside the bed. "What did she ever do to you?"

Jimmy did a passable imitation of her voice. "It's good to have family at times like this, isn't it? I'm fifty-two, not eighty-two. Do I look old enough to be your father?"

"Right now, you look old enough to be my grandfather," Robert said sincerely.

Jimmy's smile faded. "I would have been proud to have a son like you, Robert. You know that."

"Hey, there's no need for that sort of talk. I'm proud to know you too. You've taught me so much. In fact, I was thinking only this morning . . ."

"Was there drink involved in this thought?"

"Not a drop. And just as well, since I ended up driving in a snowstorm at two o'clock in the morning."

Jimmy's eyes widened. "This has to do with Stephanie?"

"Bingo. I'll tell you about that in a minute. First, let me tell you what I was thinking."

"Go on."

"Next year, I need to get my act together and crack this independent production nut. I really need to settle down and get some solid work done. You know, when I started out in this business, I had such big dreams; I was going to do cutting-edge, controversial documentaries, hard-hitting exposés. . . . And what have I ended up doing?"

"Anything and everything that puts food on the table, gives you practical experience, and that you're not ashamed to put on the résumé. I told you that."

"I remember. I didn't agree with you when I first heard it. Then you told me that Ridley Scott started out in advertising."

"Shot the famous Hovis ad. Boy pushing a bike up a hill."

"What's Hovis?"

"Bread. YouTube it. Fabulous advert."

"I'm going to need a partner, someone I know and trust, someone who can look after the business while I concentrate on getting in some new work. If this music video takes off, it could be massive and bring us in a lot of new business. I won't be able to handle it on my own."

Jimmy lay in the bed and watched him, saying nothing.

"We've collaborated well in the past. I was thinking it might be time to formalize our relationship and go into partnership together. We could set up a new company: Walker-Moran—has a nice ring to it. Well, say something," he added, when Jimmy didn't respond.

"I'd like . . . I'd like that very much," Jimmy Moran said, a catch in his voice. "But, Robert, I'm damaged goods. There are a lot of people in this city who'd cross the road to avoid me."

"And many more who cross the road to ask your advice," Robert persisted. "Will you at least think about it?"

"I'll think about it," Jimmy promised. "But only on condition that the name is Moran-Walker." He smiled. "Have you spoken to Kathy about this?"

Robert stretched his forearms out on the bed and locked his hands together. "Not yet," he sighed. "I'm going to try to buy Kathy's piece of the company off her."

"That doesn't sound good," Jimmy mumbled. He reached over and hit the light switch, plunging the room in deep gloom. "The light was hurting my eyes," he explained.

The two men remained silent while the room gradually brightened with a dull, metallic light reflected back off the snow outside. A streetlight cut a bar of warm amber high into the corner of the room. "Tell me what's happened, Robert," Jimmy said finally.

"Kathy found out about Stephanie. The three of us had a . . . meeting yesterday in Stephanie's living room. If you'll pardon the expression, I thought I was having a heart attack when I walked into the room and found the two women there."

"Been there, worn that tee shirt. It can go two ways—screaming or icy politeness."

"We had icy politeness."

"Oh, that's the worst sort. Nothing beats a good screaming match for clearing the air."

"And then Stephanie rejected me, told me to go back to my wife." Robert shook his head; he was still not entirely sure why she'd done it.

"And Kathy took you back?"

"Yes."

"Always said she was a good girl. Takes guts to do that."

Robert remained silent. He remembered that Maureen had said exactly the same thing. Funny, he'd never thought of his wife in those terms before.

"That is what you want, isn't it?"

"Well..." Robert let the word linger in the air between the two friends.

Jimmy reached out and squeezed Robert's arm. "You've been given a second chance, son; don't screw it up. Look at me—learn from my mistakes."

"I know, I know I've got this second chance... but I want to take that chance with Stephanie."

"You don't throw away eighteen years of marriage so easily."

"I'm not. Six years ago, Kathy accused me of having an affair. I think that's when our marriage started to fall apart."

"Bollocks. You're the one who had the affair, Bob. Kathy stayed faithful to you."

Robert stood up and walked to the window, stuck his hands in his pockets, and stared down onto the broad expanse of white below. His breath plumed a perfect circle on the glass.

"I'm forty-nine, Jimmy. I've been given a chance to start again with a woman who loves me. I'd be an idiot not to take it."

"Kathy loves you. Loves you enough to fight for you. If she didn't want you, it would have been so easy to let you go to Stephanie."

Robert rested his forehead against the chill glass. He knew that. Even when he had been making his New Year's plans, that was always at the back of his thoughts: Kathy loved him.

"So, I take it you haven't talked to either Kathy or Stephanie about this plan?"

"Not yet. Stephanie... Stephanie vanished after our encounter yesterday. I nearly drove myself crazy trying to find her—including driving out to her house in the middle of the night—but I managed to speak to her this morning. She's at her parents' home."

"I thought she was spending Christmas in Boston?"

"That was the plan, until Kathy ended up on her doorstep. Apparently when we left she decided she wasn't going to stay here on her own and managed to book herself a flight to Wisconsin."

"Ah, shite. The Midwest in the winter. It must be feckin' freezing. Might as well go back to Dublin." Jimmy shifted uncomfortably in the bed. "You know, once you even hint to Kathy that you're still interested in Stephanie, she'll throw you out."

"I know."

"So you need to be very, very sure of yourself and, even more important, very sure of Stephanie's reaction before you do anything drastic. You shouldn't be even thinking about this right now. Emotionally, you're all over the place: Your affair has been discovered; it's Christmas; you're worried about Stephanie . . . and of course, now I've fetched up in the middle of it all, just to add another layer of complication to the situation. Please, please, please, make no decisions. Give yourself a little time; put a little distance between you and these events."

"There's another problem. . . ." Robert looked over his shoulder. He could just about make out the shape of Jimmy Moran lying in the bed. In the gray half-light, Jimmy's eyes were glittering brightly. "Stephanie thinks she may be pregnant."

"Ah, Jayzus, Bob, and you tell me my life is a mess!"

Robert moved away from the window and started pacing up and down the small room. "Stephanie called me today. . . ." A sudden thought struck him, and he stopped. "Could I ask you a favor?"

"Anything," Jimmy said immediately.

"If you're talking to Kathy and she asks if you called the house today, would you say yes? When Stephanie called earlier, I said it was you."

"I'll tell her," Jimmy said slowly.

"Stephanie's on her way home. She wants to talk to me about the child. Make plans."

"What sort of plans?" Jimmy's voice was an exhausted murmur.

"I don't know. I doubt she'll want to keep it. I'm not even sure she'll want to carry it full-term."

"Sit down, for Christ's sake," Jimmy's voice snapped. "You're making me dizzy." Robert returned to the chair by the bed, and Jimmy reached out to grab his arm. "Now, listen to me. I've never steered you wrong before, have I?"

"Never."

"Tell Kathy about the baby."

"Tell Kathy!"

"I didn't tell Angela that Frances was pregnant. That was the single biggest mistake I made. She could forgive me everything else, but not that. Tell Kathy. She needs to be involved now."

"I can't." Even the thought of it was unimaginable.

"If you don't tell her and she finds out—and she will find out—then you're finished."

"But, Jimmy, I want to finish with her."

"What! Why?" Jimmy demanded.

"Because . . ." Robert began.

"Does she still love you?" Jimmy interrupted.

"Yes, yes, she says she does."

"Did she go to Stephanie's to fight for you?

"Yes."

"And did she offer to take you back?"

"Yes."

"Then, don't be a feckin' eeijet. You want to walk away from a woman who loves you, from an eighteen-year marriage, a business you've spent the same number of years building up, a beautiful home, two gorgeous children . . . for what?"

"For Stephanie," Robert said quietly.

"Tell me what Stephanie's ever done for you—besides bringing some jobs to the business and the sex, of course."

There was a long moment of silence, then Robert said, "She makes me feel good about myself."

"Bobby, only you can make you feel good about yourself. Let

me tell you from bitter experience, the sex is never as good when you're living with the person. Nothing beats the thrill of an illicit liaison. You've told me she's not going to be able to put any more business your way for the moment, and once you're a couple, that door is completely closed." He stopped and started to cough, deep racking barks that doubled him over in pain. "If you leave Kathy," he gasped, his breath coming in painful heaves, "you'll lose it all: wife, children, and home, and maybe the business too. Maureen will walk; she's more loyal to Kathy than she is to you. You'll be left with nothing. Trust me; this is one subject in which I am an expert."

Jimmy's affairs were legendary. Robert had realized a long time ago that Jimmy genuinely loved women, and, like most men, he enjoyed the thrill of the chase even more than the capture. Robert couldn't help but wonder if Jimmy's attitude toward affairs had colored his own mindset when he'd entered into his relationship with Stephanie. Robert remembered being almost shocked that he'd not experienced more pangs of conscience.

"Please rest, Jimmy," Robert said, becoming alarmed by the sound of Jimmy's cough. "Please. I'll think about everything you've said. I promise. Just relax now."

"Give me some water."

Robert poured a glass of water and held it to Jimmy's lips.

"Thanks."

"I won't make any drastic decisions, I promise. You've given me a lot to think about. As always," he added, attempting to smile.

"Kathy loves you," Jimmy murmured. "She's shocked, upset, confused. Telling her about the baby isn't going to be as big a blow as you might think. Be honest with her now. Tell her everything."

"I will," Robert said quickly. He would promise Jimmy anything now, just to calm him down.

"Good lad." Jimmy laughed. "You know, maybe I will go into partnership with you next year. You could be my junior partner."

"Hey—not so much of the junior!"

"I think I'd like that." Jimmy's voice was fading as he drifted into sleep. "Been alone for too long. We'd make a great team." His fingers were cool as he squeezed Robert's hand. "Don't make my mistakes, Bob. Don't walk away from a woman who loves you. . . ."

It took Robert a few minutes before he realized that Jimmy Moran was never going to speak again.

CHAPTER 32

Saturday, 28th December

"It's time to go."

Robert Walker was sitting on the edge of the small bed in his study, tying his shoelaces. His wife was standing in the doorway, wearing her heavy black down coat.

"I didn't think it was that late," he muttered.

"The roads will be icy," Kathy reminded him. "We should leave a little early. The kids have decided to stay here," she added. "They didn't really know Jimmy all that well. I think it's just as well."

Robert straightened. "Yes, yes, of course," he said distractedly. "I spoke to Lloyd, the brother in Australia, a couple of hours ago. He's not going to make it over for the funeral. He can't get the time off."

"That's a shame."

"Yes, but at least Mikey and Teddy will be here. I think Jimmy would have liked that."

Kathy stopped him at the door and brushed at the collar of his black suit, then straightened his tie. "I think Jimmy would be very proud with everything that you've done for him over the past two days," she said. Then she turned and headed down the stairs.

Robert followed more slowly, realizing that this was the first time she'd voluntarily touched him since she'd slapped him across the face on Christmas Eve on Tuesday. It felt like a lifetime ago.

It was. He sighed. It was a different lifetime entirely.

Later, when Robert Walker would try to make sense of the days immediately following Jimmy Moran's death, everything would shift and blur into a kaleidoscope of events. Trying to decide what really happened and what he imagined happened became impossible—and there were whole swathes of time for which he had no memory.

He remembered sitting in the hospital room holding the man's cooling hand in both of his, face pressed against the sheets, and weeping, not only for the friend he'd lost, but for the father he'd never known. Jimmy Moran had had such an influence upon so many areas of his life, good and bad. It was Jimmy who taught him about the business; it was Jimmy's enthusiasm and confidence that had encouraged Robert to take a risk and establish his own company. But it was also Jimmy who introduced him to excessive drinking, who used him as an alibi for his various affairs, and who had, in an odd way, even enabled him to have his affair with Stephanie.

Robert remembered being roused by a young nurse around midnight and then ushered out of the room. Nurses ran in and out, and then a doctor he'd never seen before had ambled into the room and reappeared a couple of moments later, to tell Robert the lie that he was "sorry."

Robert had no idea how he got home.

None.

Later, much later, he would find a long scrape along the side of the car, but he'd no idea how he'd gotten it or what he'd hit. One moment he was brushing his car clean of snow outside the hospital in the early hours of the morning ... and the next he was turning into the driveway in Brookline ... and the hall door was opening ... and Kathy was standing waiting for him ... and even without his saying a word, she knew what had happened. He desperately wanted her to take him into her arms, but she made no effort, and pride and shame and exhaustion ensured that he made no move either. He walked past her with just two words, "He's dead," and then climbed the stairs to his office, kicked off his shoes and dropped his jacket on the floor, fell into his chair, and was asleep immediately.

The next forty-eight hours were filled with the confusion of trying to contact Jimmy's family, such as it was. Angela was quite happy to allow Robert to make all the arrangements, and Frances was purposefully unavailable. He managed to find an address for Mikey Moran, the eldest brother, living in Vancouver. From him he got addresses for Teddy in New York and Lloyd living on the outskirts of Sydney. Mikey and Teddy immediately promised they would get home, if he could delay the funeral for a few days, but Lloyd could not give an immediate answer; he worked with the fire service and was on call over the New Year's holiday.

Robert made all the arrangements: choosing the funeral parlor, finding a church that would hold the service, picking the coffin, and arranging for Jimmy to be buried in Forest Hills Cemetery. With Angela's permission, Robert went to the apartment in the North End and found Jimmy's best black Armani suit and a white silk shirt and then chose a hand-painted Hermès tie, which Robert had given Jimmy for a Christmas present the previous year. He'd never seen Jimmy wear it.

When Robert had returned home from the funeral parlor on Friday night, he found that Kathy had set up a bed in his office so that he wouldn't have to sleep in his office chair for another night. His black suit, a pale blue shirt, and a black tie had been laid out over the back of the chair.

"Thank you," Robert said suddenly. He gunned the engine and turned the heaters to full, clearing the windshield.

Kathy glanced sidelong at him.

"For the bed . . . and getting the suit . . ."

"I thought you had enough to worry about."

"Well, thanks anyway. And thank you for coming with me."

"I knew Jimmy, I liked him even though he was a rogue, and I wanted to pay my respects. And I also want to support you."

Robert nodded, unwilling to trust himself to speak. He pulled on a pair of sunglasses. The sky was cloudless, and though the thin sunshine shed no heat, it sparkled and reflected off the banked snow and frozen water.

"How are you feeling?" she asked.

Robert concentrated on driving down the ice-locked road, conscious of the cars on either side of him. All he needed now was to sideswipe a neighbor's car to make this the perfect Christmas. "I'm a bit numb," he admitted finally when he reached the end of the road, which was glittering damply, sandy grit sparkling on the black Tarmac. "Do you know," he said suddenly, "I've known Jimmy for more than twenty-five years. Nearly half my life."

"He was at our wedding," Kathy reminded him. "That's where you introduced me to him."

"I don't remember that," he admitted.

"I do."

"There were times when I'd see him every day for a month . . . and then I wouldn't talk to him for weeks. But every time we met up again, it was as if we'd never been apart."

"There were times when I used to envy your relationship with him. I was just glad that he wasn't a woman," said Kathy, stopping abruptly, realizing what she'd said.

"Funny that, isn't it?" Robert said quietly. "A man can have a very close friendship with another man, and no one cares, but if it's with a woman, there are all sorts of questions raised."

"I used to think that a man and a woman could have a purely platonic relationship," Kathy said. "Now . . . now, I'm not so sure."

Robert carefully negotiated the traffic circle, feeling the back of the heavy car shift on the gritty road, and headed out toward the Boston funeral parlor where Jimmy Moran's body had been laid out. "And yet Jimmy had a string of female friends who were never his lovers. He used to say that once both sides realized that sex was never going to be an issue, a real friendship could develop."

"And what do you think?" Kathy asked.

"I don't know," he said truthfully. "Outside of business, I know very few women socially."

"Except your mistress!" Kathy snapped. She finally broke the long silence that followed. "I'm sorry. I didn't mean to bring that up today of all days. I know you're grieving. I'll respect that."

They drove in silence for a while, then Robert spoke. "I know we haven't had a chance over the past few days to talk about what happened."

"We'll talk about it when this is all over," Kathy said firmly. "I'm thinking we should go for couples' counseling."

Robert frowned. "I'm not sure I want to let strangers know our business. . . ."

"I'm not going to fight with you about this," Kathy said firmly. "It's not optional. If you want to stay with me—if we want to stay together—then we have to start again. I want us to go to therapy and work through those issues that drove us apart."

"Work drove us apart," Robert snapped. "Me, working all hours God sent to pay the mortgage and put food on the table. If it comes right down to it, that was the only issue. If you had been a little more involved with the business—a little more involved with me—you would have known that."

"Are you implying this is my fault?"

"I'm not implying anything," Robert snapped. "This whole sorry mess is entirely of my making. I put my hand up. I accept it." He took a deep breath, attempting to calm the bubble of rage that threatened to burst. "Let's talk about it in a day or two," he said, finally, quietly.

They drove the rest of the way to the funeral parlor without speaking.

CHAPTER 33

Robert was astonished by the number of people who turned up at the small funeral parlor near the harbor. A lot of the entertainment industry was there, familiar faces from the world of TV and movies, theater and radio. Even Angela attended, arriving on the arm of a retired game show host. She kissed Robert on both cheeks and thanked him for all that he'd done. Neither of them mentioned their last conversation when he'd called from the hospital. There was no sign of Frances.

Jimmy was laid out in his black suit, in the coffin Robert had chosen. The skin on his face had tightened, highlighting his cheek and chin bones, and he seemed almost shriveled. Robert leaned in and gently kissed his icy forehead, not caring who saw him. "Goodbye, old friend. No worries now, eh?" Then he walked away quickly, feeling the back of his throat burning fiercely. He knew if he caught anyone's eye, he was going to weep, so he kept his eyes firmly fixed on the checkerboard pattern on the floor.

Prayers in the funeral parlor were brief, and then the coffin lid was screwed down. Robert was one of the six pallbearers who carried the coffin out to the car. He knew all the others—senior figures in the Boston entertainment business, including Angela's companion—and when they stepped out into the crystalline morning air, there were a series of camera flashes as reporters and photographers grabbed interviews and images for the Sunday papers. When the back of the hearse slammed shut, he stood, suddenly unsure what to do, until Kathy caught his arm and urged him toward the car.

"Jimmy would have been pleased," she said.

Robert tucked his Audi in behind the mourning car and the hearse and glanced in the rearview mirror. As far back as he could see, a long line of cars was strung out along Commercial Street. "He would," he agreed.

"He knew a lot of people," Kathy said.

"Some came up through the business with him; and there were others—like me, I suppose—who he gave a start to in the business. I suppose there'll be more at the church, and even more at the funeral on Monday."

"I'm glad Angela came," Kathy remarked.

"She just thanked me for taking care of things. She didn't seem too upset." He was more than surprised—though not a little relieved—that Frances hadn't turned up with her and Jimmy's son. To the best of Robert's knowledge, Angela and Frances had never met, though they'd been featured alongside one another on TMZ often enough, and the last thing he wanted was a dramatic catfight over the coffin. Maybe that was why the photographers were there. Ironically, Jimmy, who had lived so much of his life in the public eye, had always attempted to keep his private life private. Without success.

"He knew everyone," Robert remarked. "I'd even thought about asking him to partner with me in the business," he added, and immediately knew that he'd made a mistake.

"Without asking me?" Kathy said, more surprised than angry.

"Well, I was going to talk to you about it first of course," he lied.

"One of the things we need to get clear is my position in the business. I do own half of it," she reminded him.

And I own half the house, he thought, but said nothing.

"Well, it's all academic now," he said.

"We're going to make some changes, Robert," she said firmly.

"Yes, we are," Robert muttered. There was something in her tone that bothered him, though he couldn't put his finger on it.

Kathy nudged Robert. "Is that your phone?" Robert looked blankly at Kathy. They were slowly making their way out of the church after the brief service in which the remains were received and welcomed by a severe-looking Jesuit, an old college friend of Jimmy's. "Something's buzzing," she insisted.

Robert patted his inside pocket and felt the vibrations through the cloth. "Oh, it's me." Gripping his left glove between his teeth, he pulled it off, then fumbled with the buttons of his overcoat before he got to his jacket pocket and pulled out the phone . . . just as the call finished.

One Missed Call.

He hit the menu and scrolled to Records, looking for his Missed Call log: Burroughs, Stephanie.

Robert felt a pulse begin beating along his jawline. Not now; he didn't need to deal with her just now. He just needed to get through this day without any more drama.

"Who was it?" Kathy asked.

"Friend of Jimmy's," he said quickly. "Probably asking about the arrangements for Monday." He was slipping the phone back into his pocket when it buzzed again. Nervously, he glanced at the screen: Private Number. Moving away from Kathy and the throng, he hit the Answer button and said very softly, "Yes?"

Stephanie Burroughs's voice was icy. "Why didn't you answer my previous call?" she snapped.

"Sorry," he whispered. "The phone was in my inside pocket, and I had to pull my gloves off to unbutton my coat. By the time I got it, you'd gone. I was just putting it back in my pocket when you called again. Sorry." He was aware that he was babbling, and conscious too that Kathy had stopped and was looking back at him, looking vaguely annoyed that he had taken the call, even though they were now outside the body of the church and making their way around the courtyard toward the exit into the parking lot.

"Did you get my e-mail, telling you I was coming home?" He

could hear background noise behind Stephanie's voice, as if she was in a car.

"No, no, I haven't checked my messages."

"Bullshit," she snapped.

"Honestly." He sighed. "Things have been crazy. Look, I can't talk now. I'll call back later."

"You'd better!"

"I'll talk to you later," he said firmly. "I've got to go. I'm at Jimmy Moran's removal," he said finally, desperately, as Kathy began to make her way back toward him.

"What? I can't hear you. What did you say?"

Robert's voice hardened. "I said I'm at Jimmy Moran's removal of remains. Jimmy's dead. He died on Christmas Day," he added, just to make it absolutely clear, and then he hung up.

"Who was that?" Kathy asked.

"Someone who hadn't heard the news."

"How did they take it?"

"I don't know," he said truthfully. "I didn't wait for a response."

It was close to noon by the time they got back to Brookline. Robert pulled into the driveway, but didn't turn off the engine.

"Aren't you coming in?"

"I want to head into the office, check up on things. Maybe do a little work, distract myself."

Kathy looked as if she were about to respond, but instead all she said was, "You could come in and catch up on your sleep. You look like shit. You've barely eaten or slept."

"No, let me do this. I meant to get in to the office yesterday, but events caught up with me. I'll get home as early as I can. I'm exhausted." It was true; a combination of the emotional trauma of the last week, coupled with the physical exertions and too little sleep, had left him feeling physically ill, with every muscle aching and a solid bar of tension sitting across his shoulders. The last thing he wanted to do was to face Stephanie's wrath, but it was preferable to her calling the house again or—worse still—turning up on the doorstep. "I won't be long," he promised.

When Kathy climbed out of the car, Robert turned around and

began the trip to Stephanie's condo. He cracked the window open to allow a little of the chill air to blow onto his face to keep him awake, and desperately began to rehearse the words he would use with Stephanie. All he had to do was to make her see sense, and he didn't think that was going to be too difficult.

Once they'd made some plans, it would take a little pressure off of him.

CHAPTER 34

—————⟨◈⟩—————

"Hi, Stef."

Even in his exhausted state, Robert recognized that the woman standing in the doorway before him looked stunning. She was wearing a cream-colored silk blouse over black trousers with her usual discreet jewelry that he knew, from having bought some of it, was platinum. She was simply and elegantly made-up, lips bright with a shade of lipstick that he hadn't seen before, eyes sparkling.

She stepped back and allowed him into the building. He forced a smile and went through number 8, the door to her condo, and walked up the flight of stairs into her living room. Was it only three nights ago he had stood in this same room, wondering if he was going to find a body waiting for him upstairs? Only the wilting flowers were missing; the balloon still lay deflated over the back of the chair. He heard her come into the room behind him, and he turned to look at her. He saw what might have been concern dart across her face.

"It's good to see you again," he said, his voice flat, emotionless.

Stephanie nodded. She looked cool and distant, completely confident, self-assured, and relaxed, and he found himself wondering, yet again, if she really had flown home for Christmas. She certainly showed no signs of it. "Would you like some tea or coffee or something stronger?" she asked.

"Tea would be great, thank you."

He waited until she had disappeared into the kitchen and then took up his usual position, leaning against the entrance, arms folded across his chest. There were tiny black spots spinning before his eyes, and it took a monumental effort of will to keep his eyes open. He watched Stephanie fill the kettle with water from the Brita pitcher and slowly came to the realization that the only question she'd asked him since he had stepped into the house was what he wanted to drink.

"You got back this morning?" he said finally, when it was clear that she wasn't going to break the silence.

"A couple of hours ago," she said shortly.

"I'm sorry I wasn't there to meet you." He felt like he needed to justify himself, although he wasn't sure she'd believe him. "Believe it or not, I didn't check my e-mails."

"I believe it."

"Flight was okay?"

"Fine. I booked a last-minute ticket and came in via Detroit, so I had to stay overnight, but I checked into the Westin and treated myself to a massage so I was able to relax a bit."

"Good. Good."

He watched as she took out a cup for herself and a mug for him—he preferred mugs to cups—and he smiled, strangely pleased that she'd take the care to make the distinction.

"How was the removal? Were there many people there?"

"Yes. I was surprised by how many. Shocked. I think Jimmy would have been too. He made a lot of enemies over the years, but far more friends it seems. They all came out today." His voice broke, catching him unaware, and then suddenly, surprisingly, for the first time since he had cried by his friend's hospital bed, there were tears on his face. He tugged a handkerchief out of his pocket and quickly patted his eyes. He didn't want her to see him like this. Then the kettle started to boil and she busied herself with that, and he was sure she wasn't aware of his breakdown.

"Tea's ready." But when she turned to hand across the mug of tea, he saw the expression on her face—a cross between pity, embarrassment, and concern—and he knew she'd heard him cry. He was glad she hadn't discomfited him further by turning around to look at him. "I've added two sugars."

"Sorry," he mumbled. "Been an intense few days; I haven't had much sleep."

He followed her into the living room and sat down on the couch, facing her. He glanced to the opposite end of the couch; only a couple of days ago, Kathy had sat on this couch with him.

Stephanie cradled a tiny porcelain cup in the palms of her hands and sipped what he recognized from its distinctive odor as licorice tea. "Tell me what happened," she said.

What had happened? Events had moved so quickly, he'd been acting and reacting without pausing to think, and it took him a few moments to put his thoughts in order.

"I got a call on Christmas Day . . . not long after yours," he added, not looking at her. "Jimmy Moran had been taken to the hospital with a suspected heart attack. I immediately went in to see him. Oh, Stef, he looked terrible. . . ." He breathed deeply and took a mouthful of tea, remembering the sight of Jimmy lying in the hospital bed. "He was awake. He said that at first he was trying to make light of it, thinking it was nothing more than indigestion. He had been cooking his own Christmas dinner and had sampled the turkey. When he got the pains, he thought that maybe the bird hadn't been cooked through. It was when he felt the pain move into his left arm that he realized it was serious and dialed 911. But it was Christmas Day, and it took the ambulance forever to arrive." He sipped a little more of the hot tea. This was the first time he had put the sequence of events into words. "They'd put him in a private room. He looked old, so old and frail . . . and the moment I saw him, I knew he wasn't going to make it. It was almost as if he'd given up. The spark had gone. Turned out he'd tried calling Angela, but she wasn't taking his calls, nor was Frances. He asked me to contact Angela. She spoke to me, but she wouldn't come in to see him. She was finished with him, she said. He'd broken her heart with his lies and his affairs, and she was afraid that this was just another one of his tricks." He fell silent; he found it hard to forgive Angela for not coming in to see Jimmy. He knew she had any number of reasons, but she should have been there. There were tears in his eyes now, but he was unaware of them. "I called Frances," he continued, his voice barely above a whisper. "She wouldn't come either. They'd had a fight, and she'd thrown him out. I think she thought it was a trick too. She told me that he was incredibly manipulative, and that this was just an act to get sympathy."

"So you stayed with him?" Stephanie asked.

"I stayed with him throughout the day and into the night until . . . until he died," he finished simply. "He died." There were tears on his face now, rolling down his cheeks. "He squeezed my hand and then . . ." He drew in a deep, sobbing breath. It was a moment he would carry with him to his grave. That, and Jimmy's last words: *Don't walk away from a woman who loves you.*

"I'm sorry, Robert. So sorry," Stephanie said coolly. "I know you and Jimmy were very close."

"He died alone, Stephanie," Robert said very softly.

"Not alone. You were there."

"But his wife . . . his mist . . . his girlfriend should have been there. Someone more . . . more significant than me. Someone who loved him."

"You loved him, Robert," Stephanie said firmly. "In the same way that he was very significant to you, then you too must have played a significant part in his life. Why else would he call you when he went into the hospital?"

Robert nodded automatically. "Yes, yes, you're right. Thank you for reminding me." Kathy had said the same thing to him, but he hadn't believed her either. Finishing his tea in one quick swallow, he put the mug on the floor. "I'm sorry, I guess I'm all over the place. Since everything that happened here on Tuesday"—he waved his hand around the room—"then frantically looking for you, then your call on Wednesday, and then Jimmy's death, it's just been an incredibly emotional time."

"Yes, I can see that. And Christmas is the most stressful time of the year too."

He smiled grimly. "There were times I thought I was having a heart attack myself." Then he pressed the palm of his right hand against his chest. "I think it was just stress."

"You should get it checked out, just in case," she said immediately.

"Jimmy was fifty-two—only three years older than I am." First thing after the holiday, he was going to book an appointment with a cardiologist. Jimmy's death frightened him more than he cared to admit.

"He lived a completely different lifestyle," Stephanie remarked.

"Not that different," he said quickly.

"He smoked."

"He did. And he liked rich food," Robert added.

"And he drank," Stephanie reminded him, "a lot more than you."

"Yes, Jimmy did that too. I'm only sorry now that we didn't get a chance to have that meal at Top of the Hub before Christmas. We had drinks around the corner in the Union Oyster House instead— You suggested that, remember? That was the last time I saw him until . . . until I saw him in the hospital on Christmas Day."

"At least you had the chance to see him."

Robert nodded. "Yes. I'm glad I did." But dead at fifty-two was simply wrong; he was determined it was not going to happen to him. Next year would be different, he promised himself. He'd already determined to make changes at work; well, he was going to make them in every area of his life. He was going to start eating healthier, drinking less. . . .

"Would you like some more tea?" Stephanie asked, breaking into his reverie.

"Yes. Thank you." He picked his mug up off the floor, handed it across, then sank back onto the sofa, resting his head on the back of the cushion and closing his eyes as Stephanie moved into the kitchen.

He was going to start exercising. Maybe he'd start biking around the Arboretum or jog along the Charles River. . . .

As if from a great distance, he heard Stephanie's voice. "Jimmy's life was also incredibly stressful, and I can guarantee you he never exercised."

He tried to respond, but all that came out was an indeterminate grunt.

"Plus, the whole situation with Angela and Frances must have taken its toll on him, and I'm sure the prospect of the looming divorce just added to the stress level."

His phone woke him with a start. There was a moment of complete disorientation when he didn't know where he was, and then he saw Stephanie's face, staring at him, and for an instant he imagined that it had all been a dream, a shockingly vivid nightmare. He pulled the phone out of his pocket, regretting now having taken it off vibrate earlier. "Hello . . . ," he began, then licked dry lips and tried again, "Hello . . ."

He heard Kathy's voice, and in that instant it all came flooding back: This was no dream, though it was still a nightmare. "Kathy . . . Yes, I'm fine. I'm at the office. . . ." He was aware that Stephanie was watching him, her eyes hard and cold in her face. "Yes, I'll be home soon," he said quickly and hung up.

"Why did you lie?" Stephanie asked what he considered to be a very stupid question.

"Well, I could hardly tell her the truth, now could I?"

"You could have said we had some unfinished business."

"I promised Kathy I would never see you again."

"And yet you're breaking that promise," she said evenly.

"Well, I made that promise before . . . before I knew about . . . about you and . . . and . . ."

"About my being pregnant?"

"Yes. That." It was over sixteen years ago that Kathy had last told him she was pregnant, and it wasn't something he thought he'd ever be hearing again.

Stephanie stood. "I'm going to make that tea now. Why don't you go grab a shower," she said briskly. "I need you awake and alert when we talk, and right now you're barely conscious. You've got some clothes in the closet, and there's a toothbrush and a razor of yours in the bathroom cabinet. Shower and change; you'll feel much better."

He was about to refuse, but suddenly the thought of a shower was incredibly inviting. "Yes, I will, thank you." He stood up and caught a hint of his own stale sweat. "Gosh, I stink," he said in disgust.

"Yes, you do," Stephanie said, and turned away quickly. He wasn't sure if she was talking about him as a person or his bodily odor.

It took an effort to lift one foot in front of the other as he made his way into the bathroom. He'd been running on adrenaline for the past couple of days and was beginning to pay the price. He'd grab a quick shower, then talk to Stephanie about the pregnancy, then head home. He glanced at his watch. He could be home before five . . . six at the latest. Then he was crawling into bed and not getting up until Monday morning.

CHAPTER 35

—— ✦ ——

"Robert. Robert."

Robert Walker opened his eyes and looked around. He knew where he was . . . in the bed of his lover. He smiled as her face leaned in toward his. "Hi . . ."

"Hi."

Then the bubble burst. The smile faded as his eyes moved toward the curtains, which were closed. "My God, how long have I been asleep?"

"A few hours. It's almost nine."

Nine. Where had the afternoon and evening gone? He remembered having a shower, the hot water an incredibly sensuous and satisfying experience. Then he'd wrapped himself in Stephanie's red flannel robe just to dry off and then . . . He'd no idea how he ended up in bed with a thick duvet over him. He jumped out of bed. "I've got to go. . . ."

"You've got to eat," Stephanie said firmly. She was sitting on the edge of the bed with a tray in her hands. It held a broad flat pizza flanked by a bottle of ginger ale and two glasses. "I ordered from Zesto's. My fridge was empty, and I didn't want to leave you."

Robert looked at the ham and pineapple pizza and started to shake his head—he had to get back; Kathy would be frantic and furious—but then his stomach betrayed him, and rumbled loudly, and he suddenly realized that he was hungry, ravenously hungry. "Just a slice then," he said with a grin.

He ate quickly, while he worked out his excuses for Kathy: He'd called on a few friends in the business, and they had ended up talking about Jimmy. That had led to a couple of drinks and then a meal. He hadn't been able to call her because his battery had run out. Would she believe it? It was plausible enough. Like all good lies.

"When did you last eat?" Stephanie asked eventually.

He shook his head. "I've grabbed a few bites on the run. When Jimmy . . . when Jimmy died, I was left to make the funeral arrangements and contact his family. Two of his three brothers are coming home. They're spread all over the world: Lloyd is in Australia, Mikey's in Canada, and Teddy's in New York. I spoke to Mikey, the oldest. He told me to go ahead with the removal, but to delay the funeral until they arrived."

"When will the funeral take place?"

"Monday the thirtieth, at Forest Hills Cemetery."

"That's just a few blocks from here."

"I know. Teddy and Mikey are coming in tomorrow morning, but Lloyd's not going to be able to make it."

"That's a shame."

"True. But they've never been close. Jimmy never really told me the full story, but I know he went to live with his mother when the family broke up, while the older brothers chose to live with his father. When his parents separated, it destroyed all their lives and shattered the family. Almost exactly like my own experience." He glanced up at Stephanie and smiled. "I'm sorry; I've done nothing but talk about me. Tell me what you did over Christmas. You went home?"

Stephanie nodded. She lifted the tray and moved around the room to put it on the nightstand. Then she leaned back against the windowsill and folded her arms. "I went home. It was a last-minute rush, and I had to go via Chicago and Milwaukee, but I made it back late on Christmas Eve, and I'm glad I went. It was good to see Mom and Dad again. They're getting old, Dad especially. I know people say that time slips by—it doesn't; it races. I'm going to try to get home regularly, maybe every second or third month, to keep in touch with them."

"That's a good idea." Robert pushed away the duvet and slid his legs out over the edge of the bed. He glanced sidelong at the clock on the nightstand. It was after nine, and the roads were probably icy. It would be after ten before he got back. "I really should be going." He tugged on his underwear, pulled on his socks, and stepped into his pants.

And then Stephanie suddenly, shockingly, exploded. "Hang on a second! We've talked about everything but the most important thing: us. Me. And the fact that I'm probably pregnant."

He opened the closet and pulled out one of the shirts he'd left there for emergencies. He was surprised by her reaction. He'd thought when she hadn't brought it up earlier that it was no longer an issue. He had assumed that she'd come to a decision. He turned to look at her as he did up the buttons. "How sure are you?" he asked.

"Sure?"

"Sure that you're pregnant."

"Almost positive. I'm nearly two weeks late now."

"Did you do a test?"

"Yes. It came back positive. That's why I came home."

He nodded as he tucked his shirt into his pants. He was no expert, but while two weeks was late, he didn't think it was *that* late. "So, let's say you are. What are you going to do about it?"

Stephanie came off the window ledge to stand directly in front of Robert. She was radiating anger. "What do you mean by that?"

Taken aback, he blinked in surprise. "I mean, you can't seriously be thinking of having it?"

"Of course I am," she whispered.

What was she thinking? Well, obviously, she wasn't. Surely she wasn't going to throw away everything she'd spent years building? Maybe it was her jet lag and a highly emotional state that were confusing her thinking. "But you can't," he said, keeping his voice reasonable. "You've got this place . . . and then there's your job. You can't have all that and a baby."

"I could if I had a partner."

At no point in Robert Walker's New-Year-New-You plan was there room for a baby. He'd had his children seventeen and fifteen years ago; he'd done all that; he didn't need to do it again. Gathering his thoughts, concentrating on his cuffs, he said carefully, "If I'm the father of this child . . ."

She cracked him across the face, the force of the blow snapping his head to one side, shocking him, the pain and the surge of her anger surprising him.

"How dare you! You are the father. There's been no one else."

"I'm sorry," he said, drawing in a deep breath, pressing the palm of his hand to his stinging cheek. This was obviously his week for getting slapped in the face—and on the same cheek too. "I'm sorry. I didn't mean to imply anything. It just came out wrong." He wasn't trying to suggest anything; he had no doubts that there was no one else in Stephanie's life. "I mean, let's be logical about this. I don't want to start again. C'mon," he pleaded. "You don't either. You're on the corporate ladder—a child would stop that dead. Neither of us can afford to have a screaming baby in our lives." If he could just appeal to her common sense, he was sure he could make her see reason. "And what would I tell Kathy and the kids?"

Stephanie remained silent, and he guessed that he was getting through to her. He knew she'd see sense in the end. He'd gotten her into this situation, so he was quite willing to help her get out of it.

"I'll pay for the abortion, of course. And we'll go on with our lives."

He smiled as a sudden thought occurred to him: He hadn't told her the news yet—that he was going to move in with her. They would be living together in January; he wouldn't have to make any more excuses. He opened his mouth to speak. . . .

But Stephanie spoke first, her voice so low that he couldn't make out what she was saying. Was she agreeing with him?

"Well, what do you think?" he asked.

And then she screamed, the sound shocking him with its raw savagery. "Get out! Get out! Get out!"

Dumb with surprise, Robert backed away from her. Stephanie reached for the nearest item—the pizza plate—and flung it at him. It missed and shattered against the wall, leaving a bloody smear of sauce. "You bastard!" she gasped. "You bastard!"

"Stephanie . . . I'm just suggesting . . ." This was a woman he did not know. This was a stranger . . . and she was terrifying.

"You've got a key to this house. Give it to me," she demanded.

There was no point in arguing with her at this point. As he tugged the key off of his key ring and dropped it on the bed, she was rummaging through the closet and flinging his shirt, his tie, and his patent leather shoes across the room at him. "Stephanie."

"Give me the key. Give it to me!" she screamed.

"Let's talk." He tried to reason with her. "I know you're upset—"

"Upset? I am way beyond upset. We're finished," she said icily. "Don't you ever speak to me again."

He'd talk to her in a day or so, he decided, but right now, her face was set in a mask that robbed any beauty from her features.

"I loved you. I loved you with all my heart. Now, I see you for what you are: an egotistical, arrogant bastard. This isn't a problem to be solved; this is a life and a future we're talking about. And you think an abortion will solve everything! A quick abortion, then we go on as if nothing has happened? I hate you, Robert. No, more than that. I despise you. Now get out. And don't come back. Don't ever come back."

Still not entirely sure what had happened to set her off like that, Robert hurried from the house, pulling the door closed behind him. He threw the shirt, tie, and spare pair of shoes on the passenger seat as he climbed in and started the car. As he pulled away, he thanked God that he hadn't told Kathy that he'd intended to leave her on Monday after Jimmy Moran's funeral.

Book 3

The Wife's Story

When I discovered the truth about the affair, I hated him.

He had betrayed me, betrayed my love, betrayed eighteen years of marriage.

But I still loved him.

And he said he still loved me.

But did I believe him?

Would I ever believe him again?

CHAPTER 36

Tuesday, 24th December
Christmas Eve

"Jingle bells . . . jingle bells . . ."

The irritatingly cheerful polyphonic version of "Jingle Bells" her son had put on her cell phone surprised Kathy Walker. She wasn't expecting any calls. Keeping her eyes on the road, she rummaged through her purse on the passenger seat; probably one of the kids wondering where she was. She fished the phone out of her bag, but before she answered, she glanced at the screen: Robert Cell.

She didn't want to speak to him.

Jingle bells . . . jingle bells . . .

At this particular moment, Robert was the last person she wanted to talk to, but she still hit Answer and switched the phone to speaker. "Yes?" she said shortly.

Her husband's voice sounded flat and echoing, the speaker robbing it of all emotion and inflection. "Hi . . . I was just wondering . . . just wondering how you are."

"I'm fine," she said shortly. Under the circumstances, that was probably the most stupid question she had ever been asked. How did he think she was?

"Where are you?"

"Almost home. Where are you?"

"In Mission Hill. I stopped to give Maureen her Christmas bonus."

"Good." Well, at least he'd had the good manners to do that. She'd been disgusted to learn that he hadn't even bothered to visit Maureen when she was out sick over the past number of weeks.

"She told me you'd spoken to her." He made the simple statement sound like an accusation.

"Yes, I have." She could understand now why he wouldn't want her talking to Maureen—or indeed any of their few mutual friends. She also understood why he hadn't invited her along on any of the social events or business dinners over the past months; he had probably been terrified that someone would say something to her about his mistress. Or, worse still, that Stephanie Burroughs would be there.

"How are you feeling?" he asked, voice popping in and out as the signal wavered.

"How do you think I'm feeling?" she snapped. "I've just been to see my husband's mistress. I've just learned some very ugly truths. We'll talk later." She hung up.

Truthfully, she wasn't entirely sure how she felt. She thought she'd feel worse, but if she could put a name to one overall emotion, it was relief. His affair was out in the open; now they could move beyond the suspicions and lies, deal with them, and go forward. And mingled with the relief was something else: shock and astonishment. And pride. She had fought for Robert.

And won.

And no one was more surprised or more proud than she was. She hadn't thought she had it in her.

The anticipation of the encounter with Robert's mistress had definitely been worse than the actual event. She'd built up an image of Stephanie Burroughs in her mind as a scheming, manipulative home wrecker who'd deliberately set out to steal Robert away from her. Yet the truth could not have been more different. If Stephanie was to be believed—and Kathy did believe her—then the woman had only allowed herself to have a relationship with Robert because she thought that his wife didn't love him. Kathy had been watching Stephanie when Robert admitted before them both that he still loved his wife; and she had seen the look of genuine anguish in the younger woman's eyes. It was at that point that Stephanie had backed away, confessed that she'd made a mistake, a terrible mistake, then told Robert to go back to his wife. . . . "If she'll take you, that is. . . ." she'd added. In that moment, Kathy had liked—even admired—the woman.

In other circumstances, Kathy thought, they might have been friends.

When she'd set out to confront Stephanie, Kathy hadn't known how the day would finish up. On the drive over she prepared herself for the worst: that Stephanie would fight for Robert . . . and that Robert would want to go to his mistress. Kathy even prepared the little speech she would give the children. Having Robert walk in on the conversation had been both terrifying and disgusting. He'd turned up at the house laden with an armful of presents. When was the last time he had taken his time over choosing a present for her, rather than just grabbing something at the last minute at the local Brookline florist?

But Kathy wasn't going to need the speech for the children— not yet anyway—because Stephanie had done the decent thing. She had walked away. The only one of the three of them who had come out of this affair badly was Robert. He'd lied to her, lied to Stephanie . . . probably even lied to himself. How did he think the affair was going to end? Was he one of those men who thought that he could have his cake and eat it too, that he'd be able to manage his wife and mistress without someday having to face the consequences? Robert hadn't been thinking—at least not with his brain.

Kathy was eager to get home; she still had the turkey to prepare for tomorrow's dinner, though she didn't think she was going to have any appetite. Her stomach had been upset from the moment she left home to drive to Robert's mistress's condo. Once they got through Christmas, she would insist that Robert go to a marriage counselor with her. A problem like this obviously needed professional help. Robert wouldn't like it, she knew that—he was an intensely private person—but she'd make it one of her conditions. If they were going to stay together, then things would have to be different. He would have to change. She vowed that she would as well. There was no denying that if she'd been paying attention, to him, to the business, to their relationship, then he would never have found either the time or the opportunity to start and then maintain an affair with Stephanie.

As she turned onto Boylston Street, Kathy suddenly smiled. A bizarre thought crossed her mind: She should be grateful. At least she now knew that there was a problem in their marriage, and she had an opportunity to fix it before the problem became insurmountable. Her late mother had always said that Kathy could find the good in every situation. Her mother had been dead for the past eighteen months . . . just about the same length of time Robert had been having his affair. Kathy wondered if the two events could, in any way, possibly be connected. Had Kathy retreated in her grief? Had it made her so selfish, so painfully blinded by her own loss that she couldn't see what was going on around her? Her therapist said that her mother's death had triggered a fear of her own mortality. Well, her therapist was going to have a field day with the new information she'd be bringing to the office next visit.

Kathy slowed as she turned down her road. Although the weather had turned bitterly cold, there were plenty of little kids running around, bundled up in thick anoraks, Bruins hats, and woolen scarves. When they were wrapped up like that, she knew all sounds were muffled and their range of vision was strictly limited. She kept reminding Robert of that every time he drove down this road—she was convinced that he drove too fast through the neighborhood. Not that he listened to her of course; in fact it had been a long time since he had sought her opinions on any subject. Her lips twisted in a smile; it had been a long time since she had volunteered an opinion. What had happened to the self-confident young woman who'd gone to Bard, and double majored in philosophy and global marketing? The self-reliant young woman who'd traveled through Cambodia with the Peace Corps. The self-assured young woman who wanted to set up her own production company and make documentaries and features? Eighteen years of marriage, children, and keeping a home together, that's what had happened.

Maybe it was time to start again.

The situation was serious, but she figured that they'd weathered the worst of it and managed to come through with a reasonable amount of dignity. There would be some tough times ahead, and although she still loved Robert—she didn't really like him right now. He'd said that he loved her. If that was true—and she had to believe that it was—then they had something they could work with; they could start again and go forward together.

There were more cars than usual parked at the curbs and in the driveways; Christmas was a time for family and visitors. As she was turning into her drive, she caught sight of a big, dark blue SUV making its way gingerly down the road behind her. Kathy's wry smile faded; it looked like she was about to have a visitor of her own, someone she would definitely not be sharing her latest bit of news with: her older sister, Julia.

CHAPTER 37

———⟨⟨⟨⟩⟩⟩———

"We have to talk."

"That sounds serious," Kathy said lightly, moving over to the sink to fill the kettle.

"It is," Julia said. She sighed dramatically as she assumed her usual seat at the kitchen table.

Although Julia was only five years older than her sister, she looked, dressed, and acted a lot older. It still gave Kathy a slightly guilty pleasure that the last time the two of them went out together, a waitress had mistaken them for mother and daughter.

Kathy's mind was racing; surely Julia hadn't somehow found out about Robert's affair? If she had, it would be just like her to rush over and break the news in person; she'd want to see the expression on Kathy's face.

"It's about Sheila," Julia said, dropping her voice to a whisper, when it became apparent that Kathy was not going to ask her the obvious question.

And Kathy immediately knew what Julia was about to tell her, knew why her older sister had driven over to see her on Christmas Eve. Julia dispensed good news on the phone, but she took perverse pleasure in delivering bad news in person. "Sheila?" Kathy said, her voice carefully neutral. "What's she done now?"

"She's seeing someone. . . ." Julia began, and then stopped.

Both women heard the hall door open, then Robert's voice drifted in from the next room as he talked to the children. He stepped into the kitchen and said, "Hello, Julia," though his eyes were fixed on Kathy's face. He walked around Kathy to stand by the sink, where he could look at them both. Was that fear she saw in his eyes? Then she realized that he thought she'd asked her older sister over to talk about his affair. Did he really know so little about her? She was half tempted to let him sweat for a while. She could see the white-knuckled tension in his fingers where they gripped the edge of the sink. But then she realized that he might say something to alert her sister. "Julia was just about to tell me about Sheila," she said, her eyes never leaving his face. She watched his features relax as the tension flowed out of them.

"Is she okay?" he asked casually.

"She's having an affair with a married man," Julia said in hushed, appalled tones, and then stopped, waiting for a response.

Kathy was observing Julia as she made the announcement. Was this how Julia—and those women like her—spread the news about Robert's affair? Would they each have the same shocked and horrified expression, but yet be unable to keep the tiniest note of glee from their voices as they passed on the news over wine and cheese?

"So?" Robert frowned, adding quickly, "What's that got to do with us?"

Kathy saw him glance at her before turning back to his sister-in-law.

"Oh, I should have known you would never understand," Julia said peevishly. "Men never do." Julia turned her full attention on Kathy. "I called her today, just to confirm that she was coming on the 26th for dinner."

Kathy abruptly decided that she did not want to go over to Julia's for the endless ritual of dinner on Boxing Day. Julia's husband Ben was British, and Kathy not only detested him, she hated his pretentious family and their peculiar, archaic holiday. She needed to spend time with Robert, and she was guessing that she would not really get a chance to talk to him tonight; tomorrow was out of the question, so she'd keep the 26th for them to talk and plan.

"Well, she said she would," Julia continued, "on one condition: that she could bring her current boyfriend with her. I was thrilled, of course. Sheila's thirty-six; it's about time she thought about settling down, and if she's going to have children, then she'd better start soon. . . . Her eggs are drying up." Julia took a deep breath and pursed her lips. "Turns out her boyfriend is not such a boy; he's actually ten years older than she is," she said breathlessly. "Ten years!"

Kathy didn't need to do the calculation: Stephanie Burroughs was sixteen years younger than Robert, ten years younger than Kathy was. She supposed she should at least be grateful that he'd not ended up with a twenty-year-old blond bimbo.

"And then she told me his name," Julia persisted. "Alan Gallagher. And I thought: I know that name. So I said to her, 'I know an Alan Gallagher—he's a chiropractor in Brookline who plays golf with my Ben.'" Julia nodded triumphantly. "And that was when she said that she didn't think she was going to be able to make it on Thursday after all."

Robert was standing behind Kathy's chair, staring out into the backyard. Kathy heard him ask, "So how do you know he's married?" She was aware of the tiniest undercurrent of anger in his voice.

Julia sighed. "The Alan Gallagher who Ben knows has boasted about his little bit on the side. I put two and two together: The 'bit' is Sheila."

"Brookline is so small," Kathy murmured. "Everyone knows someone who knows someone." She wasn't sure if she was speaking to her sister or to Robert.

"So I thought about it, and I called her back."

"Julia, you didn't!" Kathy protested.

"I did."

"But it's got nothing to do with you." When did Julia take over the role of matriarch and moral guardian of the family? Kathy was suddenly conscious that she too was beginning to get annoyed with her sister.

"Well, you may not think so, but I do, and I certainly didn't want an adulterer sitting at my table."

"Are you going to insist she stitches an *A* on all of her clothing?" Robert said evenly.

Julia looked at him coldly. "I called her. Asked her straight out. And do you know what she had the audacity to tell me?"

"That it was none of your business," Robert snapped. The irritation was clearly audible in his voice.

Kathy caught him looking at her, frowned, and shook her head slightly.

"No," Julia continued. "She admitted it. Alan Gallagher is married. So I told her straight out that she would not be welcome in my house."

"Why are you telling me this?" Kathy asked, feeling a sudden wave of exhaustion washing over her. Whether Sheila was having an affair or not was none of her business; none of Julia's either. What gave Julia the right to sit in pious judgment on Sheila? What gave her the right to spread the gossip?

Julia looked at her blankly. "Because . . . because . . ."

"This is Sheila's business. Hers alone," Kathy continued, struggling now to keep her own rising anger in check. "Who she's seeing has got nothing to do with you or me."

"But he's married!" Julia protested. "She's breaking up a happy marriage."

"How do we know that?" Kathy snapped. "How do we know the marriage is happy? Do you have some kind of psychic power that enables you to know what goes on behind closed doors?"

Julia looked at her blankly, mouth opening and closing in stunned silence. Whatever response she had been expecting from her younger sister, it hadn't been this. Color touched her cheeks.

"There are three people in an affair," Kathy said. "The mistress, the husband, and the wife. Takes all of them to make it happen."

Julia pushed back her chair and stood up. "Well, this is not the attitude I expected from you. The wives are always the innocents in these situations, always the last to know."

Maybe always the last to know, Kathy agreed, but perhaps not entirely innocent.

"I don't know why these women—these mistresses—are attracted to married men; I really don't." Julia lifted her coat off the back of the chair and pulled it on. "I just hope you never have to go through what poor Alan Gallagher's wife is going through right now."

Kathy could feel the color draining from her face as anger gave way to guilt and bitter exhaustion. She later realized that Julia must have completely misinterpreted the looks on both of their faces as anger and disgust.

"Well, I don't think that came out the way I meant it to," Julia continued hastily. "I'm sorry, I didn't mean to imply . . ." Looking embarrassed now, she turned to leave. "I'll let myself out." She paused before she stepped out of the kitchen. "You will come over the day after tomorrow for dinner, won't you?"

"We'll let you know," Robert said firmly, before Kathy could respond.

Julia ignored Robert and looked at Kathy. "We'll let you know," Kathy repeated, although she had already decided that she was definitely not going over for dinner. She glanced sidelong at Robert, wishing he would leave her alone. She wanted a little time to think . . . and she wanted to talk to Sheila. She was brought out of her reverie by the high-pitched squealing scrape of metal on stone.

"She's hit the edge of the pillar," Robert said. He was standing at the sink, pouring himself a large scotch. "She was parked at such an awkward angle. I'm not sure I would have been able to get that big SUV out of the driveway without hitting something either."

He was talking just to fill the silence, she knew, chatting inconsequentially so that he could avoid discussing the major issue. He placed the bottle on the table between them and sat down in the seat recently occupied by Julia. He poured her a glass.

"I'm thinking I might have given her a different response a couple of days ago," Kathy said quietly. "There was a time—in the very recent past—when I might have agreed with Julia. But when you become part of an affair, you discover a different perspective. There are two sides to every story, but in an affair . . . there are three. And you never really know anyone's story but your own."

"Did you know about Sheila?" he asked.

"She told me on Monday," Kathy said evenly. "We were sitting in her car outside the Boston Sports Club." Kathy held the heavy glass in both hands and looked into the amber liquid; he always poured her too much. She glanced up and saw him staring at her. She took a swig of the bitter liquor, her eyes not leaving his face. "I sat there and watched my husband kiss another woman."

That, for her, had been the defining moment.

Up until that point, Robert's affair had not been entirely real. Oh, she had known it was happening; she had the proof, but it was all hearsay and circumstantial evidence. But watching her husband of eighteen years take another woman in his arms and kiss her on the lips was like being stabbed. The pain had been physical; it was real, and it hurt. How it had hurt!

And suddenly she wanted to hurt him back, to make him pay for what he'd put her through. Something must have shown in her eyes or on her face, because Robert suddenly sat back, away from her. Kathy wondered if he thought she was going to throw the liquor in his face . . . because in that instant that is precisely what she wanted to do. But she carefully returned the glass to the table; it was part of a set from Crate and Barrel Julia had given her for a birthday present.

"I called you," she said. "I sat in a car less than ten yards away from you and called you." She saw him nod, saw the flush of color on his cheeks. "I asked you what time you were coming home," she continued, and watched him nod again. "You told me you were just leaving the office and would be home in forty minutes."

She suddenly stood and turned away from him so that he would not be able to see the tears in her eyes. She busied herself at the sink, carefully washing and drying the glass; then, when she had composed herself, she turned around and started to clear off the kitchen table.

"How long . . . how long have you known?" Robert asked, not looking at her. "About us? About me?"

"Not long. Why? Did you think I was the sort of person who would turn a blind eye to my husband's affair?" Kathy was pleased that she'd managed to keep her voice calm and without a tremor.

"No. I never thought that," Robert said.

Once she'd discovered his affair, there had been no other course of action but to confront him. She had not been prepared to let it continue in the hope that he would come to his senses. She would not have been able to live with herself, not even able to look at him, if she'd known he was cheating and she had done nothing about it.

She pulled a cookbook off the shelf and flipped it open, then pressed it flat on the table and quickly scanned the list of ingredients. This was part of the ritual of preparing Christmas dinner. The recipe book had belonged to her mother and, written into the margins, in Margaret Child's tiny, precise handwriting, were her additions and corrections to the recipes. Kathy knew Julia desperately coveted the book; every Christmas she tried to borrow it, and every year Kathy refused and presented her sister with a handwritten copy of the turkey, ham, and pork recipes. Kathy started to pull out the ingredients that would go into the stuffing.

"Will you please sit down and talk to me?" Robert asked suddenly.

Kathy didn't answer the question, but continued her previous topic of conversation. "I suspected the truth last Thursday, when I was writing the Christmas cards. Once my suspicions were roused, it was relatively easy to put it all together." She'd found the evidence because he had become careless; she knew that. He'd become just a little complacent; he'd gotten away with his affair for so long he'd stopped taking precautions. "There was a speeding ticket upstairs in your office. You got a ticket in Jamaica Plain on Halloween . . . even though you were supposed to be in Connecticut that night having dinner with a client."

Kathy started feeding bread into the blender, grinding it to crumbs, taking a certain pleasure at the expression on his face when the blades were whirling. It sounded not unlike a dentist's drill, and she knew how much he hated going to the dentist's . . . though that hadn't stopped him from having a lot of very expensive work on his teeth done recently. She wondered if that had been at Stephanie's insistence; and what about the gym, the new clothes, the extra attention he'd started paying to his grooming? Wasn't that supposed to be one of the first signs of an affair?

"Then I remembered all the other nights you'd stayed away, meeting with clients, wining and dining them," she continued. "I don't remember the company getting contracts from any of these alleged clients. You were supposed to be having dinner with Jimmy Moran at Top of the Hub last week. But when I called to check, they had no record of your reservation."

"Jimmy and I really were supposed—" Robert began, but she hit the blender again and the blades howled. She wasn't interested.

"And then I found the phone records in the file cabinet. That was priceless." Kathy turned, and the only expression on her face was one of disappointment. "Hundreds of calls, Robert. Hundreds. First call of the day. Last call at night. All to the same cell or the same house number." She remembered a time, many, many years ago, before they had married, when he would always call her late at night . . . just to say good night. She'd always thought that was so romantic. "And I couldn't help but remember the mornings you left here without speaking to me, or the days when you were too busy to call to see how I was, or those days when you got back late and I'd be in bed. Whole days would go by, and we wouldn't speak more than a few words. And yet you always seemed to find time to phone your mistress several times a day." She glared at him. "Every. Single. Day."

"Maureen told me you'd seen the phone bills," he muttered.

"She just confirmed what I already knew. She just gave me the time frame. She thinks it's been going on for a year. Stephanie said eighteen months. What is the truth?" She already knew the truth, but she wanted to hear him say it.

"June of last year was the . . . the first time."

"The first time for what?" she snapped.

She saw Robert look over his shoulder toward the family room. Brendan's and Theresa's voices were audible as they chatted happily together. She didn't even want to think of the effect this revelation would have on the children. They both idolized their father; what would they think of him if they knew he had betrayed them all?

Would they blame him, or would they blame Kathy, thinking that it must have been partially her fault for driving him away?

"Could we discuss this somewhere more private?" Robert asked.

Kathy shook her head firmly. "Right now, this is the most private room in the house. If we go upstairs, the kids will think that we're wrapping their presents and be in and out every five minutes. Right now, they know I'm prepping the stuffing for the turkey, and they've no interest in that." She caught his reflection in the glass and was aware that he was moving around to stand beside her.

"Can I help?" he asked.

"No," she said. Kathy hit the button on the blender, and it howled. When it stopped she said, "I don't know what's going to happen between us, Robert. But it's going to take me a long time before I can trust you again . . . a long time before I can even look at you without feeling sick to my stomach," she added bitterly. She saw his hand move toward her, and she jerked away. "Don't!" she snapped. She didn't want him to touch her, to lay a finger on her. The knowledge that he had kissed Stephanie, touched her, slept with her, made Kathy physically nauseous.

"I'm sorry," he said eventually. "I know it sounds like a cliché, but I never wanted to hurt you. You have to believe me—that was never my intention."

What had been his intention? And yes, it was a cliché. It was, she imagined, what every man said when he was caught. He hadn't been thinking: That was the problem. He was prepared to sacrifice eighteen years of marriage, eighteen years of memories, of love and trust, for what . . . a brief moment of passion. Was that all their marriage was worth?

"I allowed myself to enter into the relationship—" Robert began.

"Affair!" Kathy snapped. "Jesus, Robert, call it what it is—an affair!" Robert had been working in advertising too long. He was trying to spin the word into a euphemism, soften it, take the sting away from it. Well, she wasn't having any of it.

"I began my affair with Stephanie last June. I was lonely, Kath, desperately lonely. I wanted someone to talk to, someone to share

with, someone to show an interest in me. I tried to talk to you . . .
God, I tried. But you never seemed to be interested."

Kathy concentrated on the recipe, saying nothing, listening in-
tently to what he was saying. Was it true? Had she not been interested? It cut both ways of course; he had only been vaguely
interested in the house and the children. But she kept coming back
to his statement, and, try as she might, she found she couldn't deny
it. She had to admit that she had not really been interested. She had
just lost her mother. She hadn't really cared about the company or
how he was coping.

"You never asked how things were going, never seemed to be in
the slightest bit concerned with the ordinary, day-to-day minutiae
of keeping the company afloat. I'm not even sure you realized how
much trouble we were in. We came very close to going under."

Maureen had hinted at something similar, and Kathy suddenly
felt extraordinarily guilty. Had she been so wrapped up in her
world of home and children to the exclusion of everything else?

She pulled open the fridge and stared inside, looking for the
sausage meat.

But if the situation had been that serious, why hadn't he made a
point of sitting down and talking with her? She guessed that if she
asked him that he would say that he hadn't told her because he
hadn't wanted to worry her.

"I was lonely," Robert repeated. "We'd stopped . . . having sex.
When I tried, you'd turn your back on me or you'd come to me so
reluctantly that I felt like you were making love to me almost as a
duty."

There was some truth in what he was saying. After a long day of
tending to the house and the kids, carpooling, helping with homework, cleaning . . . she was often too tired.

"You didn't seem to enjoy it."

And she hated refusing him, but it had become apparent to her
a long time ago that their rhythms were different. She liked to make
love in the early morning; she loved the burst of energy it gave her.
It lifted the entire day. Whereas he liked to make love late at night
and then fall into a sound, motionless sleep.

"After a while I stopped making the effort; I'll admit it," Robert continued. "But—and please don't take this as a criticism; it's just a statement of fact—you never made an effort either."

"So you're saying it's my fault you found yourself a mistress?" Kathy asked savagely, but at the back of her mind she knew the point he was making was true. She could not remember the last time she'd initiated their lovemaking. A long time ago; too long.

"No," he sighed. "I'm not trying to score points here—I'm just trying to let you see how I ended up in this situation. I allowed myself to have the affair, Kathy, because I believed—genuinely believed—that you no longer loved me."

Kathy spun around to face him, mouth open, but he held up his hand.

"I know. I'm just telling you how I felt, telling you how I saw things. When you stood in Stephanie's living room earlier and said that you loved me, no one was more surprised than I was."

"I never stopped loving you," Kathy said immediately, though in the last couple of days she had stopped liking him.

"Even right now?" he asked, attempting a smile.

"I'm not sure how I feel about you at this moment," she said truthfully, "but the very fact that we're both standing in this room, even after all that's happened today, should suggest something."

"What?" he wondered.

"That maybe I do accept some responsibility for what happened," she said simply. "I wasn't paying attention. And if a marriage is going to work, then both parties have to keep paying attention. You stopped paying attention to me, and I stopped paying attention to you."

"Would it help if I said I was sorry, truly sorry?"

She looked at him. "Sorry for what? Do you regret the affair?" she asked lightly, though she was deadly serious.

"I regret the pain it caused you," was all Robert would say.

At least he hadn't lied and said that he regretted the affair, because she knew he didn't. She could see it in his eyes, and he'd said only a few short hours ago that he loved Stephanie. "Well, I'm glad you chose to tell me the truth."

"I would never knowingly hurt you," he murmured.

"And yet you have hurt me, Robert," she said simply. "Hurt me and humiliated me. And it's going to take me a long time to forgive that."

"What's going to happen to us?" he asked.

She'd thought about nothing else on the drive home, creating all sorts of possibilities, and she kept coming back to the same conclusion. Taking a deep breath, she said quickly, determined that her voice would not shake, "As I see it, we have two choices: We can stay together, make some new rules, start again, and really work at it this time." She finished quickly and paused before continuing. "Or I can file for divorce."

She watched him assimilate that. The thought of divorce was terrifying—she had no idea of the practicalities involved: splitting the assets, maybe selling the house and the business, moving the children to different schools. She would have to find a job. . . .

"Well, look, let's talk about this later, or tomorrow maybe," Robert said, unable to disguise the tremble in his voice. "We're both tired and probably not thinking too clearly. I know I'm not," he added. He took a breath. "I do have a favor to ask."

She was shocked by his arrogance, but bit her tongue before she said anything.

"Kath, if you decide that you want me to go—and I understand if you do—then can we keep this from the kids for a while? I don't want to ruin their Christmas."

Kathy bowed her head and looked away. She had been about to make a similar request. "I won't ruin their Christmas," she promised. "Let's try to get through the next couple of days like civilized people." If they could get through this, then the children would never have to be told.

"Thank you," he said sincerely.

"When were you going to tell me, Robert?" she asked him suddenly.

"Tell you what?"

"Tell me that you were going to leave me." She already knew the answer, but she wanted to hear him say it.

"I don't know for certain," he mumbled. "Probably over the weekend."

Something cracked and broke inside her. "You don't sound so sure."

"I'm not," he admitted.

"And yet Stephanie seemed convinced that you were going to tell me after Christmas so that you could spend New Year's Eve with her."

"Yes, we talked about that."

"Or were you going to give her an excuse and stay here?" Kathy guessed. She was surprised that she was not hearing a tremendous amount of conviction in his voice.

"Kathy, I have no idea what I would have done. But yes, the plan was to tell you, probably on Saturday or Sunday, that I was leaving."

"Bastard!" Kathy hissed. She felt a terrible rage bubble up inside her. She wanted to scream and shout and howl. She wanted to hit him and claw at his face with her fingers. How could he walk away from eighteen years together in such a cavalier way? She put her palms on his chest and pushed him hard away from her. "You callous, uncaring bastard!"

Robert stepped back. "I'm sorry, Kathy; I really am. But I made that decision believing that you didn't love me. Before I knew the truth."

Kathy turned away from him. She concentrated on the turkey stuffing, clamping down hard on her anger. When she was sure that she could control her voice, she said, "If we're going to rebuild our lives and our relationship, we're going to have to be honest with one another." She looked up and found that he was staring at her reflection in the window. "Will you be honest with me, Robert? Can you promise me that?"

"Yes. Yes, I can," he said.

"Then you have to promise me something else."

"Anything."

"You have to swear to me that you'll stay away from that woman."

"I promise," he said quickly. "In any case, I think you can tell from today that she'll want little enough to do with me." Then he turned and left the room.

Kathy continued leaning against the sink, staring out into the night, seeing only her own reflection, broken and distorted in the window. Stephanie had said that she was finished with Robert . . . but the real question was: Would Robert accept that?

Would he finish with Stephanie?

CHAPTER 38

———❧———

Kathy sat with both elbows on the kitchen table, forehead pressed into right palm, while her left hand held the portable phone pressed to her ear. "Pick up, pick up," she murmured.

An answering machine clicked in, and a polite, accentless male voice said, *"No one is available to take your call at the moment. Please leave a message after the tone. Thank you."*

"Sheila? Sheila, are you there?"

There was a click, and then Sheila's slightly amused voice cut in. "Yep, I'm here. I was just screening my calls. Julia's stalking me."

"I figured. She came over tonight."

"Shit, sorry about that."

Kathy heard a series of rustling noises, then a thump, and when Sheila spoke again, her voice was slightly muffled, "Sorry," she said. Then the sound cleared. "I'm in bed—I was just lying down. Tell me exactly what she said. But before you get to that, tell me: Did you go and see the mistress?"

"Yes," Kathy said slowly, "I went to see Stephanie."

There was a tiny pause, then Kathy heard the rustling again and guessed that her sister was now sitting up in the bed. "Oh my God . . . I can't believe you had the balls to confront her!"

"I had to." Kathy stopped suddenly. She heard the door to Robert's office close above her, then a stair creaked. "Hang on a sec," she said quickly, putting down the phone. By the time she got to the kitchen door, Robert had already stepped out the front door into the night.

Kathy stepped out into the hall. "Are you going out?" she asked, her voice carefully neutral.

"I just want to bring the car in," he said. "I parked it on the street earlier."

Kathy didn't wait for the rest of the explanation. She stepped back into the kitchen, shut the door, and grabbed the phone. "Sorry," she said to her younger sister. "I thought I heard Robert leaving, but he was just bringing the car in."

"Wait! You went to see the mistress, and Robert's still there? What happened?"

Kathy quickly filled Sheila in on the day's events. As she spoke, she darted upstairs and slipped into the bedroom. Standing well back from the net curtains, she looked down to the front of the house. Robert was slowly and carefully maneuvering the car into the drive. So he hadn't been lying. She watched him for a moment and wondered if she would ever trust him again. Could she afford to? Was she going to be constantly on edge every time he left the house? Would she end up checking and double-checking his whereabouts, noting his mileage, verifying every reason he gave to her when he stayed out at night? She couldn't live like that; no one could.

And she wouldn't.

Kathy turned and hurried back downstairs to the kitchen, then she heard the hall door shut as Robert came back into the house. The stairs creaked, then she heard his study door close and the creak of floorboards as he moved around the room.

"So you took him back," Sheila said, her voice carefully neutral.

"It was a little more complicated than I thought," Kathy said.

"It always is," her younger sister said. "In an affair, there are no blacks and whites, only shades of gray."

Kathy nodded. She was beginning to understand that now.

"So what happens now?" Sheila asked.

"I don't know," Kathy said truthfully. "Robert and I need to talk; we need to really, seriously talk. I want to go to marriage counseling. I want to get back into the business, to start taking control again. . . ." And suddenly, with the flood of words, came the tears. The sobs came from deep in the pit of her stomach, tearing at her very being, and, for a moment, she thought she was going to throw up.

"Kathy, oh, Kathy," Sheila said miserably, "I'm coming over."

Kathy attempted to compose herself. "No. I'm fine. Stay where you are. The roads are terrible. I'd never forgive myself if anything happened." She pressed the heels of her hands against her eyes and rubbed away the tears. "I'm fine," she repeated, knowing it was a lie. It was going to be a long time before she would be fine again. "I just need a little time to decompress."

"Would you rather not have known?" Sheila wondered.

Kathy's response was instant. "No. I needed to know. But I'm glad I found out myself. Discovering the truth, piece by piece, has, I think, allowed me to deal with it. I would hate to have had it sprung on me."

"The sort of news Julia would like to break," Sheila said grimly.

"Exactly." With the phone propped between her head and shoulder, Kathy started to clear off the kitchen table, loading the cups and plates into the dishwasher. She needed to start prepping the vegetables for Christmas dinner, and it would be nice to get the kids up to bed at a reasonable hour for once. She wanted them up early in the morning; Christmas Day was the one day of the year when the entire family attended church, and it was always preferable to get to one of the early masses. They were shorter. Floorboards creaked overhead, and she suddenly glanced up. Would Robert be attending church with them tomorrow?

In the few days that had passed since she had discovered Stephanie Burroughs's name in Robert's phone and begun to suspect the affair, she had found herself asking so many questions. Suddenly everything that she had taken for granted was open to doubt. All the certainties of eighteen years of marriage lay shattered about her. "Why?" she said, and didn't realize she had spoken aloud until Sheila answered her.

"Why what?"

"Why did he have the affair?"

"Because he could," Sheila said immediately.

"I keep asking myself if I could have stopped it, prevented it by being more . . . I don't know, more present," Kathy said eventually. "And, by the way, what in the world possessed you to tell Julia about Alan?"

Sheila's laugh was completely without humor. "He was here at the time. He said he was going to tell his wife that he was leaving her for me. . . ."

"Sheila!"

"Hey, I begged him not to. Alan is fun and charming and sophisticated, but he can also be just a little bit pompous and more than a little boring. He's great in bed and fun to talk to, but he's definitely not someone I want to spend the rest of my life with. Over the past couple of weeks, he's been promising me an extra special Christmas present. Guess what it was? That he was going to tell his wife about us."

"Very romantic," Kathy said bitterly.

"Tell me about it. That's the last thing I wanted. I kept telling him not to make an announcement at Christmas, where every emotion is heightened. Then he accused me of being ashamed to be seen with him. I'd never even introduced him to my family, he was saying, and right at that moment Julia called. I have no idea what got into me, but I heard myself saying that I would come over for dinner if I could bring my boyfriend. I'm not sure who was more surprised, Julia or Alan."

"But she recognized his name," Kathy said.

"I know. Brookline is so small. How many Dr. Alan Gallaghers are there? She recognized the name, obviously thought about it, and then called me back, asked me point-blank if he was married, and then started asking me if his wife knew we were having an affair, saying she wasn't going to be able to let this pass. I mean, seriously, what does it have to do with her?"

"Robert asked her the same thing."

"Anyway, she's been calling me on and off all night, obviously wanting to discuss the situation."

"Is Alan still there?"

"No, I convinced him to go home and say nothing."

"What are you going to do?"

"I have no idea. Try and stall him 'til after Christmas. And then dump him. Nicely if I can, but I'm prepared to be brutal."

"And will you bring him to Julia's for dinner?"

"Can you imagine how much fun that would be? I doubt she'd even let him in the door. Hey, Alan's calling my cell . . . d'you mind?"

"Go ahead."

"Are you sure you're okay?"

"I'm fine. I'll talk to you tomorrow."

Kathy had a lot to do before she went to bed, and she wanted to bury herself in the simple Christmas Eve routine. Talking to Sheila, knowing that she was involved in her own affair with a married man, was a constant reminder of her own situation. And right now Kathy wanted to forget about it, just for a few minutes. She wanted things to be the way they were last Christmas.

And then she suddenly realized that Robert had been having his affair last Christmas too. Pressing both hands to her mouth, she raced out to the downstairs toilet, where she knelt on the floor and retched in great heaving gulps.

CHAPTER 39

─────────⌘─────────

Wednesday, 25th December
Christmas Day

Kathy Walker opened her eyes, suddenly awake and alert. What had awakened her?

She'd gone to bed alone just after midnight when she'd finished in the kitchen, leaving it rich with the smell of Christmas—odors of spice and cinnamon, cooking and candle wax, scents that she would forever afterward equate with betrayal. Rolling over, she glanced at the clock: just before one.

The house was absolutely still and silent, and she knew, even before she rolled out of bed and pulled back the curtains, it had snowed. The world outside the window was solid white, crisp, magical, and clean. Later cars would churn the road to filthy black sludge and children would turn the paths into glistening ice sheets, but right at this moment the world had lost all its sharp edges, and everything looked gorgeous and new.

Kathy slid back into the warm bed, lay on her back, and stared at the ceiling. The room should have been in total darkness, but the snow reflected gray alabaster light onto the ceiling.

A white Christmas.

She'd been a child the last time it had snowed on Christmas Day. It should be something to celebrate—but not this Christmas, not today.

Yesterday—was it only yesterday?—she had confronted her husband's mistress.

Yesterday, she had walked up to a woman she did not know and had slapped her across the face.

Yesterday, she had drunk tea with the woman who was sleeping with her husband.

Yesterday, that woman had given up Kathy's husband.

Less than twelve hours, and yet it seemed a lifetime ago.

Kathy pressed both hands to her churning stomach. From the moment she had set out to drive to Stephanie Burroughs's apartment, her stomach started to burn with acid indigestion. When she'd climbed out of her car before the woman's house and rested her finger on the bell, she'd thought she was going to throw up.

On the drive home, she'd had to pull off the road twice and roll down the window to breathe in great, heaving breaths. The cramping pain had come back at her again throughout the remainder of the day. It had grown worse in the late evening and into the night. With the sights and sounds of the encounter with her husband's mistress running and rerunning through her head, she'd felt her stomach protest, and she'd thrown up until there was nothing left but bitter bile. In desperation, she'd drunk Pepto Bismol—which she hated—straight from the bottle, the chalky liquid coating her tongue and mouth with its milky pink residue.

Kathy glanced across the bed.

Robert's side was empty. He'd made no attempt to come to bed with her, and she guessed he'd spent the night sleeping in the chair in his study. She wasn't sure what she would have done if he'd attempted to climb into bed next to her. Got out and slept downstairs, she supposed. But she should have known he wouldn't want to put himself in a position where they would have to talk.

She knew he didn't want to do that just yet. They'd had arguments and disagreements in the past, just like every other couple. His usual tactic was to state his position and then simply refuse to discuss it further. After a few vain attempts to raise the topic of conversation, she would normally let it drop, allowing him to win by default. That was not going to happen this time; they needed to discuss the future.

If there was going to be a future.

Then she heard it: the quiet closing of a door followed by the irregular creaking of the stairs. Every sense tingling, she heard him move around downstairs, shuffling from the living room to the kitchen. There was a long silence, and then she heard the kitchen door close. Footsteps hurried upstairs, and she heard his office door open, then close again moments later. This time when the footsteps descended the stairs they sounded more solid . . . as if he had put on his shoes.

Kathy sat up, heart thumping. Surely he wasn't going out?

The chain on the front door rattled, then the door was gently eased open and pulled closed with a click.

Leaping out of bed, she watched him back the car out of the drive. He hadn't put on his headlights because they would light up the bedroom, she realized, but his reversing lights painted the snow blood red.

He was going to her.

She'd thought . . . She'd thought . . . When he'd come back with her, he had seemed genuinely contrite, and she had been hopeful that once they got through these few days, they would be able to move on. She'd asked him to promise not to see Stephanie again, and he had, but without a huge amount of conviction, she'd thought. Talking about Stephanie, he'd said, "In any case, I think you can tell from today that she'll want little enough to do with me."

He'd lied to her.

There were no tears now, just a cold anger . . . coupled with a feeling of absolute helplessness. What was she going to do? What could she do? Throw him out? Gather all his clothes, stuff them into the suitcases, and fling them out into the front garden? Call Stephanie and tell her that he was on the way and not to send him back?

Was he even coming back?

Pulling on her robe, she wandered out of the bedroom and into his study. It felt hot and stuffy, the air slightly stale with a hint of his old aftershave overlaying sour perspiration. Everything seemed in order—perhaps in a little too much order. The pile of mail on the desk was certainly a lot neater, and she guessed that if she went to it she would find that the parking ticket and the Visa bill would conveniently be missing.

She wandered down into the kitchen where she found the note beside the phone. "Office alarm has gone off; gone in to see if there's a problem."

Her first instinct was to pick up the phone and call the alarm company to confirm. She'd actually lifted the receiver when she changed her mind and put the phone down again. If she and Robert were to begin again, then she had to start trusting him. She'd been wrong about him before, when she had suspected that he'd been having an affair six years ago. Her accusations then had desperately damaged their marriage, and she didn't want to make that mistake again. Maybe the office alarm had genuinely gone off . . . but she hadn't heard the phone ring, and when she checked the caller ID, there had been no calls since one of Theresa's friends had called the house much earlier that evening. If the alarm company were calling, would they have contacted Robert's cell first, and then the house second, or the other way around? Feeling a little relieved, she returned the note to where she'd found it, then went back upstairs and climbed into the cold bed.

Lying in the silence, she heard the snow hiss and spit against the window and suddenly found herself praying for his safe return.

But at the back of her mind, faint but insistent, was the thought that he had gone to Stephanie. And if he had, she knew, then they were finished.

Finished.

She was still awake at two thirty when he returned.

The minutes had crawled by, second by agonizing second, each one accompanied by visions of an equally terrifying scenario: Robert dead by the side of the road... the car on its roof in a pileup on Storrow Drive... Robert in the arms of his mistress.

Several times she had reached for the phone to dial his number or the office number or even Stephanie's number. But each time she had pulled back. If he had gone out for a genuine reason, she didn't want him to know that she was checking up on him.

When she saw the splash of headlights on the road and heard the car slowly crunch its way down the ice-locked street, she knew it was him and experienced a wave of relief that left her shaking with emotion.

Climbing out of bed, she stood and watched the Audi approach and then the lights click off so that they would not illuminate the front of the house before he turned into the drive. Leaning forward, straightening the curtains, she watched him climb out of the car, and the look of leaden exhaustion on his face convinced her that he had not gone to see Stephanie. If he'd gone to his mistress, surely he would have spent the night, and even if he had decided to return home before Brendan and Theresa got up to open their presents, then he would be looking a whole lot happier.

She heard the hall door open and, for a moment, thought about going down and asking about the office alarm, but then she decided that she didn't want him to be aware that she knew he'd been out. Stairs creaked, his office door opened and closed, then she heard the pneumatic hiss as he sat back in his chair.

Then silence.

Kathy sat on the edge of the bed for almost an hour, then she padded out of the room, down the landing, and stopped outside his door. She opened the door and peered inside.

Still wearing his leather coat and gloves, Robert was slumped in his office chair, fast asleep. His face was ashen and, even in sleep, lined with exhaustion. He must have gone into the office, she decided. And she felt vaguely guilty then for even having her suspicions.

She was going to have to learn how to trust him again. She would, she promised. Standing in the doorway, watching him sleep in his clothes, Kathy Walker made an early New Year's resolution: She was going to work to save this marriage because, despite the pain and anguish he had put her through, despite how small he had made her feel, she still loved him.

God help her, but she still loved him.

CHAPTER 40

She dozed rather than slept for the next couple of hours.

Whenever she closed her eyes, events and incidents from the previous days came rushing back. Suddenly she would find herself remembering the look in Stephanie's eyes when she'd opened the door and found Kathy standing there. Somehow Stephanie hadn't seemed to be in the least surprised; maybe she too had been relieved that events were coming to a head.

In an affair time stopped. An affair existed in a bubble. It was only when it was discovered or ended that people could go on with their lives. In her own situation, Kathy had been trapped in a world of white lies, half-truths, and evasions, while Stephanie had been equally trapped by the same lies for the past eighteen months. And in the middle was Robert, spinning the lies, trying to balance both worlds, telling both women what he thought they wanted to hear.

She heard movement. The bathroom door opened, then slow and heavy footsteps went downstairs. Maybe Robert also couldn't sleep.

Kathy got out of bed and went to stand by the window. The front yard and road looked like a traditional Christmas card. No tracks broke the pristine snowy surface; even the tracks left by Robert's car several hours earlier had been covered over. Some of the houses had lights on, and, across the street, she could see the seven-year-old Brady triplets in their matching Spider-Man pajamas, clustered around the Christmas tree ripping paper off their presents.

She found herself remembering her own childhood, and in particular that morning when she had awoken to find that it had snowed overnight. She shared a bedroom with Sheila, and she'd shaken her little sister awake. She would have been about nine or ten, she thought, old enough to begin to suspect the existence—or nonexistence—of Santa Claus, but not prepared to question it too deeply. Just in case. Together, the two girls had huddled in the window, with the quilt pulled around their shoulders, and simply looked at the snow and the world that they knew so well, now changed beyond all recognition. They'd scanned the roofs of the houses across the street looking for reindeer tracks in the snow before finally deciding that magical reindeer probably didn't leave tracks.

She remembered, with absolute clarity, what she had gotten for her Christmas presents that year. An Easy Bake oven with miniature trays to make chocolate cakes, a Scoobie Doo Mystery Mobile that she used to cart around her Barbie dolls, a paint-by-numbers art set of Wonder Woman that she'd never finished, three Nancy Drew books, and two pairs of overalls—one of which still had a Sears tag on it . . . which she remembered thinking was a strange place for Santa to get his clothes from.

She couldn't remember the following Christmas, nor the previous one. It was the snow that had made that particular Christmas special and memorable.

Other Christmases stuck in her memory; the first Christmas after her father died, the first year she was married, the year Brendan was born, the year Theresa arrived, their first year in this house. The rest melted into one vaguely similar event, with the same rich food, the same movie marathons on TV, the same "Is that all?" feeling at the end of the day.

And now this Christmas. She would certainly be adding this to her list of memorable Christmases. This was one she would never forget and, she was afraid, would forever taint all future Christmases.

A creak on the stairs disturbed her daydreaming, and she turned away from the window and quickly slipped back into bed.

The bedroom door cracked open, yellow light from the hall spilling into the room. She heard Robert move around to her side of the bed and then the rattle of a cup and saucer as it was put down. She didn't remember the last time he had brought her up a cup of coffee. "Kathy." His voice was a hoarse, exhausted whisper. "Kathy?"

She opened her eyes. He looked wretched. There were deep bags beneath his eyes, and the skin on his face seemed to have sagged. She fought to quell her rising concern.

"I brought you some coffee," he said, then added, "Merry Christmas."

"You went out last night." It wasn't what she had intended to say, nor was it what she wanted to ask, but she had to know; she had to ask the question, and she had to hear his response. She had worked hard to keep her voice carefully neutral.

"The office alarm went off—I got a call from the alarm company. I had to go in."

She searched his face, looking for the truth. But would she even know if he were lying? He'd spent the past eighteen months lying to her, and she hadn't picked that up; he must be an expert at it by now. "You were gone for a long time," she said, pushing up in bed, pulling the covers up to her chin.

"Roads were terrible. Mine was the only car out; I crept along. And then when I got there, I had to make sure everything was okay." He'd moved around to stand by the window and look out at the dawn. Was that because he couldn't bear to look her in the face, she wondered. But no, he'd stared into her eyes countless times lately and lied to her.

"I take it there was no problem with the office."

He shook his head. "Probably snow or ice falling off a neighboring building, hitting our roof, and setting off one of the sensors. I could hear other alarms ringing out across Storrow Drive as I drove home."

Kathy nodded. It had the ring of truth to it, especially the reasons for the alarm to go off in the first place. Surely he wouldn't be able to make up that detail himself?

"Drink your coffee," he said. "I'm sure the kids will be up soon." He padded silently out of the bedroom, and then she heard his office door close.

Kathy sat up in bed drinking the rich brew, noting that he had remembered to put in soy milk for her, feeling guilty that she'd ever suspected him of sneaking off to Stephanie's in the first place.

They missed ten o'clock Mass.

When Kathy finished her coffee, she closed her eyes and then woke again at ten minutes to ten with a start, convinced that it had all been nothing more than a dream, a terrible, terrifying dream. All she had to do was to open her eyes and look around, and there would be Robert asleep beside her, and Stephanie and the last twenty-four hours, the last week would all be nothing more than a . . .

She opened her eyes.

It was no dream.

She could hear muted sounds coming from below, and although she'd been bright and alert earlier, now she felt as if she were moving in slow motion. Robert and the kids were up. Pulling on her robe, she padded silently downstairs. The kids were in the midst of opening their presents, and Kathy arrived just in time to hear Theresa say, "Thanks, Dad, how did you know I was looking for this one?"

Robert, standing beside the tree while the children scattered Christmas paper across the floor, had the grace to look embarrassed as Kathy paused by the door. "Don't you know I had a little help? As always."

Kathy turned away and headed into the kitchen and was aware that Robert was coming in behind her. He had two badly wrapped presents in his hands alongside a beautiful bouquet of flowers with a card sticking out of it. She wouldn't read the card, not for a while. Robert was a beautiful writer, and she didn't want to read what he had or had not taken the time to write. She needed her head to be clear of his charm. "Merry Christmas," he said awkwardly, holding the gifts and the flowers.

What had he gotten his mistress, Kathy wondered. She couldn't help but compare the two small items he was holding in his left hand with the carefully wrapped and beautifully presented boxes he'd carried into Stephanie's house yesterday. And where was the balloon? For a moment, she was going to refuse the gifts. Whatever they were, she would never wear or use them; she wanted no memories of this particular Christmas. But then she relented and took them from his hands. "Thank you," she said simply. She thought he was leaning in to her, perhaps expecting a kiss or a hug, but she turned away quickly. "I'll give you yours later," she said, without turning around. "It's upstairs in the closet. Now, come on, we'd better hurry or we're going to miss eleven o'clock Mass too. And midday Mass goes on forever."

Next year, Kathy promised herself, walking down the steps as she left the church, she was going to early Mass. Very early Mass. The service had been interrupted every few minutes by the blips and pips of some handheld computer game or the irritating ringtone of a newly acquired phone, and every so often a doll would cry realistically or an action figure merchandised from the latest movie franchise would fire off his laser.

As the family filed out through the gates, they bumped into Julia, who was holding court to a group of women, all of whom seemed only too delighted to make their escape when Kathy appeared. Theresa and Brendan awkwardly hugged their aunt before excusing themselves to visit with their friends.

"There you are. I was hoping to see you," Julia began, then quickly kissed Kathy and Robert on the cheeks. "Merry Christmas... Merry Christmas. And it's a white Christmas too; isn't it lovely." She made the question into a statement. "And you look lovely too— though you shouldn't have worn that outfit in this weather."

Kathy had dressed simply in her tailored black slacks, worn over black, square-heeled boots and, although she knew it made her look small and dumpy, she'd pulled on her heavy navy-blue peacoat. It was like wearing a blanket, but the open-plan, high-ceilinged church could be draughty. Julia, on the other hand, was wearing what Kathy called her country-lady look: tweed skirt, Wellington boots, a blue blazer, and a hat with a short feather in it. And this was the lady giving her fashion advice! Kathy suddenly found herself biting the inside of her cheek to keep a straight face.

"Now, about tomorrow," Julia began. "We're going to start about..."

"We won't be there," Kathy said suddenly.

Julia looked blankly at her, then turned to look at Robert. "We're starting about four...."

"I'm not sure if you heard Kathy correctly," Robert said with a smile, "but we've decided not to come over this year."

Julia's mouth opened and closed. "But it's a tradition."

"We're breaking with tradition," Robert said.

"Starting some new ones," Kathy added. "Have a Merry Christmas, Julia. Give our love to Ben." Then she turned and walked away.

Robert nodded to his dumbstruck sister-in-law and hurried after Kathy.

"Thank you," Kathy said.

"For what?"

"For supporting me."

"We should have done it years ago," he said.

"You're right. But it's time to make some changes," she said, glancing sidelong at him.

Robert nodded, eyes distant and lost. Then he blinked and tried a smile. "And what was she wearing on her head? She looks like those women . . . those princesses from the royal wedding. Bibi and Eunice?"

"Beatrice. Beatrice and Eugenie," Kathy corrected him and then she laughed, and Robert laughed with her. Climbing into the car, she couldn't remember the last time they had laughed together so easily.

CHAPTER 41

The moment the telephone rang, Kathy felt her insides twist, and the little bubble of good humor that had remained with her since Mass instantly evaporated. She moved away from the oven and heard Brendan call out, "Dad, phone!"

"You get it," came the mumbled response.

"It'll be for you. It's always for you."

Rubbing her hands on her striped apron, Kathy started to move into the dining room to get the phone when Robert—looking bleary-eyed and haggard—appeared and grabbed the phone out of the cradle. "Hello?"

She wondered who would be calling at this time on Christmas Day, and immediately thought: Julia. No doubt she'd spent the past couple of hours working herself up into a self-righteous frenzy and now had a dozen cast-iron reasons why they should come over for dinner tomorrow. At some point in the conversation she'd play the "it's what Mother would have wanted us to do" card.

"Hello?" Robert asked again.

Kathy glanced at him, eyebrows raised in a question. She saw him swallow and lick dry lips, and then he smiled.

"Sure...sure," he said, and then he added, "And a Merry Christmas to you too." He took a breath. "Let me just step out of the room away from the TV....

"It's Jimmy Moran," he said, phone pressed against his chest, "just calling to wish us Merry Christmas."

Kathy nodded as she sank the skewer into the turkey. "Don't talk too long; I'll be serving dinner soon."

Robert moved out into the hall. "I'll be just a minute."

She heard his footsteps on the stairs and knew he'd be more than a minute. He always was. Her husband had no concept of time. She glanced over at the counter, checking to ensure that everything was in place. This was the one big meal she cooked every year. When the kids had been younger she'd cooked almost every night—chicken, pasta, hamburgers, salmon. On Wednesdays, they'd always order pizza and Greek salad; anchovy for her and Brendan and Hawaiian for Robert and Theresa. On Friday night, she'd usually cook a huge chicken that they'd eat all weekend, along with Chinese or Indian takeout. It had been a family tradition for many years. But by the time the children were into their teens, and were busy with after-school activities and piles of homework, they simply had no time to sit at the table and eat, and often she found herself cooking just for Robert and herself. More recently, she found she was eating alone. Robert would come home "not hungry" or having "had a big lunch"; now she wondered how much of that was true, or was he not hungry because he'd been eating with *her?*

Kathy veered away from that thought.

If they weren't going over to Julia's tomorrow—and she was determined that they were not—then maybe they should invite Jimmy Moran to the house, and Sheila too. Kathy stopped and straightened. And what if Sheila wanted to bring her boyfriend? Kathy took a deep breath; Sheila could bring him. Kathy was in no position to stand in judgment over someone else's relationship.

She heard the door to Robert's office creak open and, when he came down, he looked ghastly. There was no color in his face, and the bags beneath his eyes looked like physical bruises.

"Is everything all right?"

"Yes, he's fine," Robert said, licking dry lips.

"Not with him—with you."

"Yes, yes, I'm fine. I'm just exhausted," he admitted. "I might try to grab a nap after dinner. If that's okay," he added.

"It's what you do every year," she reminded him.

The long table in the dining room had been opened out and covered with the Irish linen tablecloth Jimmy had given them as a wedding present, which only made its appearance one day a year. Four full place settings had been laid out, Theresa taking great care to ensure that the correct knives and forks were in the right position, while Brendan organized the soup bowls and large plates.

Robert sat at the head of the table, Kathy at the opposite end, facing him, while the two children sat at either side. Kathy looked around the table, deliberately and consciously impressing every detail into her memory. Maybe this would be their last year at home for Christmas. Every year—usually on Christmas Day and at about this time—she would come up with the idea they would go away for a vacation next year. Enjoy Christmas in some warm and sunny climate. Ever since she'd been a child, and discovered that the seasons were reversed in the southern hemisphere, she'd wanted to spend Christmas on a beach in Australia. Next year, she promised herself, next year.

She had little appetite for food—nor did Robert, she noticed, and it gave her some little satisfaction to realize that he was feeling as bad as she was—but the kids quickly finished the homemade tomato soup, and Brendan finished off his father's barely touched bowl. Kathy stood up and started to gather the bowls when the phone rang again. She caught a glimpse of something move across Robert's face—some emotion she could not identify. "Let the machine get it," she said quickly. "This is one of the few meals this family sits down to together."

Robert nodded dubiously even as he was standing up. "I'd better get it. I'll just be a minute."

Kathy sighed as she carried the soup bowls out to the kitchen. Next year they were definitely going away. She dropped the soup bowls in the sink and turned to the turkey, which she'd left cooling on the draining board. Peeling back the silver foil, she breathed in the distinctive aroma of turkey and spices.

"Hello . . . Yes, this is Robert Walker. . . ."

Half listening to Robert's conversation, she plugged in the electric knife and prepared to start slicing into the bird. Brendan would take a leg, while Robert preferred the white breast meat and sausage stuffing. Theresa was going through one of her periodic vegetarian phases and announced she was only having vegetables.

"Hi. What can I do for you?"

Kathy put down the knife and stepped over to the kitchen door, eyebrows raised in a silent question. She could tell by Robert's voice there was something terribly wrong.

"James . . . I don't know . . . Oh, you mean Jimmy."

Kathy frowned. Jimmy Moran? But Jimmy had just been on the phone to Robert.

"Is he okay?" Robert asked. He looked at her and shrugged and then said into the phone, "Today?" He quickly covered the mouthpiece and muttered to Kathy, "Mass General. Jimmy's been admitted."

"But you were talking to him less than half an hour ago," Kathy said.

But Robert had turned back to the phone. "Yes, yes, I'm here. . . . It's just it's . . . Christmas, and I'm with my family. . . ."

Kathy turned away and unplugged the knife; if Jimmy was in trouble, then she knew Robert would go to him.

"Is it an emergency?" Robert asked, then added, obviously responding to a question from the nurse, "Yes, yes, a good friend."

Kathy watched his expression change; there was something like fear in his eyes now.

"Tell him I'm on the way." He hung up and looked at Kathy. "It sounds really serious. I'm sorry, but I've got to go. . . ."

"I know. You should go. But how did he sound when you were talking to him earlier?"

She watched his eyes blank for a minute, and then he said simply, "He sounded fine."

"Go. Get your coat and gloves. I'll fill a thermos with coffee."

* * *

Kathy stood at the door and watched Robert gingerly inch the car out of the drive. She found herself waving out of habit, and then turned and closed the door behind her. She wondered when she'd see her husband again. When she got back into the dining room, Brendan and Theresa had drifted away to the television, and she didn't have the heart to call them back to the table. Having a Christmas dinner without Robert seemed wrong somehow.

As she passed the phone, she stopped and looked at the caller ID. The last call showed a 617 area code—she'd no doubt that was Mass General Hospital—but the call before that read Blocked . . . which was strange, because Jimmy Moran had an apartment in the North End, and his name always popped up when he called. Maybe he'd called from Angela's phone and it was unlisted.

Kathy stopped herself, realizing what she was doing, and feeling guilty that she was checking up on Robert. She turned away and started to busy herself cleaning up the kitchen, putting away the meats, wrapping up the vegetables, pouring the sauces—apple, cheese, and cranberry—into small containers. Just about everything would keep. Knowing that the children would be looking for something to eat in a couple of hours, she cut slices off the turkey and ham and put them onto two side plates, covered them in Saran Wrap, and left them in the center of the table.

"I've left some meat out if you want to make yourselves sandwiches later, and listen out for the phone, will you?" she told Brendan and Theresa, who were sitting on either end of the couch, playing one of the new games Brendan had gotten for his Xbox. "Your dad's gone to visit Uncle Jimmy in the hospital. I'm just going upstairs for a nap. I didn't sleep too well last night."

"When's Dad coming back?" Theresa asked, without looking away from the screen.

"I have no idea," Kathy said truthfully. "Depends on what he finds when he reaches the hospital."

CHAPTER 42

<hr>

"They took him down for tests about two hours ago," Robert said, his voice echoing slightly as if he was standing in a corridor. "I keep asking them for results or a progress report, but the nurses on duty can't tell me anything."

Kathy lay on the bed and stared at the ceiling. "And how did he look?"

"Terrible. Kathy, when I first saw him, I thought he was dead."

She could hear the genuine fear in his voice. Although Robert would probably never admit it, she knew he had come to regard Jimmy Moran as a father figure. Kathy liked the older man, but was also wary of the influence he had on Robert and had little time for his attitude toward women. Jimmy was of the generation that regarded women as objects to be conquered, bedded, and then chained to a kitchen sink. "He's tough, Robert; you know that. He's going to pull through."

There was a pause, and she could hear the ambient sound change, the echo of the corridor dying away.

"I'm sorry for ruining your Christmas," he said suddenly.

"It was ruined a long time before Jimmy got sick."

"Yes." His voice hissed and popped across the line.

"If you'd stayed at home today, we would probably have ended up fighting," she said eventually.

"Probably," he agreed.

"Maybe this time apart has been . . . useful. Allows us both to get a little perspective." Lying in the darkened bedroom, listening to the muted rumble from the TV below had been vaguely comforting. She hadn't realized just how on edge she'd been until she lay back on the bed and felt the rigid bar of pain across her shoulders that had been building throughout the day begin to ease.

"Yes, yes, you're right."

"Time to think," she added.

"I've been doing nothing but think," he said.

"We'll talk when you get home. Maybe we'll have a little dinner together, just the two of us, and talk."

"That would be nice. . . . Yes, it's been a long time since we sat down and talked. It'll be just like the old days."

Kathy sat up on the bed and looked out into the street. Heavy banks of gray-black clouds had been rolling in all afternoon, and it had started to snow again. The world outside was white and still. "Do you think you're going to make it home tonight?" she asked.

"I'd like to wait and see how Jimmy is. I don't want to leave him on his own."

Kathy frowned. That didn't sound right; Jimmy was one of the most sociable and gregarious men she knew. "Why is he alone? I thought Angela or Frances would be there. They're not snowed in, are they?"

"Maybe, but that's not the reason they're staying away. They've both refused to come. Turns out Jimmy told them too many lies over too many years; that's finally caught up with him," Robert said.

Kathy nodded. She'd always known that eventually Jimmy Moran would have to pay for a lifetime of sailing far too close to the wind with his relationships and too-close friendships with women. And his treatment of his wife and his mistress was shameful . . . not unlike Robert's, in fact, she couldn't help but add.

"I'd like to stay for a while longer . . . if that's okay?"

"Of course it's okay. It's snowing heavily here. It's probably better if you stay there, rather than getting back on the road. The hospital staff isn't going to kick you out."

"Maybe I'll try to nap on one of the empty beds."

Kathy heard a sudden, high-pitched blipping sound, and then Robert swore. "Shit, I'm down to one bar," he said quickly.

"Is there a phone in the room?" she asked immediately.

She heard movement and then a click, as if he'd turned on a light. "Here it is. . . ."

She copied down the number onto the notepad beside the bedroom phone.

"Look, I'd better go and save what's left of the battery. You've got the number; call me anytime. I'll be here for the next couple of hours at least, and if I do decide to stay here, I'll give you a call."

"Give Jimmy my love," Kathy said and hung up.

She sat for a little while longer and watched it snow. Then she opened the presents Robert had given her. The necklace and scarf were lovely, though the silver necklace with the teardrop pendant was remarkably similar to one he had bought her a couple of years ago. The flowers were beautiful, but it was the card that was magnificent. Robert had taken the time to do a series of doodles, the kind he had done when he was first courting her. They were funny caricatures of him and the children trying to get the tree through the front door, of Robert and Kathy trying in vain to talk to the kids while they watched television, and one of Julia holding court while everyone, including her husband, Ben, was sleeping. A warm feeling rushed through Kathy. This was one of the things that had made her initially fall in love with him: his humor. In between the pictures was a handwritten gift certificate for a weekend in Martha's Vineyard. Kathy smiled. Maybe they could begin again.

Then she realized that she hadn't given him his present. Opening the closet, she reached behind her long dresses and took out the large rectangular box, now wrapped in several sheets of colorful Christmas paper. Inside was a pigskin briefcase, with his initials *RW* embossed in gold onto the front. There was a Christmas card attached to the box. She'd written it before she'd discovered the affair and thought for a moment about removing it. In the card she had added a little note about how much in love she was, and thanking him for everything he had done for them all over the past year. She decided to leave it. His card to her had taken time. She couldn't just punish him for his mistakes; she had to give him credit for the effort. He seemed to be trying.

She carried the box into his office and laid it on the table alongside his computer. She glanced at the machine and, for a single moment, thought about turning it on to check his e-mails, but then she turned away, feeling disgusted with herself.

She was dozing in the family room with the TV off and the fire burned down to embers when Robert returned. Although it was not yet midnight, the children had gone to bed, and his absence had cast a pall over the day. The phone had rung twice, and she'd jumped on each occasion. Recognizing Julia's number on the caller ID, she'd allowed her two calls to go to the answering machine. But there had been no message. Kathy was definitely not in the mood to speak to her sister; it would invariably end in an argument. She thought about calling Sheila or Maureen, just to chat, but in the end called neither of them. She wanted the time to think and plan for the future, but found she couldn't do that either. Her thoughts were chaotic, and she found herself quickly shifting between anger at Robert's behavior and sympathy for his current situation, coupled with her own doubts and self-loathing. Surely there was something she could have done to prevent this from happening?

The flare of headlights against the living room window alerted her to his return, and she had the hall door open before he had climbed out of the car. And if he'd looked tired and overextended before he left, now he looked positively pitiful. His shoulders were rounded as if he carried the weight of the world on them, his eyes half-closed. When he came into the house, she wanted to gather him into her arms and hold him close, tell him that everything was going to be okay, but the look on his face was so off-putting, so forbidding that she backed away, and she knew, even before he opened his mouth and said, "He's dead," that Jimmy Moran was gone.

Robert climbed the stairs and closed the study door behind him without saying another word. She heard the double thump as his shoes hit the floor, then silence.

Kathy Walker closed the hall door, locked up, and turned off the lights. She was feeling weary, stiff, and aching, almost as if she were coming down with the flu.

Climbing the stairs, she stopped outside Robert's door, head tilted to one side, and listened for several long moments before she cracked the door open and peered inside. Robert was slumped in the chair and, although he was asleep, his brow was furrowed and his eyes were twitching furiously behind closed lids. In that moment, her heart broke for him. He shouldn't be here, sitting in an uncomfortable chair, still in the clothes he'd been wearing all day. He should be in bed, beside her, and she should be holding him, comforting him.

She went to the hall closet, found a heavy blanket, carried it into his room, and tucked it in around him. He moaned in his sleep, but didn't awaken.

Before she left the room, she looked back and came to the decision that they could—they would—put all this behind them; they would work to rebuild their marriage and relationship.

They would start again.

CHAPTER 43

Thursday, 26th December

"Thank you for the briefcase . . . and the card," Robert said, accepting the cup of coffee from Kathy's hand.

"I thought it was about time you got a new one; that old case is the same age as Brendan, and beginning to look it." She noted that he'd put her Christmas card on top of the computer screen.

Robert turned to look at the fine-grained pigskin case on the table. "I'll take good care of it," he promised.

"How are you doing?" she asked, looking around the study. As if it mirrored his mental state, the once-neat room was in disarray: There were clothes piled over the back of the chairs, the blanket she'd covered him with was tossed on the floor, and there were papers and files everywhere.

"I've been looking for addresses," Robert said, turning back to the computer and nodding at the screen. Kathy noted that he had Outlook open to the Contacts page. "Angela said she was too distraught to get involved in the funeral arrangements," Robert said bitterly, "though she didn't sound that upset when I called her yesterday and told her Jimmy was dead. There was a party going on in the background."

"It is Christmas, Robert," Kathy gently reminded him.

"And I'm not getting any sense out of Frances. The last time I spoke to her, I thought she was drunk or stoned. She didn't seem upset either by the fact that the father of her child was dead."

"Their relationship had more or less foundered though, hadn't it?"

"I think he loved her more than she loved him," Robert continued. "She lost interest in him when she realized that he was never going to make her a star."

"He spent a long time lying to her, making her promises that he could never keep."

"I know that!" Robert snapped. "I'm sorry," he said immediately. "But I would have thought that his death would change things."

"Doesn't change how you feel about a person," Kathy said. "Just because someone dies, that doesn't make him or her a better person."

"No . . . no, I suppose you're right. But he was always a friend to me, and I liked him, liked him a lot . . . despite his faults."

"I know that."

"Anyway, the upshot of it is that I'm trying to coordinate with Angela, and she's doling out information in dribs and drabs. I finally found an address and a phone number for Michael—Mikey—Moran, his oldest brother. He's living in Vancouver." He looked at his watch. "Still too early to call, I think."

"Do you know what sort of relationship they had?"

Robert shook his head. "Not really. Distant, but friendly, I think." He suddenly turned away from the computer. "Once I get him, I can plan the funeral arrangements, and then I'll start getting in touch with people in the industry. I'll write a press release, I think." He looked up at Kathy. "I'm sorry. I guess I'm not going to be much use to anyone today."

"Do what you have to do," Kathy said. "But try to get some rest. You look exhausted."

"I am," he admitted. "I'll take a nap later. What are you going to do?" He smiled. "Go to Julia's?"

"Over my dead body," she said, and then colored, realizing what she'd said. "I'm sorry. That was callous."

"Yes, but funny. You know, if you don't go to Julia's, she's more than likely to turn up at the door."

"She'd be picking a bad day for an argument," Kathy said grimly.

"Kathy? How wonderful to hear from you!"

"Maureen . . . Merry Christmas," Kathy said carefully.

"Is everything all right?" Maureen asked immediately, obviously picking up on something in Kathy's reserved tone.

"Not really," Kathy said carefully. "Jimmy Moran died yesterday."

There was a long silence, then Maureen sighed and said, "Poor Jimmy. My God," she said suddenly. "He was a lot younger than I am. What happened?"

Kathy stood at the kitchen window and watched Brendan and Theresa build a lopsided snowman in the backyard. Overhead, the sky was cloudless, the brilliant sunlight catching painfully bright reflections off every surface, but massing in the distance she could see enormous blue-black clouds boiling up out of the north. There would be more snow later.

"Kathy?" Maureen said, breaking into the long silence.

"Sorry," she said quickly. "It was a heart attack. Robert got a call yesterday, early afternoon, from the hospital. He went in, of course. He was with him to the end."

"And how is Robert taking it?"

"Badly," Kathy said simply.

"I never understood that relationship. Jimmy usually drove away younger talent. I think he was a little fearful of it, envious too, but he and Robert just . . . connected."

"I just wanted to let you know about Jimmy," said Kathy.

"I've known him for more than twenty-five years, I think," Maureen said softly. "There were times when I even liked him. We got along because I was the one woman who would never sleep with him, he said. He was so charming," she added with a sigh. "He was also the most wonderful and outrageous liar. That made him the perfect producer," she added with a small laugh. "When's the funeral?"

"I don't know yet. Robert's trying to make the arrangements.

Apparently, even in death, neither Angela nor Frances wants anything to do with him. They wouldn't even come in to the hospital."

"I'm not surprised."

"Robert's trying to contact Jimmy's brothers. . . ."

"I didn't know he had family," Maureen exclaimed.

"Three brothers, New York, Canada, and Australia, as far as I can make out. Robert's not making a lot of sense this morning. He's physically and emotionally fried."

"He came over on Christmas Eve and told me about your encounter with Stephanie. How are you?" Maureen asked softly.

"I'm okay," Kathy said quickly.

"Truthfully," Maureen persisted.

"I'm feeling a little fried myself."

"Hardly surprising. You know, if you want someone to talk to, someone who's been there and has gone through what you're going through right now, all you have to do is give me a call."

"I know. Thank you." There were tears in Kathy's eyes now, fragmenting the backyard into rainbows of bitter light. Then she said suddenly, "What are you doing this afternoon? Are you free?"

"I am," Maureen said, sounding surprised.

"We didn't really have Christmas dinner yesterday; Robert got the call before I could serve it. Would you come over? My sister Sheila's coming too—you remember Sheila? I could call her and ask her to pick you up, so you wouldn't have to drive. Say yes, please!"

"Yes, please," Maureen said without hesitation.

"Good. Thank you. I'd just really like some company," she admitted. "Someone to talk to. Robert is busy at the moment organizing Jimmy's funeral, and I think he might just crash later. It'll just be the three of us."

"I'll be there," Maureen promised.

"I'll have Sheila get you about three."

"I'll be ready."

CHAPTER 44

It was only when Kathy saw the two women standing at the door that the tears came. The racking sobs came from deep within and left her shaking with emotion. Sheila and Maureen gathered her into their arms and hugged her closely, letting her cry out her pain and terrible anguish.

Then Maureen eased them all away from the door and in toward the kitchen and sat her down in a chair. "Make some tea," Maureen suggested to Sheila, while she dug in her tiny handbag and produced a linen square, which she used to pat Kathy's eyes as if Kathy were a child.

Kathy drew in a deep breath. "I'm sorry. I don't know what came over me."

Maureen crouched beside her. "There's nothing to apologize for. You've been through a lot over the past couple of days."

"Where are Brendan and Theresa?" Sheila asked.

"They've both gone out—to different parties."

"Robert?"

"Upstairs. Asleep. At least I think he's asleep. I haven't heard any movement in the last hour or so." Kathy sat up and carefully wiped at her smudged eye makeup. "Why doesn't waterproof mascara ever work?"

"You look wonderful," Sheila said.

Kathy was wearing a simple wine-colored wrap dress that she'd bought about six months ago for an industry dinner, but which she'd never worn. Robert had been forced to cancel at the last minute. . . . She hadn't thought too much about it at the time, but now of course, she could think of any number of reasons why he would have wanted to cancel.

Sheila was wearing a silver and black beaded vest over a purple silk blouse, skinny jeans, and leather boots that made her tower over her sister. Maureen was, as always, elegant and sophisticated in black trousers and a white roll-neck sweater.

"Thank you for coming, both of you," Kathy said sincerely. "I think I was beginning to go crazy here. And, you're the only two people I can talk to about the situation. But I won't," she added quickly. "I promised myself that we'd have a little food, a little drink, but we wouldn't discuss . . . Robert and me."

Maureen pulled over a chair and sat down beside Kathy. The older woman's almost translucent eyes had taken on the gray of the afternoon sky, and it made her look older, sterner than usual. "I don't think either of us will hold you to that promise."

Sheila put a cup of tea on the table in front of Kathy. "I talked to Maureen on the way over," she said. "She knows about my situation too."

"No secrets?" Kathy asked.

"Not between us," Maureen said. She nodded her thanks as Sheila put a cup of fragrant Earl Grey down in front of her.

"I've got plenty of food," Kathy said. "I know Brendan and Theresa ended up making themselves some macaroni and cheese last night. Some Christmas dinner, eh?" She looked from Maureen to Sheila. "We can eat in the kitchen or the dining room."

"Let's do it properly," Maureen said. "Let's sit in the dining room."

The dining room smelled of Christmas tree and incense mingled with the woody tang from the logs on the fire. The three women carried in platters of cut meat, deep bowls of vegetables, and a bottle of Chardonnay from the fridge. An opened bottle of Malbec sat breathing by the fire. Kathy assumed her usual position at the table, and the two other women sat down at either side in the places normally occupied by the children. While Kathy served the food, Sheila poured the wine—red for Maureen and herself, white for Kathy—and then they raised their glasses in a toast.

"What will we toast?" Sheila asked.

"Christmases to come," Kathy said.

"Lots of them," Maureen said, "and all of them better than this one!"

"Amen to that," Kathy agreed.

They ate in companionable silence for a while. Kathy suddenly discovered that she had an appetite, and then she realized that she hadn't eaten properly since . . . well, Monday night, she thought, before she had seen her husband kiss another woman. She hadn't been able to stomach anything solid since then.

"I'm really glad we're doing this," Sheila said. "I was going crazy at home. Since I'd decided not to go to Julia's for her traditional Boxing Day leftovers, all I had to look forward to was *The Sound of Music* and a Whole Foods prepackaged turkey dinner. With stuffing," she added significantly. She glanced sidelong at her older sister. "You didn't invite Julia?"

"No. I wanted to enjoy this in the company of people I loved."

"She is your sister," Maureen reminded Kathy gently.

"As you get older, you get to pick your own family; they become more important than the family of your birth."

"Hey . . . ," Sheila said, mock indignantly.

Kathy reached over and held her sister's hand. "And sometimes, they're one and the same."

"Thank you."

"Julia feels that she has a role to live up to," Maureen explained. "She thinks you all need a mother, so that's the role she's assumed for herself. Just be honest with her. I imagine you've both deferred to her all your lives."

The sisters nodded.

"Reminds me of my own sister," Maureen remarked.

"All this time I've known you and I never knew you had a sister," Kathy said.

"My crazy sister Sue. Four years younger than I am and isn't afraid of anything. I thought of her today for the first time in ages." Maureen smiled wistfully. "She used to be a friend of Jimmy Moran's . . . a very good friend," she added significantly.

"Where is she? . . . What happened?" Sheila asked, glancing sidelong at her sister.

"She's in LA. Married twice—three times maybe—and now runs a hugely successful casting agency. When Jimmy was trying to get his Irish films off the ground, Sue was his Hollywood connection. We had a fight—not about Jimmy, but he was part of it—and just stopped talking."

"Do you miss her?" Sheila asked.

"Sometimes." Then Maureen shook her head. "I rarely think of her, to be honest. She could be such a bitch sometimes." She shook her head again. "I thought about calling her and telling her about Jimmy, but I didn't want to enter her toxic world again, or allow her back into mine." She sipped her wine, her garnet-colored lipstick leaving a perfect impression of her lips on the glass. "But Kathy's right: As you get older, the family you choose to surround yourself with can be just as important as those who are accidents of birth." She looked over at Sheila. "You'd started to tell me in the car about Alan."

"Poor Alan." Sheila laughed wistfully. "He's infatuated with me . . . or at least he thinks he's in love with me."

"For men that's the same thing," Maureen remarked.

"Apparently, I'm the great love of his life. After the Red Sox, the Celtics, the Patriots, and the Bruins. Before I finally managed to push him out the door on Tuesday, I made him promise that he wouldn't say anything to his wife. Made him swear. Told him we needed to talk and plan."

Kathy concentrated on her wine, feeling uncomfortable with the conversation. Robert and Stephanie must have had a similar chat when they were working out the best days to tell her that he was leaving her.

"So he's agreed to say nothing to his wife. I'm going to break up with him as soon as I can. Problem solved. Except . . ."

"Julia?" Kathy guessed.

"Julia! She's now threatening to tell his wife . . . who'll throw him out . . . and then I'll be stuck with him!" Sheila shook her head. "I'll talk to Julia about it. It'll cause a fight, but I don't have any other options. I promise you, I'm through with married men or men with partners, lovers, or girlfriends, ex or otherwise. I'd never really thought about the other women before." She reached out and touched her sister's hand. "But watching you . . . seeing what's happened . . . made me realize just how destructive an affair can be, how painful it can be. I'd never thought about that before. I just assumed that if the men were wandering it was because there was something wrong at home."

"There was. There is," Kathy said bitterly.

Maureen stepped in quickly. "It's a good decision," she said. "I've had my share of relationships. I've been cheated upon, I've cheated, and I've been the mistress . . . and you know something: It never works out. Never."

"Can a marriage survive an affair?" Kathy wondered seriously.

"Absolutely. And it can sometimes be stronger because of the affair," Maureen said. "But in my experience, the affair can never survive the discovery. The men inevitably go back to their wives, who invariably take them. The mistress is nearly always abandoned." She saw Sheila watching her closely from across the table and nodded. "And you don't want to get a reputation as a mistress. After a while you stop getting the invites to the parties, just in case you might try and seduce all the married men. And when you do go, all the old letches come around, thinking they've got a shot." She held up her glass, and Sheila refilled it. "Men—who needs them!"

Kathy pushed away her plate, suddenly no longer hungry. She looked at Maureen. "You know Robert. How do I . . . how do I make this work?"

The older woman rested her chin on her right hand and gazed at Kathy. "Do you want to make this work?"

"Yes."

"Why?"

"Because I love him."

"But does he make you happy?" Maureen asked.

"Yes . . . once he did. But we were younger then, with fewer responsibilities. . . ."

Maureen shook her head firmly. "With more responsibilities. A young couple, newly married, children on the way, a business to grow, a house to pay for. You should have been under even more pressure and yet, I'll bet, you were never closer."

Kathy nodded. It was true.

"But then you got used to one another, maybe a little bored. You allowed your relationship to slip into a routine."

Kathy nodded again.

"It's the routine that's the killer. Boredom." She squeezed Kathy's hand. "I know you're going to get through this. You love him; that's a start. And he says he loves you."

"He did say that."

"He just has to be honest with you now. You both have to be honest with one another. No more secrets, no more lies."

"Plus he has to guarantee that he'll stay away from his mistress," Sheila added.

"He's already promised me that." Kathy heaved a sigh. "You're right. I'd hoped we would have had a chance to talk, but so far everything has conspired to keep us apart. And he's so tired at the moment; he's just emotionally and physically exhausted. Driving into the office on Christmas Eve wiped him out."

Maureen's eyes flickered across to Sheila. "Why did he go out on Christmas Eve?" she asked casually.

"He got a call from the alarm company; the office alarm had gone off. Turned out to be a false alarm—literally—in the end: snow falling onto the roof. He wasn't gone that long, though driving in the snow on the icy roads must have been a killer. He was exhausted when he came home, and then of course, he had to go out again on Christmas Day."

Maureen sipped her wine. "Wonder why the alarm company didn't call me," she murmured. "I'm on that call list too. And my name is first." She saw the suddenly distraught look on Kathy's face and said slowly, "Robert probably had me taken off the list when I got sick."

"Probably," Kathy said, though no one at the table believed it. She stood up suddenly and started to gather up the plates. "Now, who wants some Christmas pudding?"

"With brandy butter?" Sheila asked.

"Freshly made," Kathy said, far too cheerfully.

CHAPTER 45

Friday, 27th December

Kathy waited until she heard the bathroom door close, the lock click shut, and the shower start to thrum, before she moved. She had maybe six or seven minutes at most. Moving quickly from her bedroom, she padded silently down the corridor and slipped into Robert's study. His computer was still on, a digital clock slowly rotating on the screen.

She had to know.

Previously, she'd felt guilty when she'd had her suspicions about him. No longer. Now she just needed to know the truth, and she would do whatever it took to discover it. There was a quote she remembered: "The truth will set you free." Maybe that was right, because now not knowing had her trapped like a fly in a web, and the lies, the suspicions, the doubts, and the constant questions were destroying her.

Still listening for the shower, she sat in the chair before the screen and moved the mouse.

Please enter password.

Kathy blinked in surprise. That was new. She'd never known Robert to add a password to his screensaver before. Her instinct was to turn and flee—she definitely didn't want to be caught doing this—but she sat and stared at the black letters on the gray rectangle.

Please enter password.

She knew he used his dead dog's name as the password for the machine log-on; he'd hardly use the same password for the screen-saver too, would he?

He had.

She entered *Poppykoo,* and the screen cleared. Outlook, the e-mail program, was still open, a message from Jimmy's brother open on the screen. Kathy clicked on the in-box, looking for something from Stephanie.

There was nothing.

Kathy moved the cursor down and clicked into the Sent box and then blinked in surprise. He had sent out scores of e-mails over the course of the past twenty-four hours, a simple "I am terribly sorry to inform you that our good friend . . ." They were to Jimmy's friends, colleagues, industry journalists, and scattered among them were e-mails to all three of the Moran brothers.

She finally found what she was looking for—and hoping not to find—at the bottom of the screen. An e-mail sent to Stephanie Bur-roughs on Wednesday morning—Christmas Day—at 2:43 a. m.

> Dear Stephanie,
> I don't know what's happened to you. I am des-perately worried. I've tried calling you at the house and on your cell, but it goes straight to voice mail. You've just disappeared.
> Please get in touch with me. Let me know you're okay.
> I even went over to the house earlier this morn-ing. I let myself in. I'm concerned there's no sign of you and yet I know you haven't gone away. I looked in the closets, and your clothes are still there.
> I am at my wit's end.
> I have no idea how to contact your friend Izzie, and I realize I don't know any of your other friends. If I don't get in touch with you soon, I might try to

contact Charles Flintoff. I'm half thinking I should
contact the police and report you as missing.
If you get this, then please, please, please contact me.
I love you.
Robert

Kathy looked at the screen and watched the words dissolve and fragment as bitter tears stung her eyes. Here it was: proof, if proof was what she needed that he was still in touch with Stephanie. She brushed away the tears and read the e-mail again . . . Then frowned. Something wasn't right. He'd sent this e-mail after his return on Christmas night. He must have gone to her home searching for her.

Kathy heard the water pipes clank, and then the shower was turned off. She was tempted to hit Print, but she was unsure how long it would take the printer to warm up. Scrolling back up to the in-box, she positioned the cursor on the e-mail from Jimmy's brother, then slipped out of the room. She hoped that the screensaver would kick in before Robert returned from the bathroom.

Stepping into her bedroom, she shut the door behind her and turned the key in the lock. Whatever type of e-mail she had been expecting to find from Robert or Stephanie, it certainly hadn't been this one. She didn't need to print the e-mail. Every word was imprinted on her consciousness.

I even went over to the house earlier this morning. I let myself in.

So he had lied to her and gone over to Stephanie's house on Christmas Eve night. . . . But Stephanie hadn't been there, and he had been concerned that something was wrong.

I don't know what's happened to you. I am desperately worried.

This would have been only hours after Kathy had made him promise that he would not see Stephanie again. Even as he was making that promise, he was obviously worried about Stephanie's disappearance, which suggested that he'd tried to get in touch with her earlier in the evening. He'd obviously been so worried that he'd driven to her apartment in a snowstorm to check up on her. She wondered what he had thought he'd find—a body? He was flattering himself.

Women like Stephanie didn't kill themselves over men like Robert.

Kathy was surprised by how calm she felt. She'd just discovered more evidence of Robert's infidelity, more evidence of lies. She should be angrier.... Instead she just felt sad. Sad and exhausted.

Well, since she'd started down this path . . .

Sitting by the side of the bed, she riffled through her old diary until she found the number she was looking for.

"Pro-Alarms. Tony speaking. How may I help?"

"Good morning, Tony, this is Kathy Walker, R&K Productions. We're one of your clients."

"Good morning, Mrs. Walker. Do you have a security reference code?"

"A security reference code?"

"We ask our clients to supply us with a word known only to them. When they get in touch with us, we use the word to verify that it really is them."

"Oh." Kathy looked at the diary again. There was nothing beside the Pro-Alarms number. Then a sudden thought struck her. "The only word I have here is Poppykoo."

"Thank you. We just have to be sure it's a genuine call."

"I understand. Tony, could you tell me if the R&K Productions office alarm was activated early on Christmas morning, December 25th?" She heard fingers tapping a keyboard. "Some friends were coming home from a late party and thought they heard our alarm ringing."

"I have nothing on record. No, definitely not. Could have been a nearby building."

"Probably. Before I go, could you confirm that you have Maureen Ryan and Robert Walker on your call list in that order."

"Yes, Mrs. Walker. We contact Ms. Ryan first; then, if she is unavailable, we contact Mr. Walker."

"And you have two numbers for him: cell and home?"

"Yes. It would be our policy to contact the home number first, particularly for a late-night call, then we try the cell phone."

"That's great. Thank you, Tony—you've been very helpful. Have a Merry Christmas."

"And a Merry Christmas to you too, Mrs. Walker."

So now she knew.

She'd contacted the alarm company just in case Robert had been telling the truth. He hadn't. He'd risked the dangerous drive just to check up on his mistress.

Exhaustion settled over her in a leaden blanket. She felt her eyelids close and her shoulders slump. All she wanted to do right now was to crawl into bed, curl up in a warm cocoon, and drift into a deep and dreamless sleep. But what was that going to achieve? Nothing would have changed when she got up.

Could she blame him for doing what he had done?

The sudden thought caught her unaware, and she sat, still and unmoving on the edge of the bed, looking out over the snow-locked streets.

I'm half thinking I should contact the police
and report you as missing.

He was worried about this woman. He was in love with her—she had to accept that. Love wasn't something you could turn on and off like a tap; she knew that. Even after everything Robert had done, Kathy still loved him. So, it stood to reason that Robert must also still have feelings for Stephanie. He'd admitted as much when they had spoken on Tuesday; he'd said then that he still loved Stephanie.

So he'd tried to get hold of her and failed, and then risked a drive across the city to see if she was all right. He hadn't abandoned her. Kathy had to admire that loyalty, that commitment. And then she remembered that they were the qualities of the man she had originally fallen in love with.

She heard the bathroom door open, then the door to Robert's office clicked shut.

The man she had married eighteen years ago had been kind and gentle, caring, honest, and loyal. Especially loyal. She liked to think that he still had most of those qualities. On impulse, she climbed off the bed, knelt on the floor, and pulled open the drawer under the bed. At the bottom of the drawer, buried under piles of tee shirts that she would never wear, was a small cloth suitcase. Dropping the case onto the bed, she pulled the curtains closed and turned on the lights before she turned back to the bed and opened the case. Inside there were hundreds—maybe thousands—of pictures, either six-by-four or ten-by-eight prints of every Christmas and birthday, first days of school, visits to the zoo, pictures from camp, high school, and college. For a long time, she'd been meaning to scan them and digitize them in order to preserve them for her grandchildren . . . but she'd never gotten around to it. At the bottom of the case was the white linen box that held her wedding album. She opened the box and lifted out the heavy leather-bound volume with the gilt-edge pages. A sprinkling of eighteen-year-old confetti fell to the bed covers.

Kathy didn't remember the last time she had looked at the album. A couple of years ago, she thought, when Theresa had asked out of the blue what her wedding dress had looked like.

She turned to the back of the book. The early pages, which held all the photos of her late mother and father, were filled with too many sad memories, and she knew if she started with them, she would end up weeping. The last few pages contained the images of the wedding reception.

Kathy smoothed down the slightly crumpled tissue guards and looked at the first picture she came to: the happy couple dancing in the center of an empty floor. Robert, tall, handsome, and elegant in a Ralph Lauren tuxedo, with his eyes fixed on her face, holding her as if she were a delicate piece of china. She looked so young—she had only been twenty-five, but looked maybe eighteen—wide-eyed, innocent, and ecstatic. She was wearing the wedding dress that now lay wrapped in tissue paper in a suitcase in the attic. Eighteen years later, she could only remember fragments of the day with absolute clarity: her father crying the first time he saw her come down the stairs in her dress; the moment she stepped out of the limo in front of the church; the instant she said "I do"; and then later, this particular photo, the first time she'd danced in the arms of her husband. She had never felt so beautiful, so loved.

And she had been proud to be Mrs. Walker. Robert was kind, caring, and compassionate, someone his friends and family could depend on to lend a hand when it was needed. She loved him for those qualities. When the call had come in from the hospital, he hadn't thought twice about going in to be with his friend. She understood that. It was the same quality that had driven him out of the house to see if Stephanie was all right.

But he should have said something. He shouldn't have lied to her. She smiled as she turned the page, trying to imagine the conversation. "Oh, Kathy, I know you've just discovered that I'm having an affair, but I just want to pop over to Stephanie's to see if she's okay. I'll just be a minute. She's dropped out of sight, and I can't get in touch with her." Kathy was hardly likely to have said, "Go right ahead," was she?

The next-to-last image in the back of the album was a group photo of all their friends. She was shocked to discover how few of them she could name. There was Jimmy Moran standing behind Robert. She'd met him for the first time at the wedding. On the other side, looking exotic in a navy dress that exposed far too much flesh, was Maureen Ryan. But who were the rest, and where had they all gone? The girl in the pink dress was someone she had gone to college with, and the boy with the pitiful attempt at a beard was a young director who had been working for Hill Holliday advertising at the time. He was still there as far as she could remember.

Loss of friends . . . that was one of the hidden costs of marriage. Oh, they'd all kept in touch for the first year or so, and then slowly, one by one, as they'd married or moved on to different careers, they'd slipped away.

New friends had come along, neighbors she'd grown friendly with, fellow alums from Bard, colleagues of Robert's they sometimes socialized with, but they weren't deep friendships. She'd realized that yesterday when she'd discovered that she desperately wanted someone to talk to, someone who understood the nuances and moods of an affair, someone discreet enough not to talk about it. The only names that had come to mind were Sheila and Maureen. She'd thought about asking in her friend Rose, but much as she liked Rose, she didn't think Rose could be trusted to keep her mouth shut.

The last picture in the book was a portrait of Robert and Kathy in an oval-shaped frame. They were smiling into the camera, shy, slightly scared-looking smiles. They'd promised to love, honor, and cherish one another. Kathy remembered that her mother had been scandalized that Kathy was not going to use the word "obey" in the service.

And although Robert had broken every one of those vows, Kathy still loved him and cherished him, though she was unsure if she still honored him. Whatever that meant.

But she'd never betrayed him, not in the way he had betrayed her.

Kathy closed the book with a snap and decided that no, she could not fault him for checking up on Stephanie Burroughs. The man she had married would have been concerned enough to do that, and she was pleased that that, at least, had not changed.

What she found unforgivable however, was the last line in the e-mail:

I love you.

She tried to dismiss it. "I love you" was such an overused sentiment these days. People signed off e-mails and letters with "love" and "all my love" and "xo" without a second thought. Reality TV show stars who were trapped on an island together or dancing together or singing together universally "loved each other so much" and were heartbroken when one of them was dismissed, fired, voted off. Love was just a word, often without true subtext or meaning.

I love you.

Yet, Kathy had no illusions about what her husband meant. He genuinely loved Stephanie. The only consolation left to her was her memory of her conversation with Stephanie on Christmas Eve. She'd watched Stephanie turn to Robert and say, "I love you, Robert, as much as Kathy loves you. But I cannot have you."

Maybe Robert still wanted Stephanie, but she was sure—almost certain—that Stephanie didn't want Robert.

CHAPTER 46

―――――∞―――――

Saturday, 28th December

Kathy stood in the doorway watching her husband. He was sitting slumped on the small bed she had set up in the office for him. He'd aged in the past few days . . . or maybe she'd simply started looking at him with new eyes. Looking at the photos in the album yesterday had brought it home just how much time had passed; they were getting older, heading toward middle age. She finished zipping up her black down coat and said gently: "It's time to go."

Robert looked up, eyes momentarily blank. "I didn't think it was that late," he muttered.

"The roads will be icy. We should leave a little early. The kids have decided to stay here. They didn't really know Jimmy all that well. I think it's just as well." That wasn't entirely true; she had more or less encouraged the kids to stay home, just in case Jimmy's wife and mistress turned up at the removal and there was a scene. There was another reason, one she was even more reluctant to acknowledge. She guessed that some of the people in the industry knew about Robert's relationship with Stephanie. She didn't want to run the risk that the children might overhear anything.

Robert stood up. "Yes, yes, of course," he said distractedly. "I spoke to Lloyd, the brother in Australia, a couple of hours ago. He's not going to make it over for the funeral. He can't get the time off."

"That's a shame." She kept her voice carefully neutral.

"Yes, but at least Mikey and Teddy will be here. I think Jimmy would have liked that."

Kathy stopped him at the door and brushed at the collar of his black suit, then straightened his tie. "I think Jimmy would be very proud with everything that you've done for him over the past two days," she said, before she turned and headed down the stairs. She looked in on the children.

"We're off now. We won't be too long," she promised.

"Bye, Mom, bye, Dad!" Theresa called. Brendan couldn't speak; he was too busy negotiating a busy chicane on the Monte Carlo track on his Xbox.

Kathy followed Robert out of the house, pulling the door closed behind her, then smiled as he held open the car door for her. Robert came around the front of the car and climbed in. He revved the engine and turned the heaters to full, clearing the windshield.

"Thank you," he said suddenly, surprising her. "For the bed . . . and getting the suit . . ."

"I thought you had enough to worry about." She didn't add that when she had been setting up the bed in his office when he was at the funeral parlor yesterday, she'd logged back into his e-mail. She'd found nothing.

"Well, thanks anyway. And thank you for coming with me."

"I knew Jimmy, I liked him even though he was a rogue, and I wanted to pay my respects. And I also want to support you."

Robert nodded, saying nothing, but she could see that he was touched. He pulled on a pair of sunglasses, and she fished her own out of her small black bag. She loved the wan winter sunshine, loved the myriad reflections on the banked snow and the crisp shadows. Maybe next year, instead of Martha's Vineyard, they could go away for some winter sunshine. Snorkeling in the Caymans; she'd always wanted to do that. "How are you feeling?" she asked.

"I'm a bit numb," he said, after a moment's thought. He drove in silence, then said, "Do you know I've known Jimmy for more than twenty-five years. Nearly half my life."

"He was at our wedding," Kathy said, remembering the photo. "That's where you introduced me to him."

"I don't remember that."

"I do."

"There were times when I'd see him every day for a month . . . and then I wouldn't talk to him for weeks. But every time we met up again, it was as if we'd never been apart."

"There were times when I used to envy your relationship with him. I was just glad that he wasn't a woman." Kathy stopped abruptly, realizing what she'd said.

"Funny that, isn't it?" Robert said quietly. "A man can have a very close friendship with another man and no one cares, but if it's with a woman, there are all sorts of questions raised."

"I used to think that a man and a woman could have a purely platonic relationship," Kathy said. "Now . . . now, I'm not so sure." But a woman could also have a deeply personal relationship with another woman and no one ever gave it a second thought either, she realized. Robert was right: Put a male and female together, and people talked.

"And yet Jimmy had a string of female friends who were never his lovers. He used to say that once both sides realized that sex was never going to be an issue, a real friendship could develop."

Kathy wasn't entirely sure that Jimmy had been telling the truth. As far as she knew, he had tried to screw just about every female he met. Though, to be fair, he'd never been anything but the complete gentleman with her. "And what do you think?" she asked.

"I don't know," he said. "Outside of business, I know very few women socially."

"Except your mistress!" Kathy snapped, surprised and dismayed that she'd blurted out what was obviously so close to the surface. "I'm sorry. I didn't mean to bring that up today of all days. I know you're grieving. I'll respect that."

When Robert spoke, his voice was cautious, as if he was choosing his words with care. "I know we haven't had a chance over the past few days to talk about what happened."

"We'll talk about it when this is all over," Kathy said firmly. "I'm thinking we should go for couples' counseling."

"I'm not sure I want to let strangers know our business. . . ." he said quickly.

She'd known that would be his reaction. But this was one item that was nonnegotiable.

"I'm not going to fight with you about this," Kathy said. "It's not optional. If you want to stay with me—if we want to stay to-gether—then we have to start again. I want us to go to therapy and work through those issues that drove us apart."

"Work drove us apart!" Robert snapped, genuine anger in his voice now. "Me, working all hours God sent to pay the mortgage and put food on the table. If it comes right down to it, that was the only issue. If you had been a little more involved with the busi-ness—a little more involved with me—you would have known that."

Kathy deliberately allowed a little of the bitterness that curled inside her to color her words. "Are you implying this is my fault?"

"I'm not implying anything," Robert snapped. "This whole sorry mess is entirely of my making. I put my hand up. I accept it."

She watched him deliberately take a deep breath, calming him-self.

"Let's talk about it in a day or two," he said, eventually.

She was content to leave it at that. For the moment.

Robert offered her his arm as she climbed out of the car outside the funeral parlor. She hesitated only for a moment, then took it, immediately conscious that he was the one needing support. She could feel the tremble of his fingers through the thick material of her coat.

She spotted scores of familiar faces from the world of entertain-ment—and was surprised that so many of them knew Robert on a first-name basis. She hadn't realized he was so well connected in the business. He introduced her as his wife, and, although she was sensitive to any knowing glances or untoward comments, there was nothing. Angela swept over at one point, on the arm of a famous game show host, kissed Robert perfunctorily on both cheeks and thanked him for all that he'd done, then enveloped Kathy in a cloud of cloying, musky perfume more suited to an evening at the theater than a morning removal. There was no sign of Frances.

Kathy hung back as they entered the funeral home. She'd stood in a room just like this just over eighteen months ago when her mother had died, and the memories were still fresh and raw. "You go," she murmured to Robert, and urged him forward. Standing against a wall, she watched her husband approach the coffin where Jimmy was laid out in his black suit, and was shocked when he bent over and kissed Jimmy's forehead. There were suddenly tears in her eyes. This was a side of her husband she had never seen before. She saw his lips move and wondered what last words he was whispering to his old friend. When he came back into the crowd, he was moving stiffly, like an old man, and she slipped her right arm into the crook of his arm and then held onto his arm with her left hand, supporting them both.

Prayers were brief and anonymous, and virtually identical to the prayers they had used for her mother's removal. Then Robert was called forward as the coffin was hoisted onto the shoulders of six pallbearers who carried it out of the funeral home. Kathy trailed along behind, eyes firmly fixed on Robert, watching for any sign that he was going to collapse. She saw him physically flinch when the press photographers shot some images of the coffin being loaded into the back of the hearse. When he was relieved of the burden of the coffin, Kathy immediately darted forward, caught his arm, and turned him toward the car. She was going to offer to drive, but she imagined that he probably needed the distraction of driving right now. "Jimmy would have been pleased," she said.

Robert didn't speak until he had maneuvered his Audi in behind the mourning car and hearse. "He would," he agreed.

"He knew a lot of people."

"Some came up through the business with him; and there were others—like me, I suppose—who he gave a start to in the business.

I suppose there'll be more at the church, and even more at the funeral on Monday."

Kathy glanced sidelong at Robert. "I'm glad Angela came," she said. They could both see the back of her head in the mourning car directly in front of them.

"She just thanked me for taking care of things. She didn't seem too upset. He knew everyone," Robert continued his previous train of thought, and she realized that he was rambling. "I'd even thought about asking him to partner with me in the business," he added, stopping abruptly.

The revelation stung—but all she said was, "Without asking me?"

"Well, I was going to talk to you about it first of course."

"One of the things we need to get clear is my position in the business. I do own half of it," she reminded him.

"Well, it's all academic now," he said, and she hoped he was still talking about Jimmy.

"We're going to make some changes, Robert," she said firmly.

"Yes, we are," Robert muttered.

There was something in his tone that bothered her, though she couldn't put her finger on it.

Kathy nudged Robert. "Is that your phone?" Robert looked blankly at her. They were slowly making their way out of the church after the brief service to receive the remains. "Something's buzzing," she insisted. She hadn't heard any ringtone, but had felt the vibrations through her arm, where she was linked with him. She smiled at faces she vaguely recognized and watched Robert pat his coat.

"Oh, it's me," he muttered. He pulled his left glove off with his teeth and fumbled with the buttons of his overcoat before he finally fished out the buzzing phone. It stopped.

"Who was it?" Kathy asked, watching him scroll the buttons, looking for the Missed Call log.

"Friend of Jimmy's," he said quickly. "Probably asking about the arrangements for Monday." He was in the process of putting the phone back into his inside pocket when it buzzed again.

Kathy had walked a couple of steps before she realized that her husband was no longer beside her. Glancing back, she saw him standing against one of the pillars surrounding the small square courtyard before the church, with the phone pressed to his ear. She could see his lips moving. At one point he looked up at her and smiled.

Kathy turned around and began to make her way back toward him. She could hear his voice now, bouncing off the pillar behind him, throwing back his words, and she tilted her head to one side to catch some of them. "He died on Christmas Day."

"Who was that?" Kathy arrived just as he hung up.

"Someone who hadn't heard the news."

"How did they take it?"

"I don't know. I didn't wait for a response."

Something about the reply bothered her. It was too quick, too glib. It felt wrong. If you were telling a person that someone had died, then it stood to reason that you would fill in the details.

Unless you simply wanted to get that person off the phone.

God—why couldn't she just accept the call at face value? If she didn't resolve this situation with Robert soon, it was going to drive her insane. She shouldn't be spying on her husband, checking his mail, reading his e-mails, trying to eavesdrop on his phone conversations.

She'd talk to him tomorrow. She wouldn't accept any excuses. He would simply have to make time. He'd prioritized his friend— and she understood and accepted that. It was now time for him to make her a priority in his life once again.

CHAPTER 47

The noon traffic report was just finishing as Robert pulled into the driveway in front of the house. Kathy leaned forward and turned off the radio, but, surprisingly, Robert made no move to turn off the engine. She turned to look at him, her hand on the door handle, and although her face was impassive, her voice calm and unemotional, she knew with a terrible, chilling certainty that he wasn't going to come in; he was going to give her an excuse that would take him to Jamaica Plain.

"Aren't you coming in?"

"I want to head into the office, check up on things," he said, adjusting the rearview mirror, then using the rear wiper to clean the window. Anything but look her in the eye. "Maybe do a little work, distract myself."

"You could come in and catch up on your sleep," she suggested. "You look like shit. You've barely eaten or slept."

"No, let me do this. I meant to get in to the office yesterday, but events caught up with me. I'll get home as early as I can. I'm exhausted." He added, "I won't be long."

She could have protested; she knew that. She could have insisted that he come into the house, but instead Kathy Walker climbed out of the car without saying another word.

She knew he was lying to her.

She knew where he was going.

Kathy opened the door, stepped into the hall, and closed the door behind her without looking back. She immediately checked in on the kids. They looked like they hadn't moved in the past couple of hours: Brendan was still concentrating furiously on his driving game, with Theresa crouched beside him, muttering words of advice. "Left . . . left . . . left . . . watch out for the German car on the right."

"I'm home," said Kathy.

There was no response other than a couple of vaguely welcoming grunts.

"I'm just going to pop out again for an hour. Will you be okay on your own for a while?"

That got a response. They both turned to look at her, their expressions that particular mixture of disgust and astonishment that teens perfected from about the age of thirteen.

"I'll be back as quick as I can. Your dad's gone in to the office. He should be home soon too."

Kathy turned away and snagged her keys off the hall table. Checking to make sure she had her cell, she turned and walked out of the house.

She was in no hurry as she reversed the car out of the driveway. This wasn't a race. The light car skidded a little at the bottom of the road, and she felt her heart leap; wouldn't it be wonderfully ironic to be killed in a car crash right now? That would certainly solve all of Robert's problems. There could be a brief period of mourning, and then no one would be at all surprised when the young widower married Stephanie Burroughs, who had consoled him in his grief. She supposed they'd sell Stephanie's house and move into the suburbs.

If she were killed in a car crash, she'd be sure to come back and haunt him. And his mistress.

However, there was no ice once she got onto the main roads,

and in places it was hard to tell that it had ever snowed. Traffic was unexpectedly heavy, and she was surprised by the amount of it,

She lifted her phone off the passenger seat. She quickly checked to ensure that there were no police around before she dialed Sheila's number. It was picked up on the first ring.

"I was just about to call you," Sheila exclaimed.

"Great minds."

"How did it go this morning?"

"Okay. There was a good crowd there. Jimmy's wife, Angela, turned up, but no sign of the mistress, so we were spared any unpleasant scenes. Maybe Monday."

"And how was Robert?"

"Distracted. A little upset. Hang on a sec. . . ." she said, dropping the phone onto her lap and changing gear as she spied a cop car in her rearview mirror. She then sent the call to speaker. "Can you hear me?"

"Barely. Are you in the car?"

"Yes," Kathy said shortly. "After the removal, when we got back to the house, Robert announced that he was going in to the office."

"Ah," Sheila breathed. "Do you want me to meet you?"

"No . . . no, thank you, not this time." Sheila had accompanied her the last time she had spied on Robert and his mistress. "But you can do me a favor. I know they're fifteen and seventeen, but could you go check on the kids and wait until I get back? They were talking about having a few friends over, and I don't want it getting out of hand without an adult present. I don't know how long I'm going to be."

"Of course, give me twenty minutes."

"He may have gone in to the office," Kathy said, more to herself than to Sheila.

"Maybe," Sheila said noncommittally, though neither of them believed it.

"Thanks. I'll keep in touch."

"You know you can't go on like this, Kathy," Sheila said gently.

"I just need to be sure."

"You're already sure," Sheila reminded her.

"I know," Kathy said, but she'd hung up by then and was talking to herself.

There was no car outside the office, no sign of tire marks on the unblemished snow piled up outside the door. Truthfully, she hadn't really been expecting any. Kathy stood outside the office, the keys held so tightly in her hand that they were pressing painfully into the flesh, staring at the small brass plate to the left of the bell. R&K Productions. The brass was tarnished and smudged, and the *K* was practically invisible. She sighed; she had been invisible in their relationship for far too long. Turning away from the office, she headed back to her car.

Kathy drove the rest of the way to Stephanie's house with the radio turned to a hard rock station and the volume turned all the way up so she wouldn't have to think.

Kathy pulled into a parking spot next to the post office, turned off the radio, and rolled down her window, blinking as the bitter air stung her cheeks and eyes, ears still ringing from the too-loud music. Just down the street, she could clearly see the Victorian building where Stephanie lived.

Robert's Audi was parked outside the house, alongside his mistress's silver BMW. There were lights burning in the living room, shedding a warm golden light out into the early afternoon.

Kathy knew that room well; she knew she would remember every detail of it to the day she died. Stephanie would be sitting in her chair facing the window, and Robert would be on the settee facing her. They would be drinking wine. . . . No, Robert wouldn't risk wine in case he was stopped on the way home. He would be drinking either coffee or tea, and he and Stephanie would be talking, making plans, deciding on their futures, deciding what to say to Kathy, how to tell the children.

Kathy turned off the car and continued to stare at the house, unaware that there were tears on her cheeks and that she was sobbing. After all the promises he'd made, all the chances she'd given him. She was heartsick; she'd never understood exactly what the expression meant before. She did now.

The phone rang, and she answered it without looking at the caller display. It was Sheila. "I was just checking in. I'm on my way to Brookline now, but the traffic is terrible. Where are you?"

"Outside her house," Kathy whispered.

"And is he . . ."

"Yes."

"Well, then you know all that you need to know. Drive away or, better still, let me come and get you."

"No. I need to do this. I need to see this through."

"Kathy, please," Sheila begged.

"Let me do this."

Sheila sighed. "I understand."

"Sheila," Kathy said suddenly, "you said the other night that you would never be responsible for putting another woman through what I'm going through now. Did you mean it?"

"I've already told Alan we're finished."

Kathy nodded. "Thank you. I'll call you later." She hung up and immediately hit the speed dial.

"Hello . . . hello?"

Robert's voice was hoarse and croaking, sounding slightly breathless, and she wondered what he'd been doing before she called. Her imagination—abruptly vivid and obscene—supplied all sorts of possibilities. She struggled to keep her voice light and bright, covering the mouthpiece to drown out the noise of the passing traffic.

"Hi, it's me. I'm just wondering how you are."

"Kathy . . . Yes, I'm fine."

Wondering why he had used her name, and then realizing that it was his way of alerting Stephanie, she continued. "Where are you?"

"I'm at the office."

"Don't stay too long," she said, staring at Stephanie's window.

"Yes, I'll be home soon," he said quickly and hung up before she could say anything else.

No, he wouldn't want her to ask too many questions. . . . In fact, he probably didn't want her taking up too much of his time. Because he was busy now, busy with the woman he loved. *I love you.* That's what he'd said in the e-mail. *I love you.* She remembered the last time he'd said those three simple words to her. Four days ago. She'd been standing in that house, in that same room, facing Robert and his mistress. She'd asked him straight out, and he'd said that he loved her. She believed him then.

She didn't now.

She thought that there could be no more tears; surely she was all cried out? But as she sat in the car, clutching the phone in the palm of her hand, she sobbed, heartbroken.

Time ceased to have any real meaning. The world was reduced to the front of the house behind the wrought-iron gates. It snowed again, two brief showers that coated the car in a dusting of white crystals and sent the temperature plummeting, but she didn't feel the chill. She watched, expressionless, as a light went on in the bedroom and a shadow moved behind the curtains.

Then the light went off.

And later, much later, she watched a pizza delivery boy on a motorcycle buzz up to the house, and she had a brief glimpse of Stephanie standing in the doorway, stylish and beautiful in cream and black as she took in the food.

The lights went on in the bedroom again.

So, the mistress had gotten up and ordered in some food, and now she was bringing it back upstairs to her lover.

Kathy could clearly see the shape of someone outlined against the curtains and then, a little while later, the vague shape of a second person moving around the room.

She was tempted to call again. She was equally tempted to walk up to the door and hammer and scream until they allowed her in, but she wouldn't give them the satisfaction of that type of display.

A short while later, there was more movement in the bedroom, and then abruptly the door opened and her husband appeared on the front porch. There were clothes—a shirt, ties, shoes—in his hands.

Stiff and sore, frozen through to the bone, Kathy turned the key in the ignition and pulled away as he climbed into his car.

She'd seen enough.

Jimmy Moran's Funeral
Forest Hills Cemetery

CHAPTER 48

Monday, 30th December

"I thought you spoke very well," Kathy said shortly, as they followed the hearse as it wound its way through the graves in Forest Hills Cemetery. They moved slowly, picking their way over the muddy, puddle-spattered ground. A long snaking column of dark-suited men and fashionably dressed women trailed behind.

"I was just hoping I could get through what I had to say without breaking down," Robert said, ducking his shoulders against the icy wind that whipped across the graves.

"You did." Kathy didn't add that she found the eulogy almost painfully embarrassing in places.

Robert tilted his head slightly and glanced back over his shoulder. "Looks like most of the entertainment industry in Boston is here," he said proudly. "I heard someone say that Ben Affleck had come home for the funeral. Apparently he and Jimmy used to play cards together."

"I didn't see him," Kathy said.

She had seen Stephanie Burroughs however.

There had been a single instant when they were driving out of the small church parking lot when she'd spotted Stephanie. The woman had been sitting in the passenger seat of the latest model Mercedes, alongside a handsome older man Kathy vaguely recognized. She wasn't sure if Stephanie had seen her or not, but Kathy was glad Stephanie was there; she was determined to catch up with her today, and the graveyard was as good a place as any.

It had rained during the Mass, a combination of ice and sleet battering the church, tip-tapping off the stained-glass windows, and when the mourners had finally filed out of the church, they had found that the ground was littered with tiny pebbles of ice that crunched underfoot and made walking treacherous. As the long, winding cortège made its way from the church, it rained again, battering the cars in sheets of icy sleet that the windshield wipers, even on high speed, had difficulty coping with. Perfect funeral weather.

Only the hearse was allowed into Forest Hills Cemetery. The mourners were forced to follow on foot.

Charles Flintoff parked across from the graveyard and stepped out of the car. He opened the back door and pulled out a midnight-blue umbrella and then moved around to the passenger side to help Stephanie out of the car, always keeping her covered beneath the large umbrella. She smiled her thanks and linked her arm in his as they entered the cemetery. She picked her way along the irregular path, regretting wearing heels now and wishing she'd opted for boots and slacks, rather than heels and a black pencil skirt. She felt vaguely uncomfortable on Flintoff's arm, and she knew people were looking, first at him—because everyone knew Charles—and then at her, many of them wondering who she was, and no doubt drawing erroneous conclusions. She was beginning to regret accepting his suggestion that he pick her up and drive her to the church and graveyard.

Stephanie had listened to Robert speak in the church. She'd thought he looked exhausted, and guessed he'd had little sleep since she'd thrown him out on Saturday night. His eulogy had been a little too saccharine for her taste; according to Robert, Jimmy had been one of the finest specimens of humanity to walk the earth. She'd caught some of the cynical smiles and even sniggers as

Robert had gone on and on about Jimmy's good qualities, and guessed that many of the people crowding the small church knew the real Jimmy Moran.

Mikey Moran, Jimmy's eldest brother, had spoken briefly and elegantly about their early years together, and he thanked Robert for everything he had done to organize the funeral. Stephanie remembered craning her neck at that point, wondering where Angela was. She didn't see her in the church, and yet she guessed she must be there.

"Neither of them turned up," Charles murmured, peering at her over the top of his half-frame glasses.

Stephanie looked at him blankly.

"Neither Angela nor Frances," he continued. "Both probably thought the other would be here and didn't want to share the limelight. I understand from a colleague that the only reason Angela turned up at the removal of the remains on Saturday was because she knew that Frances wouldn't be there."

Stephanie nodded. She thought it sad that the two women who had loved Jimmy the most had chosen this particular occasion to abandon him.

Directly ahead of her, moving past the nineteenth-century marble memorials and granite monuments, she spotted Kathy walking alongside Robert. Stephanie thought that the woman looked wretched, ashen-faced, her eyes huge and dark in her head. She was bundled up in a three-quarter-length black coat and lost beneath an oversize umbrella. Stephanie noted that she didn't seem too eager to share it with Robert.

Robert Walker was livid.

He was desperately trying to hold his emotions in check. The funeral was bad enough, and having neither Angela nor Frances there was a slap in the face to his old friend. But seeing Stephanie turning up on the arm of her boss, that had been the real sickener. She hadn't waited long, had she? Maybe she'd try to claim that the baby was Flintoff's, he thought vindictively. He shook his head quickly, the sudden movement surprising Kathy.

"What's wrong?"

"Nothing," he mumbled, "Everything. This weather." He shook a water-logged shoe. "We're all going to catch pneumonia."

Kathy didn't remind him that she'd told him to bring his boots. She looked around. She loved this cemetery; it had a much different feel than the cemetery where her parents were buried. She used to come here as a girl and read on the grassy slope near the waterfall. She loved the tranquillity of the place: the odd juxtaposition of the dead spirits with the thriving arboretum. When she died, if she changed her mind about being cremated, this was where she would be buried.

She didn't care where Robert went.

Jimmy Moran was to be buried near fellow Irish immigrant Eugene O'Neill. O'Neill was one of Kathy's favorite playwrights. She remembered learning that he had been born in a hotel on Broadway... which was now a Starbucks. She shuddered to think that the multitudes of New York City tourists ordering their overpriced double nonfat lattes were walking on such a sacred birthplace. O'Neill had been married three times, and his first wife's name had been Kathleen. Kathy looked sidelong at Robert.... How many times would he be married, she wondered.

The hearse stopped behind the open grave, and when Robert Walker moved forward to help shoulder the burden of the coffin, Kathy stood stock-still and allowed the crowd to ebb and flow around her until she was almost at the back of the throng. Latecomers hurried up, creating a semicircle about ten deep around the grave. She didn't want to stand on the edge of that gaping hole and look down. A year and a half ago when she'd stood beside her mother's open grave, she'd felt as if she were being pulled in, and it was only Maureen's strong hand on her shoulder that had kept her upright.

Kathy turned away... and spotted Stephanie on the edge of the crowd at the same time that the other woman turned and looked in her direction.

The two women stared at one another, then Stephanie began to move through the crowd toward Kathy, who turned off to the right and started to walk down a narrow, muddy path. She stopped and stood by an ornate marble monument and waited for the younger woman to catch up with her.

Standing on the edge of the open grave, which was raised a little higher than the rest of the ground, Robert Walker turned just in time to see the two women stop and face one another. He felt his stomach twist, and for a moment he thought he was going to throw up.

And there was no possible way he could leave what he was doing and get to them.

CHAPTER 49

Kathy Walker spoke first, her voice as icy as the weather. "I'm glad you're here. I was hoping you would be. Saves me a visit." She shifted the black umbrella to include Stephanie, and the two women huddled together.

Stephanie looked at her, saying nothing.

"I wanted to give you this," Kathy said. She reached into her pocket and passed across a plain brown envelope.

The younger woman looked at it, feeling something solid move and shift in the paper. Holding the envelope in her black-gloved hands, she tore open one end and shook the contents out into the palm of her right hand.

Nestling in the soft black leather was a slightly worn gold wedding ring.

"I don't want it anymore," Kathy said, unable to control the tremble in her voice.

"Are you kidding? I don't want this!" Stephanie exclaimed, horrified.

"You want Robert," Kathy snapped. "You've got him. And you'll need this to go with him."

"I don't want him," Stephanie protested venomously. "I wouldn't have him if he were the last man in the world!"

Kathy blinked in surprise. If she hadn't known better, she would almost have been inclined to believe Stephanie.

A hundred yards away, Robert was in an agony of indecision.

He wanted—he desperately needed—to get to the women, to talk to them, to . . . what? What could he do? What were they talking about? Was Stephanie telling Kathy about the baby? What in God's name was going on?

He saw Kathy hand something to Stephanie. What was that?

He could feel his heart rate increase, and he was conscious that he was sweating profusely.

"I know he came to you on Saturday," Kathy snapped.

"Yes. I asked him to."

Stephanie's answer stopped Kathy cold. She blinked. "You admit it!"

A sudden gust of rain whipped in under the umbrella, and Kathy and Stephanie automatically turned. Now they were facing the funeral, with the rain coming at them from behind. They could both see Robert standing alongside the priest. His face, white and desperate, was turned toward them.

"He can see us," Stephanie remarked. "And we're probably the last two people in the world he wants to get together."

"Good," Kathy said emphatically. "You were together for most of Saturday afternoon. I sat outside. I watched you. I saw the bedroom light go on. I saw the pizza guy come. I watched my husband drive away with his clothes in his hands."

"That's all true." Stephanie turned to Kathy, and the older woman was shocked to see a wry smile on the younger woman's face. "I had to see Robert yesterday. I told him I was pregnant."

Kathy, who had believed that she was beyond any more pain, felt this new revelation like a physical blow. She reached for a headstone, convinced that she was going to fall down. Stephanie reached out and caught her arm.

Kathy's lips formed the word, *pregnant,* but she never uttered it.

"When he got to my place, he looked terrible. And I felt sorry for him, because I knew how close he was to Jimmy. Initially, all we spoke about was Jimmy, and I told him to take a shower, because I wanted him awake and alert when we discussed the baby."

The temptation was to leave the graveside, push through the crowd, shove his way to the women. But there were photographers present. They would be sure to capture anything out of the ordinary. He'd seen how Stephanie was now holding onto his wife. From the distance, he suddenly noticed for the first time the extraordinary physical similarity between them; they could easily be mistaken for sisters.

What were they talking about?

Stephanie's eyes were firmly fixed on Kathy's face. "He took a shower, and when I went up to talk to him, he had fallen asleep. I didn't have the heart to wake him up." She was still holding onto Kathy's arm, and she squeezed it firmly. "I swear to you, Kathy, that was it. I didn't sleep with him. I'd just flown in from Wisconsin."

"So that's why he couldn't get you."

Stephanie nodded. "I went home on Christmas Eve. I came back when I found out I was pregnant."

"Pregnant." Kathy licked dry lips, tasting icy rainwater on them. A half brother or sister for Brendan and Theresa. This wasn't something she would be able to keep from them, and with that disclosure would come the revelation about their father's affair.

The priest's voice droned out across the winter graveyard, and in the distance, black and stark against the morning sky, a trio of birds took to the air in an explosion of wings. Stephanie turned to follow their flight. Still watching them, she continued. "I let him sleep. My fridge was empty, so I ordered in some pizza. He wolfed it down as if he hadn't eaten in days."

"He hadn't," Kathy admitted.

"We finally got to speak about the baby." Stephanie suddenly turned back to Kathy, and her eyes were huge, and her face was a mask. "He wanted," she whispered, "he wanted me to . . ." She was crying now, rain mingling with the salt tears on her cheeks. "He wanted me to have an abortion." Her breath began to come in great, heaving gasps. "He gave me a bunch of clichéd, ridiculous reasons—business reasons, personal reasons, stupid reasons. He offered to pay; suggested that we could have a quick abortion and then . . . and then return to our lives."

And suddenly Kathy had her arms around Stephanie and was holding her close, while the young woman sobbed.

"I loved him, loved him with all my heart! He didn't want children. He had his family, he told me. He thought I'd just get rid of the kid, and then life would go on as normal. He was happy to have the affair, but he didn't want to face the consequences. I hate him! I hate him."

Seeing Kathy hugging Stephanie was the final straw. Excusing himself, Robert backed away blindly through the crowd, apologizing automatically, desperate to get to the two women.

Stephanie still sobbed as Kathy supported her. "I shouted at him, screamed at him. Demanded my key back, flung his clothes at him, and threw him out. I never want to see him again." She drew in a deep, shuddering breath. "I thought I knew him. I don't."

"Neither do I," Kathy said very softly. "This isn't the man I married." Still holding onto Stephanie, she raised her head and watched her husband stumble his way through the graves toward them.

Robert came wheezing up. "Kathy . . . Stephanie . . . I . . ." he began, and then his voice trailed away as both women turned to look at him, their expressions identical, a mingling of disgust and contempt.

"You wanted Stephanie to have an abortion?" Kathy practically spat the word onto the ground.

"Now hang on a second. . . ." he began to bluster. "Is that what she's telling you?"

"She is. And I believe her, Robert."

"I haven't seen her. . . ." he said desperately.

"I followed you on Saturday, Robert." His eyes flashed, but Kathy pressed on, ignoring him. "I saw the e-mail you sent Stephanie—you said you loved her. You promised you'd stay away from her, but you lied to me then, and you've continued to lie. Your every waking moment is a lie. Jimmy Moran didn't call on Christmas Day either, did he?"

"He did...."

"I called on Christmas Day," Stephanie said. "Early afternoon Wisconsin time."

"You didn't go in to the office on Christmas Eve night. The alarm company has no record of a call," Kathy continued relentlessly. "And Saturday, you weren't going in to the office; you were going to see Stephanie, determined to convince her to have an abortion because it didn't suit you to have a baby!"

"Fine. I went to see Stephanie. And yes, I suggested she get rid of it. I thought it would be what she'd want."

Kathy ignored him. She turned to Stephanie. "I was sure he was in bed with you on Saturday." Stephanie opened her mouth to reply, but Kathy pressed on before she could speak. "I know he wasn't. I know that now. I was going to finish with him then because of that. But now I know the truth."

Robert started to relax.

"And it doesn't change a thing."

Kathy took the wedding ring from Stephanie's hand and tossed it at Robert. He fumbled with it, but it fell into the dirt at his feet. "We're finished." She watched him trying to pick up the delicate gold band with his gloved fingers. "A couple of days ago, I swore that next year would be different. I guess I didn't realize just how different. Don't come home, Robert. I don't want to see you ever again. You'll be hearing from my lawyer. I want a divorce."

Kathy turned and walked away, her arm through Stephanie's. As they wound their way among the graves, they saw a distraught young woman with long dark hair plastered to her skull hurrying toward the graveside, a bunch of wilting flowers in her hands.

"Frances," Kathy remarked, "Jimmy's lover." She looked over her shoulder.

Robert was still where they had left him, staring after them, completely stunned.

* * *

Robert pulled off his gloves, and the wedding ring was cold against his flesh. He kept looking from it to where Kathy and Stephanie were fast disappearing through the trees.

What had just happened?

Yes, he'd lied to Kathy about visiting Stephanie, but surely she could understand why? He couldn't exactly tell her he was visiting his mistress . . . well, ex-mistress. And how would she have reacted if she had known that Stephanie was calling the house on Christmas Day?

Anyway, he was now finished with Stephanie. . . . Why, she'd even arrived on the arm of another man. But like every scorned woman, she'd had her revenge: She'd turned Kathy against him.

He shook his head and walked away, heading back to the graveside. He was shaking so hard he could barely walk. A divorce? He attempted a laugh, but it stuck in his throat, and came out as a ragged cough. It would all blow over; Kathy would come to her senses. He was sure of it.

"He'll try to come back, you know that?" Stephanie said.

"He'll try, but not today. He'll probably sleep in the office tonight. But I'm sure he'll come home tomorrow for New Year's Eve, or maybe Wednesday. When he does, he'll find the locks have been changed. When I discovered that he was having an affair, I gave him his chance. All he had to do was be honest. But he couldn't even do that. We could have started again."

"Maybe . . ."

"You don't sound so sure?"

"There would have been another affair with another woman in a couple of years' time," said Stephanie. "Once a man cheats . . ."

"I know." Kathy glanced at the younger woman. "We need to talk about the baby," she said.

"I'm having it," Stephanie said emphatically.

"Of course." Kathy smiled. "And the baby will have two wonderful half siblings." Kathy paused. "And they're going to want to know him or her."

"Really?" Stephanie said nervously.

"Really."

"So, you'll be in my life?"

"Whether I like it or not. We're family now." Kathy linked her arm through Stephanie's. "So we both begin a new year without a man—the same man." Kathy smiled.

"Interesting times ahead."

"Especially for you," Kathy said.

"For both of us," Stephanie said supportively.

"It'll be tough," Kathy admitted. "I've no illusions about that. But I stood outside the office on Saturday and looked at the sign that read R&K Productions . . . and I've been thinking about the young woman I used to be. I was so passionate. So smart. So brave. I had huge dreams, but I allowed them to be swallowed up by my husband." She stopped walking and looked at Stephanie. "Half of R&K is mine, and I'm thinking . . . I might set up my own independent production company; I know Maureen will come with me, and I'm sure we could make it a success. What do you think?"

"I think it's a fabulous idea."

The two women walked toward the entrance of the cemetery before Stephanie shyly looked at Kathy.

"So . . . would you consider taking on a partner?"

The Consequences

Colette Freedman

About This Guide

The suggested questions are included
to enhance your group's reading of
Colette Freedman's *The Consequences*.

Discussion Questions

1. Stephanie asks herself, "What attracted a thirty-three-year-old, single, unattached, attractive woman, with her own mortgage and car, to a man with the ultimate baggage: a wife, two teens, and a struggling business?" Why do you think she's attracted to a man with so many complications? Have you ever been in her position? What does she see in Robert that makes him so attractive to her?

2. Stephanie says, "All men lie. But let's be honest, we wouldn't want them to tell us the truth about everything, would we?" She similarly believes that all women lie as well. When is it okay to lie to a spouse or partner? Have you ever lied to your spouse? Can a lie be justified?

3. As technology changes, so too does the nature of an affair and, indeed, all relationships. Stephanie checks her e-mail and finds an urgent message from Robert. She also gets an instant message from him. How do you think technology has played a role in affairs? Are relationships stronger or weaker now because we are almost always connected?

4. Stephanie's father advises her that "love is the only thing worth fighting for." Is love always worth fighting for—even if it's with the wrong person?

5. Are you surprised by Stephanie's coldness when she learns about Jimmy's death? Does it make her a bad friend that she did not immediately console Robert? How would you react if your lover's best friend had just died?

6. Should Stephanie tell Robert she is pregnant with his child or should she keep that information to herself? Why?

7. Maureen tells Robert that it is time for him to choose between Stephanie and Kathy. Yet, do you think the choice is still his to make? Is it really now the women who are making the decisions in this situation?

8. When Kathy confronts Robert, she accepts some responsibility for what happened. How culpable do you feel Kathy was? Can you fault her for his affair?

9. Robert worries that Kathy will spy on him for the rest of their relationship. When trust is broken, how long do you feel it takes for that trust to be rebuilt? Indeed, is it ever possible for trust to be rebuilt? Could you trust your partner if he or she had betrayed you by having an affair?

10. Kathy wonders if a man and a woman can have a purely platonic relationship. Do you think it's possible? Do you know any male-female friendships that are completely devoid of sexual tension?

11. Kathy's sister Julia immediately rushes to judgment over their sister Sheila's affair. Have you ever jumped to a conclusion about a relationship before hearing both sides of the story?

12. When the truth about an affair comes out, women usually side with women and men with men. Have you ever stuck with a friend even though you knew he or she was behaving in an inappropriate manner?

13. Sheila says, "In an affair, there are no blacks and whites, only shades of gray." But is that true? Or is an affair always black and white and simply wrong? Where are the shades of gray in Robert's affair?

14. Robert and Kathy's children are present throughout the book and are a major factor in both Kathy's and Robert's thoughts. We never get to see their side of the story. How perceptive

would teenage children be to a situation like this unfolding around them? Whose side do you think they would take?

15. Until Kathy discovers Robert's ultimate betrayal of lies, she still has hope that they can rebuild their relationship. Can you understand her actions and is she right to fight for Robert even after the betrayal of the affair? Do you agree with her?

16. At the end of the book, the two women discuss going into business together. Given that they are very alike in many ways (Stephanie has acknowledged that she is a younger version of Kathy), do you think the women would be good business partners?

17. Statistically, men often have affairs with women who look like a younger version of their present partners. Women never have affairs with men who look like their partners. Why is this, and what does this tell us about the sexes?

18. Where do you think Robert will be in a year's time? He is about to lose his wife and family, his home, and probably his business. Can he start again or will he end up like Jimmy Moran?

19. All affairs begin in the mind. But at what point does an affair begin? Is it with flirtation, a kiss that is more than a peck on the cheek, sexual texting or salacious e-mails? Or does the affair really begin the moment the couple end up in bed together?